THE PANNELL WITCH

BASED ON A TRUE STORY

MELISSA MANNERS

MELISSA MANNERS PUBLISHING

For all those women whose lives we have forgotten

1

ARREST – ELIZABETH

Kippax, West Yorkshire, 1593

Elizabeth knew Mary was hiding something. From the smile plastered over worried eyes to her bitten lip and fidgeting hands; she was terrified. But Elizabeth wouldn't force the truth out of her.

'We can slow down if you like. It's no rush,' Elizabeth said. She needed to help Mary calm down.

'No.' Mary's breaths were quick. Shallow. 'I'm fine.'

She sighed. 'If you say so. Follow me.' With every step she had to lift her foot up high, over the mass of leaves covering the ground. 'Why here?'

'What do you mean?' Mary asked.

'When you left Ledston Hall, why did you come here, to the woods? Why didn't you go home?'

Mary cleared her throat. She was struggling to keep up. 'Something happened. And I couldn't face Mother Pannell.'

'Why not? My mother would want to help—you're family.' It wasn't strictly true; she had married into the Pannell family, whereas Elizabeth was born a Pannell. Elizabeth untucked her hair from the back of her collar. It was itchy in this heat, and she didn't need to be Eli right now.

'It's complicated,' Mary muttered.

Underneath the thin layer of dried leaves, the ground was wet and muddy. With every step Elizabeth had to unstick one foot from the ground and let it fall in front of her with a squelch. There were lots of tree roots to step around and Elizabeth was worried Mary would trip. She kept looking back to check on her. 'Do you need me to slow down?' She called.

Mary didn't respond.

It was a sunny day and climbing over the uneven ground as fast as they were only made them more exhausted. Mary was walking slowly, placing her feet into the spots where Elizabeth had stepped. Elizabeth was glad—she didn't want her to trip.

'What happened at Ledston Hall? What's got you so shaken up?' Elizabeth asked.

Mary was dripping with sweat, her face red and blotchy. She had been crying. What had happened back at the house?

'Please, talk to me?' Elizabeth tried again.

Mary forced a smile. 'I'm fine.' She carried on walking.

Something was worrying her. Mary closed her eyes and inhaled. Elizabeth copied her, taking in the comforting earthy smell of the forest and listening to the birdsong.

Elizabeth stopped at a small clearing, shielded from the sun by a circle of tall trees. It was perfect for sitting in because of all the large tree roots sticking out of the ground. They hadn't been to this place for years, but Elizabeth would never forget it.

Mary leaned forward and put her hands on her knees, panting. 'I always liked it here.' She wiped the sweat from her forehead and pulled off her cap. 'It's private.' The only people that lived nearby were themselves and Mother Pannell, in their huts at the edge of the woods.

'Mother used to take me swimming here.' Elizabeth said. She took Mary's hand and led her to a flat area on the edge of the lake. 'Do you remember coming here with me?'

Mary took a second to catch her breath. 'Of course. This is where we used to...' Her cheeks reddened with embarrassment and she looked at the ground. Elizabeth reached over and tucked a stray hair behind Mary's ear.

'Sit here. Let's try to unwind, forget about everything.' Elizabeth lowered herself down, one hand on her back, rolled up her trousers and took off her shoes. Then she dangled her feet in the water. She flexed her feet, one at a time, making small splashes.

'Isn't it cold?' Mary asked.

'See for yourself.' Elizabeth patted the ground next to her and gestured for her to sit.

Mary squealed as her feet touched the surface but lowered them in anyway. 'Ah, that does help. My feet are so sore from the walk here.' Mary did a lot of walking most days, and she was not a young woman. She sighed and lay her head on Elizabeth's chest.

Elizabeth smiled and kissed her on top of her head, which was at the perfect angle. She untied Mary's long black hair and let it fall down past her shoulders. Finally, Mary had taken a moment to relax.

'Anyway, it's time for a swim!' Elizabeth stood and began to undress.

'No! It's too cold!' Mary said.

'You're still sweating from the walk! Come, join me.' Elizabeth threw her work trousers over a nearby tree branch and unfastened her linen shirt.

Mary's breathing quickened. 'You make me feel like a child sometimes!'

Elizabeth smirked. She ran her fingers through her hair and shook her head from side to side. Mary was watching her, but avoided looking directly at her.

Mary grinned and placed her woollen skirt over the same branch.

'Come on, then!' Elizabeth called.

Mary's eyes widened as she surveyed Elizabeth's long, bare legs. The dark, dense hairs on her lower legs grew more sparse at her knees and became fairer on her thighs. Mary took a deep breath and unfastened her bodice.

'Ready?' Elizabeth ran towards the lake and dived in. The cold shocked her system all at once and she was glad she hadn't lowered herself in gradually. She disappeared under the surface, the water closing over her head, before emerging with a cry.

'The water is cold, isn't it?' Mary had undressed, but now stood with her arms wrapped nervously around herself, pacing.

'No,' Elizabeth lied, and she swam to the far side of the lake.

'I think I'll lower myself in.' She sat on the edge of the lake and dangled her feet in the water.

Elizabeth held her breath and swam underwater towards Mary. She brushed Mary's toes with her hand as she swam to the water's edge, then threw her head above the surface.

Mary gasped.

She always pretended not to be ticklish, but Elizabeth knew better.

Elizabeth jumped out of the water and wrapped her arms around Mary. 'Surprise!'

Mary giggled. 'Elizabeth, it's cold. Let's dry off while the sun is still out.' Mary's expression darkened once more. What was she hiding?

She distracted Elizabeth with a kiss on the cheek. 'Come here.' She patted the ground next to her, then spread her linen under-skirt over them both, shielding them from the wind. They stretched out to dry on the grassy bank of the lake.

Elizabeth shivered. Goosebumps had formed on her legs. The grass was hot from the sun, and it warmed her aching back.

'I like it here.' Mary said.

'Me too.' Elizabeth stroked Mary's dark, wet hair, streaked with silver. 'I wish we didn't have to go back to Ledston Hall.'

Mary stiffened next to her. 'But you like working there, especially as Eli.'

She twirled a strand of Mary's hair around her finger. 'Just because they don't make me cook and clean, doesn't mean I'm not still a servant.'

'What else would you want to be?' Mary asked.

Elizabeth didn't have an answer. 'Forget it. Let's just lie here for a while.' She closed her eyes.

The trickles of water running over the rocks and crashing into the banks grounded her in that moment. Mary settled once again onto her side, her head leaning on Elizabeth's chest. It was much warmer with Mary this close. Before long they both fell asleep.

THE CRACK of a branch sounded from behind them.

Elizabeth's eyes snapped open. She shivered—the sun was no longer overhead. A darkness enveloped them in their small clearing. Mary was already awake—she pushed Mary off her and sat up straight. Her mind was racing as she ran through the possibilities in her mind. It was probably nothing, a rabbit that had been scared off at the sight of them both.

More branches cracked—they were closer this time. This was no rabbit.

A horse whinnied in the distance. Who could it be? The villagers would not normally travel this far. Maybe it was a wild horse, or even a group of wild horses?

A louder crack sounded from right behind them. It had to be heading towards them, whatever it was.

'Quick, get dressed.' Elizabeth whispered to Mary. 'Do not make a sound.'

Mary did as she was told. While she dressed, Elizabeth kept a lookout. She was trying to catch sight of whatever or whoever was nearby, but in such deep woodland it was impossible to see very far around them.

'Hurry,' Elizabeth urged Mary. Elizabeth too reached into the pile of her clothes, not taking her eyes off the trees where the sounds of cracking branches had come from.

Both women were standing partially clothed when the man appeared. Mary wore a linen slip, and Elizabeth had on a shirt.

'Ahem.' He cleared his throat.

Mary squealed and grabbed her skirt to cover her body. The man was younger than Mary and Elizabeth, probably in his thirties. The sound of footsteps made Mary look around, to see ten men waiting and watching them.

Elizabeth addressed Mary. 'Don't worry. We'll sort this out. Get dressed.' Mary's eyes widened.

'My name—' the man began.

'Excuse me,' Elizabeth interrupted and spoke loudly and

clearly. 'We were just bathing in the lake. Please allow us a minute of privacy to dress.'

He coughed and sputtered over his words, not used to this sort of directness coming from a woman. 'Ah, yes. Yes, I suppose.' He gestured to the other men, who turned away. Mary pulled on her bodice and her heavy woollen skirt. Elizabeth brushed off the dried mud from her feet. Specks of mud were stuck in the hairs on her legs, so she rubbed off what she could. She thrust her legs into her trousers and they both put their shoes on.

'Who are these men?' Mary muttered, breathing fast. 'Why are they here?'

'Don't worry. Whatever happens, we can sort it.'

'Elizabeth, I think this is about me.' Mary's cheeks reddened, more in anger than in embarrassment. 'But you have to trust me. I have done nothing wrong.'

Mary had pulled on her cloak just as they turned back around.

'Ahem.' The man who had spoken before looked disapprovingly at Mary. 'My name is Sir Henry Griffith of Burton Agnes, Justice of the Peace and High Sherriff.' He wore a bright red, tightly fitted jacket. It matched his trousers, which were tucked into white socks. His clothes set him apart from the plain-clothed group gathered behind him.

Tears welled up in Mary's eyes—she was scared. Elizabeth shook her head at her. Mary held her breath to calm down.

'I seek to arrest Mary Pannell, née Tailor, on suspicion of witchcraft.'

Mary's eyes widened and she let out an involuntary gasp.

Elizabeth stepped in front of Mary. 'Stay behind me,' she said under her breath.

Sir Henry took a roll of parchment from his inside jacket pocket. He frowned as he read from it.

'The charge is that you did place a charm on Sir William Witham, of Ledston Hall, taking him to your bed, and that you did bewitch him to death.'

Mary stifled a sob.

'No.' Elizabeth shook her head. 'No!' Why was he saying these things? 'You've got it wrong; Mary wouldn't do this.'

'I hereby place you under arrest. You shall be imprisoned and interrogated for up to three days, during which time we shall seek a confession and thereafter bring you to trial.'

Elizabeth turned around but Mary avoided eye contact. She couldn't hold on any longer. She sobbed, tears streaming down her face. Elizabeth squeezed her hand. 'Mary, tell them.' She gritted her teeth, trying to stay calm. 'Tell them they've got the wrong person. I know you didn't do this.'

'I'm sorry.' She dug her fingernails into Elizabeth's palms. 'I didn't think they'd find us here.' Her sobs punctuated her words. 'I'm innocent. I promise.'

Sir Henry nodded to two of his men, who approached Mary and grabbed her by the shoulders. They pulled her from Elizabeth's side.

'Stop!' Elizabeth shouted. She elbowed the man next to her in the chest and he doubled over. 'Let go of her.'

A man grabbed Elizabeth from behind and threw her to the ground.

Mary screamed. 'Leave her alone, she has nothing to do with this!'

'Mary? Mary!' Elizabeth tried to stand up, but the man kept his foot firmly on her back, burying her face in the mud, and she couldn't move. She couldn't even see her as they dragged her away.

2

POISON – MARY

That morning, Mary couldn't have known what was going to happen. She never meant any harm. In fact, she did all she could to heal the boy. How could she not? She was only a servant, but still—she had rocked him to sleep as a baby and helped him take his first steps as a toddler. But out of nowhere this illness took hold of him, attacking him from inside until he was all skin and bones, that awful cough echoing through the corridors of Ledston Hall. Mary was sure the concoction would cure him—she couldn't have known that his mother was going to cry 'witch'.

For now, she tried to push the worries out of her mind. Mary leaned forward, then dragged the brush back along the floor and sat on her heels. She scrubbed forwards and backwards. Forwards and backwards. Again and again. The floor wasn't dirty, not really. But if it wasn't washed every day, it would build up. And it was important that Ledston Hall always looked perfect. Mary dipped the brush in the bucket of soapy water, shuffled along on her knees and started again. Scrub forwards, scrub backwards. The familiar ache crept into her upper back so she rested on her heels. She blinked, trying to keep sweat from dripping into her eyes, and wiped her forehead with her damp sleeve.

Lady Witham cleared her throat, making Mary jump.

Mary got back to work, eyes firmly on the floor. She did not want to be whipped.

Lady Witham was on the floor above, at the top of the grand staircase. Mary glanced up, out of the corner of her eye, while continuing to scrub the floor. Ledston Hall had tall ceilings where cobwebs seemed to form in the upper corners almost daily. She would have to clean those today. She tutted. Mary hated heights.

She looked over at Lady Witham. It was barely noon, but there she was, leaning on the banister and gulping down something from a glass bottle. Mary shook her head, trying to ignore her. She thought of Elizabeth—she must be around here somewhere. What would she be doing right now? Polishing the silver? No, it was too early for that. It was dry out today—maybe she was in the grounds. Chopping firewood? Feeding the horses? When she got the chance, Mary resolved to find her.

Lady Witham came stumbling down and around the curved staircase, mumbling something to Mary. The side of her body slid along the banister as she couldn't hold herself up straight. Her feet thumped down the stairs one at a time until finally she reached the bottom. She bared her black teeth into a grimace and groaned.

'Yes, ma'am?' Mary sat up straight, wincing as a bone in her back cracked. That couldn't be good. She should get Mother Pannell to have a look.

'I said, get up. Did you give Mother Pannell my letter?'

'Yes, ma'am.' Mary nodded and threw the scrubbing brush into a bucket of water. She reached into her skirt pocket and pulled out a small package, complete with a wax seal to ensure Mary hadn't opened it.

Before Mary had a chance to ask what it was, Lady Witham grabbed it out of her hands. 'I will have some wine.'

Mary gestured to the other servant girl who was working the floors today. She would finish up here.

Lady Witham clicked her fingers at Mary, and then at the large oak door to the drawing room. 'In here.' She looked her up and down, frowning. 'And clean yourself up.' It was dark in this house, with its small, high-set windows and few candles on the walls. Mary was sure she looked fine, but this was not the time to argue.

9

'Yes, ma'am.' Mary stood up but immediately took a step back, trying to avoid the stench of alcohol that surrounded Lady Witham. 'Please, there's something else.'

Lady Witham ignored her.

'Please, ma'am. I wanted to give you—'

'I don't have time for this. Go.'

Mary sighed. She should have realised then that something wasn't right. After working at the house for years, she knew it was not the housemaid's job to serve drinks. But all she could think about that day was the boy. He would have to wait. She hurried into the kitchens. Her brother, the butler at Ledston Hall, was sitting outside talking to one of the kitchen maids, Dorothy.

'William?' She called.

He ignored her. Dorothy was laughing at something he had said. Why did these young women ever show any interest in him? He was overweight, gambled away all his money, and he was married.

'William?' Mary called, more loudly this time. She walked outside and stood in the doorway, arms crossed. 'Shouldn't you be working?'

He winked at her. 'Bit busy right now. Come back later?' Dorothy was still standing close to him so Mary scowled at her. She knew William was married.

'Lady Witham wants some wine.' Mary said.

William sighed. He knew he couldn't deny the lady of the house, so gave Dorothy an apologetic look. 'You heard her; in we go.'

Mary followed them inside where Dorothy reported to the Head Cook, while William set about polishing the silver. Mary stayed out of the way and looked around the kitchens. She was proud to have always been a housemaid. Even when she was young, she was never confined to the kitchens. The kitchen staff were running around frantically, getting the rest of the day's meals ready.

'Why did she ask you to bring it to her?' William asked, raising an eyebrow.

Mary shrugged. 'How should I know?' But she did have an idea what this could be about. Lady Witham had long suspected her husband of having affairs with the servants, even servants as old as Mary.

William poured some wine into a jug and placed it along with a couple of wine cups on the tray.

'She didn't say Sir William would be joining her.' Mary said.

William smirked. 'She'll get someone to ask him. But he probably won't come. He hates her.'

Didn't they all?

'She'll want sugar.' He gestured to a small dish in front of Mary, where there were a number of small white cubes.

'I don't understand why she likes these.' Mary picked up one of them, held it to her nose and sniffed. 'What's so special about sugar?'

William shrugged. 'All I know is it's not worth the hassle. There's only one or two men in the country who sell it, and half the time they've got no stock anyway.'

She nodded and took everything to the drawing room.

Mary knocked three times, but there was no response. She tried again.

'Come in!' Lady Witham called.

The woman sat scrunched up, tiny in comparison to her tall-backed chair in the centre of the room. Her chest bones protruded over the low neckline of her dress, making her look less than human. The edge of her lip turned up in a wicked smile that exposed her blackened teeth. She wasn't ashamed of her teeth— they made her think she resembled Queen Elizabeth.

'Mary, finally. Right there. That's it.' She pointed to the table in front of her.

'Yes, ma'am.' Mary put the tray down and poured a cup of wine for Lady Witham. 'Do you have a minute? I wanted to talk to you about something.'

Lady Witham untangled the bones of her body to sit up straight on the edge of her chair. 'No.' She raised her voice. 'Fetch my husband. Tell him I would like him to join me.'

Mary should have noticed the change in Lady Witham's demeanour by this point. But still her mind was consumed with worry about the boy. Mary sighed. It was clear Lady Witham wasn't interested in what she had to say. 'Yes, ma'am.'

At least Sir William might listen to her. As soon as she knocked at his open door, he invited her in.

'What is it?' He kept his eyes on the stack of papers in front of him, which he was scribbling on with a long feather quill.

'Lady Witham has asked for you.'

He sighed and waved her away with a gesture of his hand. 'Tell her I'm busy.'

Mary took a deep breath. 'How is young Master Witham?'

He frowned and put down his quill. 'No better. We've had the doctor over and he thinks it's something to do with the humours, not that he had any idea how to treat him. What business is it of yours?'

Mary hesitated, wondering where to begin.

'I don't have time to sit here talking to you. If you have something to say, please do.'

'Sir, I apologise for disturbing you, but—'

'Well? Out with it!'

'Have you tried the medicine I gave you?'

He narrowed his eyes. 'Well, no.'

'It will help, I promise.'

'Com- something, wasn't it?'

'Comfrey, sir. The mixture needs to be rubbed on his chest every day until he shows signs of improvement.'

Sir William reached for the small bottle on his desk, exactly where he had placed it when Mary gave it to him. He turned it over in his hand. 'I'm not sure about this.'

'It should only take a week, maybe two.'

'You've done this before, have you? Given children medicines you've mixed up yourself?'

Mary nodded. 'Yes, sir. I actually delivered William, if you remember.'

'Oh yes. He was early, wasn't he?'

'Yes, sir. The physician couldn't get here in time so I assisted with the birth, but when I saw the yellow tinge to his skin, I knew he needed some milk thistle.' Mary remembered the day well: it was not long after Mother Pannell had explained the use of this particular herb, and though she hadn't quite believed it, she herself saw it bring the boy's complexion back to life.

'You mixed up a potion for my son?' Sir William raised his voice.

Mary tried to keep her voice steady. She had already explained this to him, but evidently he hadn't taken her seriously. 'Not a potion, a medicine. Mother Pannell told me—'

Sir William stood out of his chair, towering over Mary. 'That old woman from the village? The gypsy who lives in that rat-infested shack in the woods?'

Mary had to be careful. Though most people in Kippax thought of Mother Pannell as the one who saved the town, there were some who didn't trust her. 'Please, sir. I used it to save his life. Let me do it again.'

Sir William shook his head. 'No thank you, I don't want to be using any'—he made a face when he said the word—'remedies.'

'Please trust me. My brother died at the same age, and I've helped countless people with the same issue. Your son can barely keep down any food or drink, and it's not good for him. He's losing weight every day.'

He looked her in the eye, trying to make up his mind.

'It's simple, you take some of this on your finger and rub it on young William's chest every day. I promise you; he'll feel better in no time.' She smiled but Sir William still seemed unsure.

'Rub it on his chest?'

'Yes. Once a day, every day. It will help him, I promise.'

'You say you've used this before? Even on those as young as my boy?'

Mary nodded.

'Well, I should see what my wife wants.'

Mary followed him to the drawing room and waited to be dismissed.

'Close the door.' Lady Witham called.

Mary put a foot out of the door but was interrupted.

'No—don't leave yet. Close the door but stay inside.' Lady Witham rolled her eyes, and then under her breath, muttered,

'Stupid.' Mary stood up straight, eyes on the floor. She was determined not to anger Lady Witham.

'I'm not staying. I just came down to tell you, Mary has brought—'

'Sit down, please.' She interrupted. 'Have some wine.' She showed all her teeth, but not in any way resembling a smile. Mary wasn't sure Lady Witham was capable of smiling these days.

Sir William raised his voice and threw his arms in the air. He did not sit down. 'What is this about? I have a lot to deal with right now. What do you want?'

'Please, calm down. Have a drink with me.'

Groaning, he picked up one of the full cups of wine from the tray. After gulping it down in only a few sips, he dribbled down the sides of his mouth and then slammed it back down on the tray. 'There. I've drunk my wine. Now I'm going back upstairs. Don't call me down here again.'

Sir William turned towards Mary but her stomach dropped when she saw his face. Foam was forming at the edge of his lips. His cheeks grew pale and his knees gave way. He was a tall man, so when he fell to the floor there was a loud crash.

Lady Witham screamed. 'What have you done?'

Mary stared at Sir William. What was happening?

Lady Witham fell to her knees and let out strange noises that sounded like sobs, but without tears. She cradled her husband's head in her arms.

'Lady Witham, turn him over. He might choke. His life could be in danger.' Mary tried to cut in.

She wailed even more loudly, drowning out Mary's words.

'Please, let me. I might be able to save him.' Mary urged.

Lady Witham's head whipped up to meet Mary's gaze, and her eyes glared at her with such victorious hatred that Mary knew exactly what she had done.

Mary gasped.

'My dear husband!' She shouted. 'What have you done?'

Mary knew what Lady Witham was insinuating. She had to get out of there. There was no time to make a plan. She had to go. Right now. She ran.

3

RUMOUR – BESS

Bess hurried towards the Middletons' farm. She was fit enough that it wasn't difficult, and she knew it would warm her up. At this time of night, she was glad for every bit of warmth. Besides, she was excited to see Matthew. She saw him most days at work of course—he was a farmhand—but it was different when she could sneak a visit at night.

Tonight she had to see him. She had to talk to somebody, and he would know what was going on. He would be on her side, too. He always stood up for her. There were lots of other girls on the farm, many of them prettier than Bess, but he only had eyes for her. She arrived at the farm out of breath but ran straight to the barn where he lay sleeping. She shook him awake.

'Matthew?' She whispered. She didn't want to wake the others.

He blinked his eyes open and let her lead him outside.

'What is it?' He rubbed his eyes. Bess was holding a rushlight and as soon as his eyes adjusted, he cleared his throat and blushed red. 'Bess! You're not dressed!'

Her eyes widened, and she clutched her arms over her chest. She hadn't thought to put on her work clothes, so she was only wearing her nightdress. 'Oh. I'm sorry. I came because—' She blushed too.

'Please.' He stood up straight with his eyes fixed firmly on hers. 'Do not apologise. What do you need?'

He looked so put together, even though he had only just woken up. He had smoothed his hair and straightened his shirt. Was he trying to impress her? Bess pushed the thought from her mind. She shouldn't assume.

'Y-yes. I wanted to see if you...' She trailed off. She wasn't imagining it. His eyes were lingering on her. This wasn't the first time she had seen him in the middle of the night, but it had been a while. Normally when they were together, there were lots of other people around. They rarely got the chance to be alone.

Still keeping his eyes on hers, he added, 'I'm glad you came to see me, Miss.'

'Miss'? Nobody ever called her 'Miss'. He was trying to impress her. Why? Where was he going with this? She had to respond. What should she say? Bess didn't know how she was supposed to talk to a man.

'I—I was in bed. And I thought of you.' What? Bess thought. Why did she say that?

He coughed in shock.

Oh no. No, no, no. This was dangerous talk. What was she doing? Her mother would kill her. She would tell her that—Bess stopped herself. Her mother. That was why she was here.

'Bess, I would like to talk to you.' His awkward smile reached his eyes, lit up by the torch Bess held.

'I'm sorry. Forgive me. I should not have said that.' Bess added.

'No, it's fine. I wanted to say—' Matthew tried, but Bess cut him off again.

'Please. I came about my mother. She didn't come home last night, and I heard—well I heard a rumour. I know you know people from up at the house. Ledston Hall. I thought you might know what happened.' She blurted out.

'I'm sorry, I don't remember. Your mother's name is...?'

'Mary. She's Mary Pannell. Please, tell me if you know anything.'

Matthew's expression was blank, unreadable. Did that mean something was wrong? Or did he not know anything at all?

'Please, Matthew.' Taking his hand in hers, she continued, 'My mother is a housemaid there. She cleans, looks after the house, sometimes helps with the children. Mary.'

A flicker of comprehension reached Matthew's face, but he frowned. 'Oh no, Bess. I'm sorry. Someone said something, but I don't know if it's true. And I don't know if it was about your mother.'

'What? What is it?' Bess raised her voice.

'Shh, you'll wake the others. We can't let anybody find us alone out here in the middle of the night.' He was right, that would be bad.

He took her hand and led her some distance from the barn until they were out of earshot from anyone who might still be awake.

Bess shivered and whispered, 'what did you hear?'

Matthew's face was lit from below, where Bess held the rush-light. 'There's a witch. At Ledston Hall, one of the servants.'

Bess gasped. She let go of his hand.

'She tricked the man of the house into her bed. She put a charm on him. And when he tried to stop her, she killed him.'

'No. That's nothing like Mother. That can't be about her.' Bess insisted.

He continued, 'they're saying she has run off into the woods. She lives there with a group of women. They put spells on men and plot their deaths together.'

'What? That's not what happened!' But Bess could see there were elements of truth to the story.

Matthew sighed. 'Look, I don't know. This may only be a rumour. But if it's not, you need to be careful.'

'Don't worry about me. Who did you hear this from? We can find the source, explain that they've got it wrong.' Bess nodded.

'That wouldn't do any good.' He looked her in the eye. 'I think they have evidence.' He took a deep breath. 'They mean to take the witch to court.'

'The witch?' Bess raised her voice. 'You mean my mother? My mother is no witch!'

'Please. I didn't mean to offend, but you need to think about what this means.'

She knew what he was getting at. She bit her lip. 'You think I could get mixed up in this?'

'I think you need to plan to leave Kippax—just in case.'

4

HONESTY – ELIZABETH

E lizabeth stirred to the smell of freshly baked bread. Mmm. She took a deep breath in through her nose and rolled over onto her side, resting on a thick, woollen blanket. She patted the space next to her but it was empty. Empty? She blinked her eyes open and sat up straight.

'Mary?' Elizabeth called.

'Oh! What is wrong with you?' Agnes cried. 'You scared the life out of me.' In the kitchen area of their hut Agnes was stoking the fire. It was a small space, so the kitchen area was only a few steps away from where Elizabeth slept with Mary. The bed Agnes and Bess shared was about the same distance away, on the far side of the kitchen area. Both beds were nothing more than bundles of straw, covered in blankets, but it was enough for them.

Elizabeth tutted. 'Why would you bake bread today of all days? Mary always bakes bread. I thought...' She trailed off. 'For a second, I thought...'

A harsh chill slivered in through the gap around the edge of the door, so Elizabeth wrapped the blanket tightly around her chest.

'I don't know why I bother. Every time I try to do something helpful!' Agnes tore off a piece of bread and took some lumps of cheese to have with it. The chickens clucked noisily from their corner, hungry now.

'Ignore her, Agnes. She doesn't mean it,' said Bess, who was sitting by the fire. 'She misses Mother, that's all.'

Elizabeth avoided Bess's gaze. With one hand supporting her lower back, she used the other to push up into a seated position. She was getting older every day, and these early mornings were becoming more difficult.

'Agnes, feed the chickens, please.' Elizabeth said.

Agnes mumbled something that Elizabeth ignored. Agnes had lovely pale skin and a healthy, rounded figure. Unlike Bess, Agnes had soft facial features, undamaged by the sun, and she curled her hair into such tight ringlets that she looked almost like a lady. It was her manners that gave her away.

'Elizabeth? Please tell us what's going on. Where is Mother?'

'Not now, Bess.' Elizabeth sighed. 'Your mother is not here, but she's fine. Nothing has happened to her. Not yet, anyway.'

Elizabeth had to stay calm. She knew that. But what was she going to do? They had arrested Mary—for witchcraft. She had never dealt with anything like this before.

'Leave it to me.' Elizabeth said. 'I'll figure it out.'

Bess raised her eyebrows.

'What are you talking about? Just because she's not home yet, it doesn't mean something is wrong. She'll still be at Ledston Hall. Stop worrying.' Agnes said. She tucked a stray hair behind her ear.

Bess rolled her eyes, picked up an empty bucket and went outside.

Agnes groaned. 'The fire's gone out. Again.' She stood next to the fire pit, which was right under the gap in the thatched roof, the coldest part of the hut. It wasn't too windy today though.

Agnes was still in the throes of youth, just eighteen. Her work as a scullery maid to the Beale family kept her out late, but she still preferred to sleep at home. Elizabeth was glad to have her close. It wasn't far to walk and the Beales' house wasn't much better than their own hut. It was no warmer, anyway.

'Agnes, get up, please. Relight the fire.' Elizabeth said.

'I only just lit it.' She groaned, but obeyed anyway. 'Why is Bess so worried?'

Elizabeth snapped at her. 'No talking back. Do as I say.'

Bess yawned loudly from the doorway, stretching one arm above her head. She wrapped her other arm around the bucket of water she had filled up. 'Elizabeth, do you need me to do anything?'

Bess was a hard worker too, spending long hours at the Middletons' farm, working at the dairy. She was strong, and at twenty-four was protective over her younger sister. Elizabeth knew she was distracting her, trying to stop her from scolding Agnes.

'Thank you, Bess.' Elizabeth noticed her slight smile, her bright eyes—she had slept well. But that wasn't all, Elizabeth thought. She must have snuck off to see Matthew last night. Yes, that must be it. He was utterly in love with her, and Elizabeth suspected Bess felt the same way about him.

Although Elizabeth hadn't asked, Bess poured her a cup of ale and handed her a piece of bread.

Agnes was still trying to light the fire.

'Here.' Bess bent down to help her.

'It's fine, I can do it.' Agnes insisted.

Not particularly skilled at housework, she had remained a scullery maid for years. It was the lowest of all the domestic servants and she wished she could quit altogether. Sometimes she talked about doing exactly that. She was sure her family would continue to support her even if she lost her job. Still, Elizabeth hoped she could stick it out. There was no telling how long they would be around to support the girls. This wasn't something Agnes took the time to think about.

Agnes groaned, gritting her teeth as she struck the piece of flint repeatedly.

The naivety that plagued her was no issue for her sister. Bess had grown up fast, ever since the traumatic experience of the fire that killed her father when she was only six years old.

Although Bess still had that sort of glow, her expression was solemn, lit by the fire Agnes had finally got working. Had she heard about Mary? Had Matthew told her? She caught Elizabeth's eye, and they exchanged a look which Agnes didn't see.

Elizabeth sighed. Bess always had a way of figuring things out, and it wasn't because of Matthew. Bess would always know what questions to ask, which people were best placed to answer them. And Matthew of course, would do anything for her. Despite their closeness, Bess had shown no interest in marriage. Elizabeth suspected this had something to do with Bess's father. After all, it was only when he finally became a father that he became violent. Elizabeth could understand this—she herself had never seriously considered marrying any man. What was the point?

Agnes looked from Bess to Elizabeth, who were staring at each other over the fire in silence. She threw her hands up in the air. 'I give up.'

Elizabeth bit her lip, but Bess said nothing.

'It's that wretched woman, isn't it?' Agnes asked. 'Lady Witham?'

Agnes had lived her whole life poor and fatherless and she was tired of it. She wanted a husband, and a rich one at that. She could not get her head around why Lady Witham would be miserable when she had a husband able to give her anything she could want.

Elizabeth shook her head. 'It's not what you think.'

Agnes searched her face, trying to work it all out.

'So it is Lady Witham?' Agnes asked again.

Elizabeth sighed. Was it wrong to keep this from them? Or was it worse to worry them when this could all blow over in a couple of days' time?

Bess sat next to Elizabeth and pulled her into a hug. 'Don't worry. Nobody is going to take her seriously.'

Agnes nodded in agreement. 'Yes, Elizabeth. Everyone knows Lady Witham has always been jealous of Mother. It's not even as if Mother is young! If Sir William wanted somebody else, he would hardly pick somebody old!'

Bess scolded her sister. 'Agnes, I love you, but do shut up. Mother is in serious trouble. And it's not because of any suspected love affair.'

Since their father had died, Bess had helped raise Agnes, and her mothering instinct had never really gone away. Elizabeth took a deep breath. Bess appeared to know the truth already. Or at least, part of it. It was only a matter of time before Agnes found out too.

'Girls, I need to tell you something.'

Bess moved to sit next to Agnes on their bed of rushes. She wrapped a blanket around them both and Agnes warmed her hands on the fire.

They waited.

'Sir William Witham has been killed.' Elizabeth said.

Agnes gasped. Both girls were full of questions.

'When did he...'

'Who would have...'

'Have you spoken to...'

Elizabeth raised her voice. 'One at a time, girls.'

As the eldest, Bess began, 'How did he die?'

Agnes rolled her eyes and answered, 'Lady Witham killed him, evidently.'

Bess tutted at her sister. 'But how?'

'I don't know, how do wives usually kill their husbands?' Agnes gave an exaggerated shrug of her shoulders. 'How would I know?'

'Maybe it wasn't her,' Bess said.

'Who else would have done it?'

'What about his children? They hate him as much as his wife does. I mean, did.'

'No, I still think it was her. It's always the wife,' Agnes insisted.

'However it happened, I'm glad he's gone,' Bess said.

'Why would you care? You don't even know him.'

'I know he was violent. Not just to her, but to their children too. He'll get no sympathy from me.' Her voice faltered.

'Please listen, both of you,' Elizabeth urged. She knew this was a sensitive topic for Bess. She was strong, but the memory of her own father was painful. Agnes was too young to remember, fortunately. 'That's not what I need to talk to you about.'

Agnes ignored her. 'No one knows what their relationship was really like.'

'What relevance does that even have?' Bess shook her head. 'No matter what their relationship was like, he had no right to hurt his own family.'

'I didn't say he did,' Agnes insisted. 'You're twisting my words. Elizabeth, isn't it true that Lady Witham was just as awful to him as he was to her?'

Bess raised her voice. 'How can you say that? You know once, I heard he—'

Agnes interrupted, 'I'm just saying—'

'Girls!' Elizabeth shouted. She hesitated and then rested her head in her hands. 'Please—let's not gossip. That's not what I wanted to talk to you about.' She took a deep breath. 'Lady Witham has dismissed your mother from her post.'

Agnes groaned in indignation. 'She's taking out her anger on Mother? It's not fair to fire her for no reason. She'll have to give her back her job.'

Bess was a few steps ahead of her sister, as usual. She whispered, 'so it's true?'

Agnes sighed. 'What are you talking about now?'

'It is, isn't it?'

Elizabeth didn't know what to say.

'Agnes, look around. Mother isn't here. They've arrested her, haven't they, Elizabeth? She's the one everyone is talking about.'

Agnes shook her head. 'No, that makes no sense. Why would they think Mother did anything?'

'Lady Witham has somehow blamed her for Sir William's death. They arrested her, and everyone's saying she's a witch.'

'A witch?' Agnes pulled a face.

'I'm serious. That's what happened isn't it? They arrested her and now she's locked up somewhere. Will they take her to court? Surely they can't do anything without evidence?'

Elizabeth did her best to keep her voice steady. The girls needed her to be strong for them. 'I won't lie to you. The Justice of the Peace, Sir Henry, has arrested her. But please don't worry. Everything will be fine. We'll figure this out. What's important now is that we stick together.'

She walked over to Bess and Agnes and lowered herself to sit between them. She put an arm around each of them and pulled them into a hug. 'I love you two. As if you were my own daughters.' She kissed Bess, then Agnes, on the tops of their heads. 'I love you more than anything. I will get your mother back.'

Bess sat stiffly in the hug, clenching her fists. 'I love you too, but I'm worried. We can't let Lady Witham hurt Mother.'

By now, Agnes had tears in her eyes and she let Elizabeth hold her. 'They won't hurt Mother, will they? While they have her locked up?'

'Don't worry about that. Shh, it will all be fine.' Elizabeth kept hold of the girls, trying to convince herself as much as them.

'I hate Lady Witham.' Agnes muttered.

'No,' Elizabeth scolded. 'None of that, please. The village will hear about this soon enough, if they haven't already. I need to know you won't spread any gossip.' She directed this comment at Agnes. 'I don't want it coming out that you have been speaking out against Lady Witham. Do you hear me?'

The girls looked towards the fire.

'Girls?'

'Yes, Elizabeth.' They replied in unison, begrudgingly.

'Good. You don't want Lady Witham as your enemy.'

5

WORK - BESS

Bess told her sister, 'get back inside.'

Agnes pulled on her boots silently.

'You can't go to work today,' Bess said. Sat cross-legged in front of the fire, she rubbed her hands together, trying to warm up.

'Actually, I can.' She took a piece of stale bread from the sideboard but Bess reached up, grabbed it and threw it to the floor.

She stood up and spoke firmly. 'How can you even think of going back to your normal life?'

Agnes sighed and put her hands on her hips. 'If I don't work, I won't get paid. I can't put my life on hold to stop my big sister worrying about me.'

Bess pulled her back inside by the wrist. 'Don't you see how this works? This is so much bigger than us.'

She rolled her eyes. 'You and I are irrelevant to the whole situation. We don't even matter. Lady Witham will end up getting what she wants, and it's Mother who will pay the price. Is that what you want me to say?'

'Of course not. All I'm saying is that we have to be careful. You haven't heard the gossip about her. About all of us.'

Agnes frowned. 'What do you mean?'

'They're calling Mother a witch.'

'You mean Matthew called her a witch,' Agnes corrected her.

'Will you listen to me for a minute? This is serious. I thought you understood that. Yesterday it seemed like you did.'

Agnes sniffed and tucked her hair under her cap, determined to appear unaffected. But her cheeks were red and puffy—against her usual porcelain skin it was obvious she had been crying. 'Elizabeth was overreacting. They wouldn't hurt Mother. She just wanted us to be careful. It won't help anyone if we all lose our jobs as well. Besides, where is she today? I bet she went to work.'

Bess shook her head. She couldn't understand how Agnes could be so ignorant. 'Even if she did, she'd be a lot more careful than you.'

Agnes groaned and this time when she headed out of the door, Bess didn't stop her. She sank back onto the floor, dropped her head into her hands and let herself cry.

It wasn't until she felt Matthew's hand on her shoulder that she looked up. 'I—I'm sorry,' she said. She was so distressed that she hadn't even heard him arrive.

He sat next to her on the floor. 'Don't apologise.'

She didn't dare move any closer to him, but she was grateful he hadn't moved his hand. Just having him there made her feel better. A moment later she realised how unusual this was. 'Wait.' Bess turned and looked around. He had left the door open so she could see all the way down to the river. There was nobody else there. 'Has something happened?'

'No, nothing like that. Well, I don't think so.' He hesitated for a second too long.

'What is it?'

He scraped his hair back and sighed. 'You must know what people have been saying.'

'Who? What are they saying?' Bess could feel her heart beating faster. She wished he would say whatever it was he came here to tell her.

'All I mean is, there's been a lot of talk about your Mother. People have heard what happened.'

Bess frowned and pulled away. 'Nothing happened. It's all a mistake, you know it is.'

'Someone actually saw them throw her in the old lock-up by St Mary's.'

'My mother will come home soon. I know she will. She's innocent.'

He shuffled closer to her again. 'I know. I trust you and I'll do what I can to keep you safe, I promise.'

She let out a deep breath.

Matthew ran his fingers through his hair again.

'There's something else. Please, just tell me what you're so worried about.'

'I'm sorry. It's just—I heard the Middletons talking this morning. They're worried about how this looks for them.'

'What does it have to do with them?'

Matthew fiddled with his fingers again. 'Nothing. It has nothing to do with them, I know that. But it sounds like they're worried they'll be dragged into this. If someone finds out they've employed a—well, the daughter of a—'

'Go on, then. Say it.' Bess raised her voice and stood up. 'A witch. If my mother's a witch then so am I. So they don't want me working for them anymore. That's it, isn't it?'

Matthew's face went pale.

'You can tell them they don't have to worry about me. I won't be back to their precious farm. There's no reason I can't find another job. I'll figure something out.' She stormed out of the door and headed straight for the Beales'.

It didn't take long to find Agnes. Bess found her engaged in a shouting match with Mr Beale.

'Please, just take it and go.' He was trying to give her a small coin purse.

'I'm not going anywhere. You can't rush me out of my job because I haven't done anything wrong. Just wait—you'll see. They'll release my mother and this will all be forgotten.'

Mrs Beale cowered behind her husband, brightening up when she caught sight of Bess. 'Hello, dear. I'm so sorry.'

'Don't talk to her!' Agnes scowled at her sister. 'You didn't have to come here. I can take care of myself.'

'What's going on?' Bess asked Mrs Beale.

Mrs Beale took her hand and apologised again. 'I am sorry, but we can't afford to fall out of favour with Lady Witham. Do take this, it's all we could get together.' She took the purse from her husband and handed it to Bess.

'Thank you, Mrs Beale. Mr Beale, I'm sorry. We'll be on our way.' Bess grabbed Agnes by the hand and marched her home.

6

GAOL: DAY ONE – MARY

Mary was glad Elizabeth had not been to visit. She didn't want her to witness this. The lock-up was small, much smaller than the hut they lived in. It was near pitch-black, with a sliver of daylight coming in through the slits in the large wooden door. The cold stone ground only got colder at night. Several planks of wood formed a hard, uncomfortable bed, though it was not long enough even for Mary to fit without having to curl her body into a ball. There was a length of wood on top of a large stone that jutted out from the wall, to be used as a bench. A bucket in the corner served as her chamber pot. Regardless of the conditions, when they threw her in here last night, she thought she could handle it. After all, she had slept on cold floors before. She had slept in rat-infested basements. As a servant, she rarely got to have a full night's sleep, and it was never somewhere warm.

Nothing could have prepared her for the first night. As soon as she shut her eyes, she was woken in shock. Freezing cold water all over her. She looked up. A man cackled before re-bolting the door shut. At first, she thought it was a cruel joke. He was abusing his power temporarily, that was all. Unfortunately, it seemed to Mary that whenever she was close to sleep, there was another bucket of cold muddy water to wake her again. The misery of the night intensified when she realised they were not going to give her any food or water. She didn't dare speak to the man in charge of flinging the water at her. No. She didn't want to give him the satisfaction.

Mary let out a sigh. She sat on the makeshift bed and let the ache of her eyelids pull them closed.

————

HER MIND FLITTED BACK to years ago, when her girls were young and her husband was still alive. It was soon after Mother Pannell had first offered to teach Mary about herbal remedies and medicine.

Mary knocked firmly on the door to Mother Pannell's hut.

'In you come,' she said. 'Put the girls down over there.'

Mary frowned at the mass of dirty hay pushed into the corner. There were little flies and insects everywhere in here, and she almost changed her mind and went home. Mother Pannell didn't give her the chance.

'Get on with it,' she ordered. 'I don't have all day.'

'Right.' Mary stepped over a pile of small bottles and a pile of rags to get to the corner. She motioned for Bess to follow her, and after rearranging the hay into a sort of baby-sized seat, lay Agnes down there. Bess sat next to her, happily comparing the size of each of her tiny fingernails to her own.

'First, I'm going to show you a few of my plants. Then we'll come in here and I'll talk you through these.' Mother Pannell gestured to the pile of small bottles on the ground.

'Where does your daughter sleep?' Mary asked, looking around. There was barely enough space for the two of them in the hut.

'Don't worry about that. She's out anyway, working. Now, follow me.' Mother Pannell took a woven basket outside and led them to her garden. She sat by a group of pink flowers spread out sparsely in the grass. 'I first learned about this in Italy—they called it holy thistle.'

Mary knelt down and picked one of the flowers. It had milky

white veins on the leaves, and the pink flower resembled a daisy, though it was covered in spikes. 'What's it used for?'

Mother Pannell took out a leather-bound book, filled with messy scrawls and with some extra pieces of paper stuffed inside. She leafed through it until she found what she was looking for. 'Here you go. I call it milk thistle. Have a read.' She passed the book to Mary.

Mary bit her lip.

'Don't tell me nobody taught you to read?'

Mary said nothing.

She sighed. 'Give it here, then. I hope you've got a good memory.' She put the book face down on the grass, saving her page.

'I do. I've memorised all my recipes.'

Mother Pannell looked her up and down, apparently still trying to form an opinion of her. 'Well, take your flower and snap open the hollow stem.'

Mary did so, then let out a groan in disgust. 'What's that?' A thick, white substance oozed from the stem.

'Don't waste it! Here, collect it in this,' she said, handing over a small bottle from the basket. Then she knelt next to another group of plants and collected some of them in her basket.

Mary poured in as much as she could get out of the plant and then pushed a small cork in the top to seal it. 'What's it used for?'

Mother Pannell picked up the book and read from the open page. 'If someone presents with yellowing skin, that's liver problems. Give them some of this, and as long as they're not allergic, they should be fine.'

Mary turned the bottle over in her hands, not sure if she believed her. She put it in the pocket of her skirt.

Right then, an old woman shouted over to them, 'Mother Pannell! Do you have a moment?'

She pushed herself up to standing and brushed some dirt from her skirt before replying. 'I'm here, I'm here.'

Mother Pannell was around twenty years older than Mary, but she moved like a much younger woman.

'Who's this then?'

Mother Pannell introduced her. 'This is Mary. John Pannell's wife, you know?'

She nodded, though it didn't seem like she recognised John's name. 'Lovely to meet you. I'm Maggie.' She shook Mary's hand. 'Here to learn from the best?'

Mother Pannell brushed away the compliment. 'You exaggerate, Maggie. Now, what do you need?'

Maggie shook her head. 'Oh, I'm not exaggerating. You'd be too young to remember,' she told Mary, 'but when Mother Pannell first came to Kippax, she saved us from the Plague.'

Mary had heard the stories. 'Is it true?'

'Simple remedies, that's all I brought with me. Along with a good dose of hygiene and common sense.'

Maggie smiled at Mary again. 'It's true. After that we couldn't let her go—she's been with us ever since.'

'That's enough of that,' Mother Pannell insisted.

'Listen to her—we'll need someone to take over from her one day,' Maggie added.

'Nonsense,' Mother Pannell said. 'I'm going nowhere.'

———

MARY WAS BROUGHT BACK to harsh cold reality when the door swung open and Sir Henry Griffith threw a bucket full of cold water on her. She screamed in shock.

'Hello, witch. How was your first night in lock-up?' He smirked.

The brightness of the daylight made her squint, and she held her hands up to her eyes.

'Grab her.' She couldn't see who he was addressing, but suddenly there were men either side of her, taking her by the armpits. Mary was vaguely aware of people in the street and outside the church. Were they staring at her? Were they laughing? She couldn't tell. She kept her eyes closed; it was easier that way.

The men sat her on the cold ground. She blinked. They were inside a barn. There were no animals in here, but it smelled distinctly like cows.

'You are Mary Pannell, are you not?' It was Sir Henry that spoke, the two other men standing either side of him.

She nodded.

'Mary Pannell, being of sixty years of age or thereabouts?'

'I'm fifty-five.'

They ignored her.

'Tell us, how long have you been a witch?'

She screwed up her eyebrows, unsure how to respond. 'I am no witch, sir.'

He nodded to a man next to him, who immediately punched her right cheek. It happened so fast. Her hands rushed up to touch it. That only made it sting more. Blood trickled down her face. She whimpered.

'Let's try that again. How many years has it been since you first practised witchcraft?'

She shook her head vigorously, blinking to stop tears from falling.

Sir Henry sighed. 'You should work with me, you know. The longer you take to confess, the longer I have to keep you here.'

She looked towards the ground. It would only get worse. She had heard horror stories of what they did to accused witches, and they had brought their 'instruments'. Mostly made of wood but some with metal components, she tried not to look at them. They might not even use them on her. Besides, they could only hold her for three days. She could handle three days.

'What familiar do you keep?'

Mary had heard about witches before. They were said to keep a familiar close to them. This could be a cat, or another small animal, but it would change form and encourage the witch to perform black magic. She supposedly enacted curses and would even let the familiar suck blood from a teat on her body. The familiar was a creature sent by the devil himself. If the witch allowed it to suckle on her skin, she was giving her soul to the devil.

'I would never. I am a good, God-fearing woman.' Mary insisted.

Sir Henry nodded to the other man. He pushed her onto the ground. Unsure of what to do, she remained there.

'Get up, witch,' he snarled at her.

She did as she was told.

'Have you lain with the devil?'

Her jaw dropped in shock.

'Has he appeared to you as some man or creature, that you have lain with?' He tried again.

Shaking her head more vigorously this time, she only hoped they would believe her.

'You know, we have ways of making you talk. I thought a Christian woman would admit her wrongs sooner rather than later.'

Mary kept her gaze downwards.

'One last question for today. Who are the others? If you name the rest of the witches with whom you are acquainted, you may be treated with more kindness.'

Kindness seemed the last thing on Sir Henry's mind as he pushed her to the ground himself.

'Right. If you won't tell us anything today, it's time for the examination. If any teat is found on your person, it will be taken as evidence of your illicit deeds.'

7

WORK – ELIZABETH

lizabeth shivered as she waded through the wet grass in the grounds of Ledston Hall. She tucked her hair behind her ears, still tangled with flecks of mud from swimming and lying down in the woods with Mary. That felt like a lifetime ago.

The whinnying of the Withams' horses made her jump. She liked horses, but right now she didn't have time to check on them. They had their thick blankets on but no doubt they still felt the cold.

Elizabeth wondered if Mary was cold wherever they were keeping her. She shook off the thought—it was no use worrying. Besides, she had already decided: the best thing she could do for Mary would be to go to work as normal and find out what she could. Elizabeth made her way up the servants' steps and through the tall oak doors, where the grandfather clock read 6:30. It was time for her to report to the butler, William.

She pulled off her muddy trousers and pattens and left them by the door. Kneeling down, she took a piece of cotton from her pocket, spat and rubbed each of her shoes, brushing away the flecks of mud, until they were shining. She noted that the sole of one shoe was coming away, and she would need to fix it soon. In the kitchen, the staff were busying themselves preparing breakfast. Elizabeth stood by the door next to the second footman, hands behind their backs. Today was a Saturday so the family would take breakfast alone in their bedrooms. The cooks had put out some trays, and on each was a selection of cold meats, slices of bread and butter and a cup of milk. The bread made here was much better quality than they could make at home. It was something to do with the grain—Mary would know more about that. Sometimes they took home the leftovers, if they were stale or mouldy. It didn't bother Elizabeth—stale bread could be toasted and mould could be scraped off. William came over and looked the two footmen up and down. They both stared straight ahead.

'Nice, clean uniforms.' His eyes lingered on their shoes. 'Excellent job on your shoes, Eli.'

Elizabeth smiled back at him in thanks. William was the reason Elizabeth originally got the job here. As Mary's brother, he knew that 'Eli' was a woman, but he turned a blind eye. She did a good job as a footman anyway, so he saw no problem with it. She wanted to get him alone, ask if he knew anything about Mary, but now was not the time—there were servants everywhere.

The cooks summoned the footmen one by one. Elizabeth took a tray first and looked to William, who was speaking with the Head Cook. He then turned back to Elizabeth and addressed her again.

'That one is to go to Lady Witham's room, please.'

She made her way out to the grand staircase which opened up to the two separate bedrooms on the first floor. She looked at the closed door to Sir William's room and wondered if it was the same in there as when he died. Had somebody tidied away his things? Or did Lady Witham prefer to keep his bedroom as it was? Elizabeth shivered and looked around to see if she was alone in the corridor. She was. Nobody would know if she went in.

As she was still holding Lady Witham's breakfast tray, she pushed open Sir William's bedroom door with her hip. It was clean and smelled fresh. The windows were open though the fireplace was cold. The bed had been made. Elizabeth wondered who had cleaned the room. Normally this would be Mary's job.

Lady Witham snapped behind Elizabeth, pulling her out of her reverie.

'What are you doing in there? That's my husband's bedroom! Don't you have work to do?'

She stormed past her and into the room, almost knocking the tray out of Elizabeth's hands. The stale smell of alcohol followed her like an invisible cloud. Her narrowed eyes surveyed the space, looking for anything out of place. 'Hmm.' She picked up a medicine bottle from the oak writing desk and put it in her pocket.

As much as she wanted to, Elizabeth couldn't ask Lady Witham about Mary. If she suspected any link between the two of them, she could have Elizabeth arrested too. It would be best to wait and see what information she could get from the rest of the family.

Lady Witham pushed past Elizabeth again and made her way into her own bedroom, slamming the door behind her.

Mr and Lady Witham had married almost twenty years ago and had never, since Elizabeth had known them, slept in the same room. They had eleven children, common enough among aristocratic families, but spent their time apart wherever possible.

Elizabeth knocked on Lady Witham's door, but heard no response. She paused before pushing open the door and found her sprawled across her bed, blankets kicked to the floor. A bottle of wine was open on her bedside table. Lady Witham was staring at the wall, ignoring Elizabeth. The fire had not been lit, and the room was cold and dark. The smell, far from the fresh breeze of her husband's chambers, was musty and stale. Not wishing to speak to her, Elizabeth placed the breakfast tray on the table. She grimaced at the odour of wine—Lady Witham must have spilled some nearby—and swiftly made her way back to the kitchen, closing the door behind her.

The young children had already had their breakfast taken to them, so now it was down to Elizabeth to tend to the two eldest daughters. Elizabeth had never really wanted to be a mother, but Mary was the opposite. She loved the Witham children almost as much as her own, and that was part of why she kept working here, despite Lady Witham's treatment of the servants. The stairs led first to Anne, sixteen years old, who was up early every day, just like her father. Elizabeth knocked three times but there was no response. Pushing the door open, she saw the girl sitting up in bed, her nose stuck in a book. Anne was a plain girl and Elizabeth thought she could do with a wash. Her face was dotted with spots and her limp hair fell in pieces down the sides of her face.

'Good morning, Miss Witham.'

'Hmm.' She called out in a half-response. Anne's bedroom was clean; she never denied the servants access, but there was a mess of books in piles next to her bed. Elizabeth had built a beautiful desk for Anne, at Sir William's instruction, this time last year.

'You should read at your desk.' She nodded towards the grand, hand-crafted dark oak desk. 'You don't want to hurt your back.'

'Mm-hm.' She turned the page, barely noticing Elizabeth.

'I'm sorry about your father.'

'Thank you,' Anne replied absent-mindedly. Elizabeth didn't know much about Anne's relationship with Sir William, but Anne tended not to show her emotions. This attitude didn't necessarily mean she was unaffected by his death.

Elizabeth tried again. 'Do you know how it happened?'

Anne closed her book with a finger inside, keeping her place. She narrowed her eyes, like her mother often did. 'Mother has had a servant arrested for his murder.' She paused, trying to read Elizabeth's expression. Anne was clever. 'Was she a friend of yours?'

Elizabeth bit her lip. 'She's an acquaintance, Miss Witham. That's all.' Her heartbeat quickened, but she had to take this chance. She needed to find out more. 'Do you think she's guilty?'

Anne sat up straighter in bed. 'Why do you care what I think?'

'I just wondered.' Elizabeth was normally so confident, but her voice faltered and gave her away. 'Do you think the courts will find her guilty?'

'Ah. So you are not asking what I think. You are wondering not about who committed the crime, but whom they will punish for it.'

Elizabeth did not respond; she kept her eyes on the ground.

Anne sighed, impatient. 'I apologise for my directness. It sounds like you two were close?'

'Yes, Miss.' She thought it best to keep her responses brief.

Anne narrowed her eyes. 'I see. Look, you should know that Mother does normally get her way. Besides, in a case like this, a woman of her standing is more likely to be believed than a servant.'

Elizabeth felt a lump in the back of her throat.

Anne explained further, 'as I understand it, there is not a great deal of physical evidence, so the courts will rely heavily on testimony.'

'What does that mean?'

'It means your friend doesn't stand a chance. Sorry.' She opened her book again and waved a hand in dismissal.

Elizabeth put her breakfast on the desk and headed out. She let out a deep breath. Could Anne be right? Would Lady Witham be able to convince the courts to believe her? Even without physical evidence?

Elizabeth took the last tray to Molly's bedroom. In a stark contrast to her sister, fourteen-year-old Mary Witham, known to her friends and family as Molly, was naturally pretty. She had a healthy, rounded face and was blessed with her father's strong jawline, which closely resembled Elizabeth's. Molly had a fair complexion but her frequent laughter gave her a redness in her cheeks that, other than today, never seemed to disappear. Elizabeth walked straight into her room, knowing she would still be fast asleep. She was lying flat on her back, with curlers in her hair. It was as if, even when asleep, she knew to keep her hair neat. She reminded Elizabeth of Agnes. When she awoke, a maid would bring her face to life with those bouncing dark brown curls of hers. Elizabeth put the tray down on the small wooden side table beside her bed. Daylight poked through the curtains, illuminating a tapestry that Molly must have hung on the wall recently. She had a keen eye for design. With a quiet moan, Molly stirred. 'Mm...'

'Good morning, Miss Witham.' Elizabeth left the bedroom door open. She was supposed to be a male servant, after all.

She yawned. 'Eli! It's so good to see you. What's for breakfast today?' She stretched her arms in the air and reached for the tray, pulling it onto her lap. A warm smile spread across her face, but her eyes were red. She had been crying.

'I believe this meat is new. The cooks have been curing a particular piece of pork for a while.' Elizabeth pointed at the pink piece on the edge of the metal dish. She had never eaten cured pork before, but had learned about various foods like this from her time in service. She would like to try them herself, but it would not be appropriate to ask Molly—even though they were close, she was still a servant.

Molly picked at the meat absent-mindedly.

'Are you quite well, Miss Witham?'

'It's nothing. I'm fine. I just miss Father.' Molly's voice cracked as she spoke, as if she were about to cry. Elizabeth didn't want to push her.

'I understand.' She didn't pretend to understand Molly's relationship with her father, but she could see she was upset and wanted to make her feel better. 'Your sister misses him too. You should talk to her.'

Molly scoffed. 'Anne has no interest in talking to me.'

'Well, you should talk to someone. It might make you feel better.'

She shook her head. 'I won't speak to Mother. And the other servants are all so tiresome.'

Elizabeth tried to smile back but her smile didn't reach her eyes. All she could think about was Mary, but she didn't know how to ask about her tactfully. She bit her lip.

Molly didn't seem to notice her awkwardness. 'Eli? May I ask you something?'

'Of course, Miss Witham.'

'Will that man be coming again?' She held the bedsheets around her chest and brought her knees up to kneel on them.

She was speaking of the visitor from the day before. Thomas something. Molly Witham had the unfortunate tendency to flirt with any young man she met. This visitor was an important man who lived at Cudworth, an estate near Ledston Hall. It was important to the Witham family that she not behave inappropriately.

'Miss Witham, eat your breakfast. It's good for you. And don't you have to catch up on your music studies today?' Elizabeth narrowed her eyes to appear stern.

'Oh, please tell me what you know. I promise I won't tell Mother.' Molly pushed her breakfast tray aside. She didn't seem to have any interest in eating right now.

'Miss, you know I mustn't.' Her mother, Lady Witham, worried about Molly's conduct around young men; she considered her too young for that sort of thing.

She looked up at her with wide eyes as Elizabeth sat on the edge of the bed. How could she say no? Now that her father had died, she needed something to distract her from the pain. She indulged her.

'None of this gets back to your mother. Do you hear me?'

She sat up straight and nodded forcefully.

'He told a servant that you were beautiful and he is going to think up an excuse to come and visit you again.'

Molly squealed with excitement. If it weren't for her swollen eyes and cheeks, nobody would have known how sad she was.

'Shh, be quiet, please, Miss Witham!' Elizabeth reached for the tray and put it back on Molly's lap. 'Now eat your breakfast.' Elizabeth made her way to the door.

'Wait—don't go. I can't stand being on my own at the moment.' Molly's eyes widened.

'Very well, Miss Witham. Why don't you take some time to eat and get dressed? I will send someone in to do your hair and when you are ready, I will come and join you on a walk.'

She smiled once more. Molly knew how to get what she wanted.

From outside the bedroom door, there came the sounds of the household getting ready for the day. The youngest Miss and Master Witham were in the nursery with the nursery maid, Alice. They were screaming and running around, making far too much noise for this time in the morning. Elizabeth sighed. Alice was terrible at controlling the Witham children, even after all these years. Most people found Alice difficult to talk to—her face made others uncomfortable—but children didn't treat her any differently, which was probably why she was a nursery maid.

Anne would continue to read in her bedroom for a few more hours, as she had recently completed her schooling, along with Molly. The other children would be in the schoolroom by now—

today's lessons would have already started. From here, the staircase and large hall were not visible, but Elizabeth could hear the servants making their way up and down the stairs, talking to each other and slamming doors. They knew they wouldn't get in trouble for anything today. Lady Witham would be in bed until afternoon, and Sir William was no longer in a position to scold them.

'Eli? Come in!' Molly called.

Elizabeth pushed open the door. 'You look lovely.'

'It's not too much, is it?' Molly twirled on the spot and her skirt flowed out into an upside-down tulip shape.

'Not at all, it's very respectful.' She wore all black, from her shoes to her dress to her cap. 'The dress suits you—it accentuates your waist.'

'Good. You know, you are very observant, for a man.' Molly winked at her.

Unsure how to respond, she cleared her throat. 'Here.' She offered her arm and Molly looped hers around it.

Elizabeth thought now might be a good time to ask about Mary. 'Miss Witham, I wonder—'

'Shh. Not here. Let's wait until we get outside to talk.' This would have been suspicious if it were anyone else, but Molly always seemed to have secrets to tell.

Elizabeth grinned. 'Of course.' She led them down the staircase and when they got to the front door, Elizabeth and the other footman opened the double doors for Molly.

'Thank you.' Molly was always polite. She linked arms with Elizabeth once more. Still she said nothing, until they reached a small corner of the gardens, away from prying eyes. She jumped up to sit on the stone wall that faced the large set of fountains. Her dark brown curls framed her face beautifully, though her normally pale complexion was still red and blotchy from crying.

She tapped the space next to her. 'Come up, join me.'

Elizabeth did so. 'These fountains are beautiful.'

'Oh yes. They're new—I worked with Father for weeks to get the shapes exactly right.' She pointed to one part of them. 'You see here, how each circle sits exactly on top of the next one up?'

Elizabeth nodded.

'As you go upwards, each circle halves in circumference, until you get to the top. That's what makes the cascading effect so powerful.'

They watched the flowing water for a while, listening to the whoosh as it cascaded down, only to be brought back up again.

Molly looked up at Elizabeth. 'I have a favour to ask of you.'

'Of course, what do you need?'

She reached into the pocket of one of her many skirts and pulled out a letter. 'I need you to get this to Mr Jobson.'

Elizabeth raised an eyebrow.

'And you cannot tell Mother.'

'Ah, I see.'

'Please, Eli. You're the only one I can trust here.'

She took the letter.

'Thank you! I can't wait to see what he says. He will reply, won't he? Do you think he likes me?' She scoffed. 'I sound so childish. Was I childish when I met him? Would he disapprove of me? I am younger than he is.'

'Please, Miss Witham. You are a beautiful young woman and from what I hear, you conducted yourself perfectly. I'm sure he will reply to you soon.'

'Oh, thank you so much! I owe you.'

'Not at all.'

'Oh, go on. Is there anything I can do for you? Everyone always needs something. What's going on with you?'

Elizabeth hesitated. 'No, no, it's fine. I'll be fine.'

'There is something, isn't there? Go on. Please. I need something to distract me from everything happening at home.'

She bit her lip.

'It's a woman, isn't it?'

Elizabeth blushed. Of course, Molly believed her to be a man. At least, if she suspected otherwise, she had never mentioned it. She paused before answering. 'Yes. It is to do with a woman.'

'Eli, tell me everything!'

'It's not good news. I'm afraid.'

Molly's face fell.

'I don't have anyone I can talk to. There's nobody I trust.'

'You can talk to me.' She tilted her head to the side reassuringly.

'I have a sort of... relationship with her. But something happened and I'm not sure what to do next.'

Molly squealed. 'Is it another servant? Does she work here?'

'I can't tell you that. All I can tell you is the situation has become complicated. She has had to go away; I don't know for how long.' Elizabeth's tone became higher and she spoke more quickly. 'This changes everything between us. The future we thought we could have is now impossible. We are not young, so there is no way out for us. We don't know anyone who can help. There is nothing we can do. Oh Miss Witham, I can't stand it.'

'Come here, come here.' She pulled Elizabeth into a hug and whispered in her ear. 'Is it Mary?'

Elizabeth's body went stiff.

'I knew it! I've seen your stolen looks in the corridors. You think you've hidden it well, but nothing gets past me.'

Elizabeth pulled away and got up. 'I shouldn't have said anything.'

'No, don't leave—you can trust me. Do you love her?'

'Yes.'

'Does she love you back?'

'Yes.' Elizabeth blushed.

Molly squealed. 'You're just like me, deep in love. It's not a crime, you know.'

'You don't understand. Yesterday, Mary was...'

'Arrested, I know.'

'You know?'

'Yes, yes. It was my wretched mother. I know full well she is responsible for the death of dear Father.'

Elizabeth let out a deep breath she hadn't realised she was holding. 'So you don't blame Mary?'

'Of course not. No. It was all Mother. Father was no saint, but he didn't deserve to be killed. And she's going to get away with it! She has known Sir Henry—the Justice of the Peace—for years. It was she who sent for him. I hear he gathered up a group of men to accompany him for the arrest, is it true?'

Elizabeth nodded grimly. 'It's true. They all came. I don't know how they found us; we were in the middle of the woods!'

'What rotten luck. They all hunt you see; I'm sure they can track somebody in the woods. But what happens now?' Molly got up and walked around the fountain, motioning for Elizabeth to follow her.

Elizabeth cleared her throat. She stood up and paced back and forth. 'Well, he said he's going to question her for three days. Is that allowed?'

She shrugged. 'I've heard worse than that. In London, Queen Elizabeth had Mary, Queen of Scots, imprisoned for nineteen years before having her beheaded. And she was her own cousin!'

'Nineteen years? Beheaded? Surely Mary's in no danger of that?'

'You never know. Especially when witchcraft is the charge. My advice is to find her, and run.'

Elizabeth sat on the edge of the fountain, dipping her finger-tips in the water. The trickling was louder now, so she had to speak up.

'Miss Witham, I have family here. I can't leave.'

She came to sit next to Elizabeth, fanning out her skirts and leaning backwards to rest on her hands.

'Eli, this is your choice. You must decide whether your love for Mary is true.'

'Real life isn't like stories. You're too romantic.'

She grinned. 'Probably. But you know I'm right.'

Elizabeth took a deep breath, choosing her words carefully. 'I love Mary more than anything. I'd do anything for her. Even if it means abandoning our home.'

8

HENRY – BESS

Bess crept along the side of the house—she wasn't sure whose house it was—until she got to a window. Hushed voices inside were just about audible because the window was open. She crouched underneath and listened as best she could.

'Your sister wouldn't understand,' said a deep voice.

'But she knows something's wrong. If I could just explain—'

Bess recognised the second voice. It was Agnes.

The man interrupted her, 'no. We agreed, this stays between us until we get married.'

Bess gasped.

Agnes raised her voice, 'Henry, please. She's so worried about Mother. She won't work, and she even made me quit my job. How am I supposed to go on with no money?'

'Shh,' he urged. 'Here, take this. I can take care of you. Trust me.'

Bess gritted her teeth. She didn't believe a word out of his mouth, but she didn't want Agnes to know she had followed her. She stayed hidden.

'I do.'

There was the sound of lips against lips, and Bess rolled her eyes. She couldn't understand why her sister hadn't told her about this man. If they really were going to get married, what was the need for secrecy?

'I trust you,' Agnes went on, 'but I don't want to keep hiding away like some kind of criminal. Once you've made them release Mother, promise me we can tell people about us?'

Bess put her head in her hands. How could Agnes be so foolish as to fall for the same Henry who had arrested their own mother?

'Of course,' he assured her. 'As soon as the suspicion surrounding your mother has gone, we will be free to get married.'

After a few more nauseating minutes of kissing, they said their goodbyes and Agnes left. Bess didn't have time to creep round to the back of the house so Agnes saw her.

Bess tried not to look so guilty, but it was no use. Agnes stormed past her toward their home. Bess ran after her and as soon as they were out of earshot of Henry's house Agnes shouted at her.

'You followed me! You don't trust me at all, do you?'

'I'm sorry. I was worried about you. And I was right to worry!'

Agnes shook her head, her curls bouncing as she walked, hiding her expression.

'Please talk to me. What do you think you're doing, getting engaged to the man who arrested Mother?'

'It's more complicated than that.' She bit her lip. 'And I'm sorry. I wanted to tell you, but I thought you might overreact. Like this, actually.'

Bess took a deep breath. 'I'm calm. I won't overreact. Explain it to me, because there must be something I'm not understanding.'

Agnes stopped in her path and looked her sister in the eye. 'I don't love him. I'm not actually planning to marry him.'

Bess frowned. 'But you said—'

'I know what I said. You should have trusted me. He's been working with Lady Witham—this plan to blame Mother, it's not new.'

Bess took her sister's arm, and they walked together.

Agnes continued, 'he thinks I'm utterly in love with him, so his guard is down. He tells me things he wouldn't tell anyone else, and I've been able to make him delay this plan for weeks.'

'What changed?'

'He says Lady Witham got impatient and went ahead without him. He couldn't tell her no, so he's arrested her, but it's only temporary. Once the three day legal limit has passed, he's going to tell Lady Witham he couldn't extract a confession and all this will be over.'

'Do you really believe that?'

'Well, I'll have to come up with a reason to break off the engagement, but that's all.'

'How do you know you can trust him?' Bess was wary of her sister's plan, but also impressed that she had come up with it by herself.

Agnes shrugged. 'I don't. But it's the best plan I've got.'

'What was all that talk about when Mother is released? Why did you keep asking him if he can tell people about you?'

They were walking alongside the river which Agnes looked over to before she answered. 'I'm not stupid. I know he doesn't want anyone to know about us. Not now, not ever.'

'But why...?'

'He keeps saying everything will change in three days, when he releases Mother. I'm not sure what he's got planned, but I know that's when it will happen.'

Bess's eyes widened. 'That's clever. Really, it's a good point. But what does he get out of this?'

Agnes looked at her sister as if she were stupid.

'Oh.'

'Look, I'm not like you. I want to get married one day. And for that you have to take risks.'

'Who says I don't want to get married?'

'Come on, if that's what you wanted, you would have married Matthew years ago.'

Bess bit her lip. She didn't want to admit that Agnes was right.

Once they caught sight of their hut, Elizabeth called out to them. 'Where have you been?'

The girls looked at each other quickly before Bess called out, 'nowhere.'

Agnes exhaled audibly and whispered, 'thanks.'

'Elizabeth,' Bess called, 'I have something to tell you.' She sped into a jog and when she was close enough she said, 'it's Mary. Matthew told me where they're keeping her.'

9

THE CURE – MARY

Mary lay on the cold, hard planks of wood that made up her bed in the lock-up. She was on her side, hugging her legs in a tucked-up position because they wouldn't fit lengthways. Mary wasn't even tall. Her arms were shaking from the cold. She hoped that Sir Henry wouldn't come back to get her soon. It was pitch black except for the slither of light coming under the door, but she couldn't fall asleep. Instead, she fell into a daydream, replaying the events that brought her to this place. She replayed her last day at work, the last day that all had been well. The day that everything had gone wrong.

Mary sighed and rubbed her forehead with the back of her hand. Her long black hair was tied up and tucked under her cap, but wisps fell down her face and restricted her vision. She pushed the stray hairs to the edge of her face. It was almost lunchtime, but she had been working since the early hours of the morning. Her woollen skirt weighed her down, and she had to lean against the wall for a quick rest.

She was glad to work at Ledston Hall. The family was kind, mostly, and the work of a housemaid was not too difficult, but the hours were long. For a woman of her age, it was becoming too much of a struggle.

She was dusting the parlour, which Thomas of Cudworth had visited the previous day. The solid oak furniture was beautiful.

The fireplace matched the table and bench. When lit, it was such a warm and cosy room, but they weren't expecting visitors today so there was no need for a fire. Anyway, the sunlight from the large glass windows shone on Mary's back. After sweeping the dust from the floor, she admired the hand-crafted wooden ornaments, crafted by Elizabeth. Mary hoped that when she had finished work, she might bump into her—there was time for them to sit down and have a drink together before their afternoon duties. She got to the top of the stairs and through Sir William's open door, saw that he was still in his bedroom. He noticed her looking and called over to her, not taking his eyes off the paperwork on his desk.

'If you have something to say, you'd better come in and say it.' There was a harsh edge to his voice that made Mary's blood run cold.

'Yes, sir.' She entered and gave him a small curtsey.

Although he was younger than Mary, he looked much older. He had a tall, imposing figure, obvious even from his seated position. He leaned back in his chair, so that the light coming from the window illuminated his strong, square jawline and mostly bald head. Other than his lack of hair, he was the spitting image of Elizabeth, though he was nothing like her in personality. Mary wouldn't want to get on his bad side.

'What is it?'

Mary cleared her throat. It was important that she spoke confidently. 'Sir, I wanted to ask, how is young William?'

He sighed and pushed his books aside. Despite Sir William's faults, nobody could claim that he didn't love his sons. He rubbed his temples and hesitated before answering. 'The same.'

'I've brought some medicine for him. Here.' She handed him the small glass bottle.

He turned it round in his hands. 'What am I supposed to do with this?'

'It will help him. These chest problems he's been having—this medicine will ease his symptoms and give him the best chance of recovery.'

Sir William narrowed his eyes and looked closely at her. 'You mixed this yourself?'

'Yes, sir.'

'You've mixed up some herbal remedy and expect me to trust it?'

'Please, sir, I'm a mother myself. He's only a child, and he's in such pain. I promise it will help. I've seen it.'

He shook his head. 'You know, there's a word for women like you.' He held the bottle out for her to take, but Mary stepped back.

'Whatever you think of me, I beg you to try it. It's called comfrey, and it's made by crushing the leaves of the plant and mixing them into a poultice.' Mary couldn't stand seeing a child so ill, especially when the condition was treatable. But people didn't always trust these sorts of remedies.

'He has been ill for a long time now. I suppose there's no harm in trying.' Sir William rubbed his right temple. 'You say you've used this before?'

Mary nodded. Technically speaking, only Mother Pannell had used it before, but she had taught Mary exactly how to make it so she was confident it would help him.

Sir William shrugged. 'How does it work?'

Mary breathed a sigh of relief. 'It's very simple. Rub it onto his chest every day for a week and you'll see an improvement.'

'Very well.'

Before Mary could say anything else, Sir William's bedroom door swung open and banged against the doorframe. Lady Witham stood there, a thin woman with hollow cheeks and dark circles under her eyes, forcing her eyebrows together in anger.

'What is she doing in here?' Lady Witham glared at Mary.

Mary kept her eyes on the floor. 'Sorry, ma'am, I just wanted—'

Sir William interrupted her. 'We need to give our son some medicine.' He held up the bottle. 'Why haven't you dealt with this? You're his mother, for goodness' sake.' He raised his voice again and grabbed his wife by the wrist.

Mary looked to the floor—it was probably best not to speak.

'Out. Out with you,' Sir William commanded.

Mary hurried out of the room. She didn't want to get involved in their argument. Maybe she should have gone to Lady Witham with the comfrey, but she didn't think she would have listened to her or trusted her to use it on William.

The shouting from his bedroom followed Mary as she ran over to the stairs to get on with her work. She should have kept going, but her curiosity betrayed her.

The loud crash of hand against cheek made Mary jump. She gasped. There was silence for a few seconds until Sir William shouted once more. 'Your behaviour is not good enough. This household is your responsibility, and I don't have time to organise everything for you.' Another crash sounded from their room, but this time it sounded like the smashing of a bottle. 'And stop drinking at all hours of the day.' The door slammed as he pushed Lady Witham into the hallway.

Mary ran down the stairs but she was not fast enough. When Lady Witham came out, she looked at Mary with a look of such hatred that Mary froze. Was she going to have her whipped? She had done it before. Mary stood, feet on different steps, her arms gripping the handrail behind her tightly.

Lady Witham staggered to the top of the staircase without breaking her harsh glare. Mary did not move. Lady Witham descended the stairs until the whiff of alcohol made Mary wince. She came up close. Her face was inches away from Mary's. It was flushed red, her temples throbbing. Quick, stale breaths engulfed Mary in a cloud of decay. Those black teeth, rotten from all that sugar she loved so much. She spoke in a whisper.

'Stay away from my husband.'

Mary said nothing. Her heart was racing. She nodded quickly.

'I know about you, you know.'

Mary's eyes widened.

'People talk.' There was something in her expression, even in her drunkenness, that told Mary she knew something. Mary's breaths were shallow and quick. What was she talking about? Elizabeth? No. How would she know? They were always so careful to hide their relationship. Mother Pannell then? Did she find the medicine? It was not proper to be mixing up remedies. Why would she deny her own son something that was sure to cure him? Her mind ran through all the possibilities. Did she still think she was Sir William's mistress? At least she could never prove this point.

She held her gaze. It was best not to respond. What was it Lady Witham suspected of Mary? The two women stayed still, urging the other to be the first to look away. Eventually Lady Witham gave up and staggered down the rest of the stairs.

Mary must have dozed off because she was pulled harshly out of her daydream when another cold, muddy bucket of water was thrown at her. She let out a cry and sat up straight. She wiped her eyes dry just in time to see the door of the lock-up slam shut again. Sir Henry laughed as he walked away.

10

GAOL: DAY TWO – ELIZABETH

When Elizabeth arrived, she looked up at St Mary's Church, over five hundred years old, and shivered, pulling her woollen cloak tightly around her. The church had brick walls and long oval stained-glass windows all around. At the west, there was a tower which could be seen for miles when it wasn't so foggy. Trees framed the church, but with no leaves, the scene looked eerie. Elizabeth hadn't attended a service in a long time, but as a servant, she wasn't expected to. The path she now found herself on led to an old stone wall. It was about the same height as Elizabeth, so she could just about see over the top, but Mary wouldn't have been able to. Further along the stone wall she saw the old pillory. The wooden posts, connected by a wooden panel with holes cut out for a head and wrists.

She had been here once before, almost thirty years ago. She could still see the look of shame on John's face as he was walked to the pillory. This punishment was designed to humiliate. He knew he had done wrong and was ashamed that the entire village now knew about it. Their friends and neighbours expected Mary, as his wife, to lead the charge against him, but she didn't have a taste for this sort of thing. Instead Alice, who would soon become nursery maid to the Witham children, took charge. She stood at the front of the crowd and shouted, 'Pelt him!'

A cheer arose from the crowd of women, where peddlers pushed through, offering rotten eggs and vegetables for a price. One woman bought a rotten egg, and before she threw it she spat on the ground, 'This is for all the men who indulge in filth!' John had a full head of hair, and the egg landed right on his head. A clump of yolk got tangled in his hair, while the rest dripped down his forehead and onto the ground below.

A group of older women were digging their long fingernails into the ground and throwing the damp mud at him. At this point Alice walked to a neighbouring field and stuck her hands straight into a cowpat. Cupping her hands in front of her, she walked back and chucked it in one swift movement at Mary's husband. 'Men like you make me sick. How many times? Since you got married in the house of God, how many times have you been to see your whore?'

John whimpered in the background. Mary and Elizabeth stood and watched him together. Elizabeth had no sympathy for John, but she didn't like to see Mary's life ripped open for the whole town to see. In fact, Elizabeth cared less about John's preference for prostitutes as she did his tendency to beat his wife. Apparently she was in the minority.

Alice antagonised the crowd. 'Pelt away!' She had never married or had children, possibly because of the extensive burns to her face. It was said that as a baby, her mother had become so sick of her that she threw her into the fire. She didn't die, but she ended up permanently disfigured, and those who were sceptical about the story of her mother assumed the devil was involved somehow. Either way, Alice had grown bitter and angry and spent days like this taking out her frustration on whomever she could. It was she who had found John with a prostitute and reported him to the authorities. Mary had begged her not to, but she paid no attention.

After his hour had passed, the Justice released John from the pillory, and Mary helped him home. Elizabeth offered her help which Mary gratefully accepted. John stumbled out of the pillory and stretched one arm around each of them. Since he had such a small build, they were able to get him back to the small house he shared with Mary, though it took them a long time. Mary stayed with him while Elizabeth ran over to Mother Pannell's hut. She brought her over to help Mary tend to John's wounds.

Elizabeth pushed the memory out of her mind. This was not the time. She had to focus on Mary.

Further along the church's tall stone wall was the lock-up. It was familiar—she had walked past it before, but never paid it any attention. The stone wall led to the rounded stone walls of the lock-up. A wide, dark wooden door was bolted shut, and the roof was a pointed spire, made of the same stone as the walls. It gradually narrowed up into a sharp point at the top. There were no windows. She took a deep breath.

'Mary?'

There was no answer. She banged on the door and raised her voice. 'Mary? It's me. Are you in there?'

A groan sounded from inside.

'Oh! I didn't mean to wake you, I'm sorry.'

She paused.

'Elizabeth?' She spoke in a whisper, her voice trembling.

'Yes. Yes, it's me. I'm here. I'm so sorry I didn't come last night. How are they treating you?'

Mary cleared her throat but still spoke in a whisper. 'I'm thirsty.'

'Have they given you anything to drink?'

No reply.

'Did they give you something to eat?'

Still nothing. There didn't seem to be anyone around, so Elizabeth couldn't ask them to release her early, and even if she could break down this door, it might attract attention and get her in even more trouble.

'Mary, please talk to me.'

'How much longer?'

The pain in her voice sent a shiver down Elizabeth's spine. 'You've been here for two days. It's only one more day. I know you can do it.'

She groaned.

'What is it like in there? Is it cold? Did you sleep last night?'

Mary said nothing.

'Mary, please. Talk to me.' Elizabeth sighed. Maybe it would help if she spoke first. 'I'm so sorry this happened. They'll question Lady Witham, I'll make sure.' It was all her doing. She had to tell Mary. 'She's responsible for this, I know it. Her daughters know it too. We are all here for you. Your brother loves you too. William will help however he can—he's covering for me at work today.' She paused briefly to think. Mary's parents died long ago. Her brother John had died as a child, and the only other relative was her sister Ellen, who had moved away when she married. Even if Ellen agreed to help, Elizabeth would not have the slightest idea where to find her. No, Mary had no other relatives. What about her own family? Elizabeth didn't know who her birth mother and father were, and she doubted that Mother Pannell could help. 'I'll find a way. I promise I will. Please get through this.' She paused but Mary did not respond. 'Mary, can you hear me?'

She murmured something Elizabeth could not make out. A pain formed in the pit of her stomach. She pushed it aside. Mary would be fine. She had to be.

11

THE WISE WOMAN – MARY

Still stuck in the lock-up, Mary kept flitting in and out of consciousness, weakened by hunger and thirst, unable to think clearly. Her mind flashed back to when she first put her faith in herbal remedies.

After Mary had healed the Witham boy with the milk thistle, she was grateful to Mother Pannell for her help. It was the first time she had saved somebody's life. Soon after the boy was born, his skin was yellow and so Mary gave him the milk thistle until he had fully recovered. It was a great feeling, of being useful to others in a way she had never been before. But it wasn't the first time she had used medicine to her advantage.

It was soon after the birth of her youngest daughter, when her husband's violence had been getting worse. Mary hurried along the Lin Dike, the river that ran past Mother Pannell's hut, until she found her sitting cross-legged on the riverbank. Her long white plaited hair was hanging down her back. 'Hello,' she said, without looking at Mary.

'I want to learn,' Mary said breathlessly. She didn't want to give away her true motives right away.

Mother Pannell offered a sideways smile. 'What do you mean?'

'You've got to teach me. Tell me more about your remedies. They really do work, don't they?'

She raised her eyebrows. 'Of course. But it's difficult. It will take time to learn.'

Mary sat on the damp grass next to her. 'Please. I need your help...' She trailed off.

'For what?'

Mary bit her lip.

'Very well. Since you're so eager, let's start with this.' She pulled out of her skirt pocket her black leather-bound book.

'Is that where you write your recipes?'

'Recipes?'

Mary corrected herself. 'I'm sorry, I meant—remedies.'

'Yes and no.' She opened the book to the beginning and showed Mary the page. It was a mess of scribbles. 'As you can see, it's not all written in English.'

Mother Pannell had an unusual accent and darker skin than most others in Kippax, but Mary had never asked her about her family or where she was from. 'Was it your mother's?'

She nodded. 'She left it to me when she died. It's the only thing I have left of my family.' She offered the book to Mary who flipped through the pages. Certain pages had a different shade of black ink scribbled on them.

'Are these notes you made on her remedies?'

'Yes, I've added translations here and there, or noted which plants aren't actually available in England.' She looked sideways at Mary and sighed. 'It's a shame you can't read.'

'I have an excellent memory,' Mary said. 'I promise.'

'Good.' She flipped through the pages until she came upon one filled from top to bottom with scribbles and diagrams. 'Ah, anaesthetics. Have you heard of them before?'

Mary shrugged.

Mother Pannell pointed to a drawing in the book of a small plant. 'This is hemlock. The white flowers and red-brown markings on the stem are unique—I'll show you where I grow it.' She pushed herself up to a standing position and Mary followed her to a patch of her garden with several small white flowers.

'What's it used for?' Mary asked.

She held up a hand. 'Slow down, my child. We'll get there.

Next, I'll show you some henbane.' Again she pointed to a drawing of a flower, this one with spikes on its leaves. 'Follow me.'

Mary repeated the words to herself, trying to lock them in her memory. 'Hemlock, henbane. Hemlock, henbane.'

'There it is. Henbane. You can identify it by its pale yellow, bell-shaped flowers combined with the purple veins.'

Mary reached out a hand to touch it but Mother Pannell pushed her hand away.

'Don't touch—only touch a plant if you're confident you know what it is.'

'Yes, of course. Sorry, Mother Pannell. Is it dangerous?'

'It can be. See the small hairs on the leaves? They'll stick to your skin, so make sure you wear gloves.'

Mary nodded. 'So hemlock and henbane are both types of'— she paused, trying to remember the word Mother Pannell had used—'anaesthetic?'

'Not quite. On their own they are essentially poison.'

Mary's eyes widened. She thought about her husband.

Mother Pannell went on, 'but they are also ingredients of the most common type of anaesthetic—dwale.'

Mary nodded.

Mother Pannell looked again into her book and ran her finger down the page. 'Some of these items you already know. This one depends on who needs the anaesthetic. If it's a man, you need the bile of a boar, or for a woman, that of a sow. Then hemlock juice, pape—ah, yes. You may know pape as the white poppy.'

'You mean opium?'

'That's it. Can you see it anywhere?'

Mary walked up and down the flowerbeds until she saw the white poppies. 'Here they are.'

'Well done,' said Mother Pannell. She walked over while reading down the page. 'Then we need some vinegar and wine. And I should mention something else, too.' She put the book back into her skirt pocket before continuing. 'I've travelled through many countries, and everyone seems to have a slightly different recipe for dwale.'

Mary nodded. She knew Mother Pannell and her family did a lot of travelling before they came to England.

'Around the Mediterranean, they add a plant called mandrake to dwale. It's a powerful root in the shape of a man. It's often used for fertility rituals or in childbirth and can be a powerful drug, but it doesn't grow in England.'

'Because of the climate?' Mary knew enough about plants to guess this.

'Exactly. But not everyone knows that. Bryony looks very similar to mandrake, but it's an English root, so you sometimes get tricksters selling it as mandrake. Even if they picked mandrake abroad and transported it over here, it would be as useless as bryony. Always use fresh ingredients.'

Mary nodded. She followed Mother Pannell into her hut. Not big enough for more than two adults to stand up in at once, they leaned over a pot to make the dwale. Bottles of herbal remedies took up most of the space inside, covering every inch of the benches that ran alongside the edges of the rectangular hut. Mother Pannell kept the floor covered in rushes to keep it fresh, but she kept some herbs on the ground too. She often got bugs inside. Mary would hate living here. She winced at the idea of cooking on a surface covered in mouse droppings. Mary liked to keep her own home tidy. She stored all food in closed containers, and in case of spillages, she soon replaced the rushes on the ground. After all, her bed of rushes was on ground level, and she didn't want rats climbing all over her at night. Mother Pannell was apparently less fussy. Mary glanced over to a pile of rushes at the edge of the hut, which must be where Mother Pannell slept, and next to it but closer to the ground was another mound that must be where Elizabeth slept. Mary wished Elizabeth were here with them, but surmised that she must be at work.

Mother Pannell first put into the large pot 3 spoonfuls of each of the fresh ingredients: hemlock juice, pape, henbane, vinegar and what she assured Mary was the bile of a boar. Into this she poured a great quantity of wine, before putting the pot over the fire to boil.

'Did your mother show you how to do this?' Mary asked.

'Oh no, I was very young when she died. I picked up bits and pieces on my travels, and some things I learned from my mother's book.' She sighed before adding, 'I suppose my aunts and cousins talked me through some of this before I got married. What's with all the questions?' She gave the pot a stir and sat next to Mary.

'Where are they now? Your family?' Mary was much more interested in learning about Mother Pannell than she was in waiting for the pot to boil.

She shrugged. 'I wouldn't know. I haven't seen them since I was about twelve years old.'

Mary frowned. 'Twelve? But I thought you said you spoke to them when you got married?'

She broke eye contact. 'Oh, right. Well, I suppose...' She trailed off.

'You got married at twelve?' Mary's mouth dropped open.

'That's quite enough questions for today!' She raised her voice.

'Sorry, I only meant—'

'I know what you meant. Look, my family is complicated. It's not worth talking about.'

'Elizabeth said when you took her in you didn't have any family at all.'

Mother Pannell sighed but didn't reply.

Mary shook her head. 'I don't understand. Your family arranged for you to get married while you were still a child, and then they just left you? Where did they go?'

'Mary! Stop asking so many questions. It's rude.'

She stood up. 'I'm sorry, I just wanted to know why your own family would—'

Mother Pannell rubbed her temples, and when she spoke her voice was gentle. 'They didn't have a choice.'

'You mean someone forced them to leave you?'

She took a deep breath. 'They called us Egyptians. Gypsies. I don't know why they called us that—I've never been to Egypt, so it never made sense to me. Anyway, it wasn't abnormal for us to marry so young, but the plan was for me to stay with my family for a few years before I moved in with my husband. And that's exactly what we did—for a few months.'

Mary tried to match the soft tone of her voice and said, 'what happened then?'

Mother Pannell sniffed, fighting back tears. 'The King passed the Egyptians Act. My whole family had to leave the country, had to leave me. I was alone, married to an old man whom I barely even knew.'

Mary stared at her, lost for words.

Mother Pannell cleared her throat. 'Anyway, what's done is done. Just don't go telling the whole town my business. Especially not Elizabeth.'

Mary argued, 'but Elizabeth loves you. Why can't you just say—'

'I said no. Elizabeth is all I have. She may not be interested in these herbal remedies, and I'm happy to share them with you, but she's my daughter. She's my only daughter, and she has been since the day I took her in as a baby. I won't have you telling her all sorts of things about me. It's my business and my right to keep it quiet. Don't make me regret having you over.'

Mary nodded quickly. She didn't want to appear ungrateful. 'Of course. I'm sorry. Thank you for everything you've taught me so far. I won't mention anything to anyone.'

'Good.' She glanced into the pot and nodded. 'Now that it's been boiling for a couple of minutes, we can pour the mixture into small glass bottles and seal each one with a cork. This will keep them fresh, and we only need to use a small dose at a time. I'll label each so that I know what they are.'

12

GAOL: DAY THREE – MARY

S omebody was shaking Mary by the shoulders, slapping her across the cheek. She blinked her eyes open and immediately regretted it. Daylight was streaming in through the open gaol door and for a moment Mary wondered if Elizabeth had come to get her.

'Witch,' Sir Henry spat at her.

Mary knew it was the last day they could keep her for, but a whole day seemed impossibly long and she doubted she would last until evening.

Someone threw an ice-cold bucket of water over her. She let out a yelp. Sir Henry and the two men beside him laughed. It was a croaky, wicked laugh that came from deep in their throat.

'Grab her.' Sir Henry commanded.

They took her by the shoulders and led her once again through the muddy fields to that awful barn. She tried to walk, but the tiredness was so bad that she didn't have the energy. Instead, they dragged her along, and without her shoes this meant they were scraping her feet along rocks, through the wet mud and cow pats. Her mind was foggy so that part of her wasn't even sure this was real. Why would people treat her this way?

'Throw her on the ground there.' The deep voice of the man she had come to hate was enough to convince her that Sir Henry was really here.

They did as he commanded, and she felt the cold, hard spikes of a piece of farm machinery digging into her back. She rubbed her lower back, only to find it wet with blood—it had cut her. The men saw the blood but just laughed, again. Mary turned around and with horror realised that this wasn't a piece of farm machinery at all; it was some kind of torture device. She gulped.

Over the past two days in this barn she had been punched, kicked, stripped and pricked. They called her names and took her dignity, laughing at her pathetic naked body. When she had asked for food and water, they said that a woman as fat as she was could do with being starved. In fact, they were doing her a favour, they said. But all of this was nothing compared to today.

Mary looked at the men from her position, curled up on the floor, bleeding and sweating, wearing only her underdress.

'Today is the third day we've had you here.' Sir Henry began.

Mary didn't respond.

'If you've reached day three without confessing, we have to step up. Do you understand that?' His voice had a sarcastic, high-pitched tone that made Mary scowl.

'It's not something we want to do, but we have to do this until you confess. At any time today if you would like us to stop, all you have to do is confess. Would you like to confess?'

Mary was sick of that word. 'Confess'. Why would she confess to something she hadn't done?

One of the men whispered something to Sir Henry.

'Yes, I'm getting to it. Light that fire,' he commanded. Then, turning back to her, he said, 'to summarise our results so far: we have, in evidence, the body of a man whom you poisoned and killed; we have the first-hand account of Lady Witham; we have even found a witch's teat on your person.'

Mary furrowed her eyebrows.

'You have nothing by way of response?' Sir Henry stroked his chin in a way that made him seem bored. 'Nothing to confess, even in light of all the evidence?'

'The evidence?' Mary kneeled up and looked him right in the eye. 'You know as well as I do, none of that is solid evidence.'

He smirked. 'I assure you, people have been hanged for less.'

MELISSA MANNERS

'You have nothing against me.' Mary felt suddenly confident, defiant. If he was trying this hard to extract a confession from her, did that mean that she had all the power here? Perhaps she had been thinking about this all wrong. If she could just get through today, this would all be over.

Sir Henry nodded to one of his men who kicked her back down onto the ground, where she stayed, eyes fixed on the barn door. She just had to survive the day without confessing. Just one more day.

He motioned towards the spikes that had cut into her back. 'Do you know what this is?'

Mary turned to inspect the object. It looked like a chair, made of metal and covered in razor-sharp spikes.

Sir Henry pushed her out of his way and pulled the chair upright. 'We haven't used this for years.' He rubbed his chin, as if recalling a fond memory. Mary felt sick. 'Here, let me explain. Do you see this compartment?' He pointed to the space below the seat of the chair. 'We light a fire here. As the chair is made from metal, it's great at spreading the heat around. You sit in the chair, the spikes digging into you, and wait for the fire to roast you, slowly, to death. Like a sort of chicken!' He laughed.

Mary couldn't help but imagine the horror that people had gone through when sitting on this very iron chair.

'Oh, you don't need to worry. We tend to use this on the relatives of the accused. It's hard to predict when death will come, and we wouldn't want the accused to die before trial. In your case, I suppose we would put your youngest daughter in the chair and make you watch.'

Mary ran at him and screamed, 'don't you touch her!' but his men restrained her before she could reach him.

'Agnes, isn't it?'

Mary screamed.

'I've seen her around town. Pretty girl. It would be a shame if she got hurt just because her mother refused to confess.'

'Leave her out of this.'

'I would enjoy having a young girl in here for once. If she were in here instead of you...' He trailed off, getting lost in the thought.

'I swear to God, if you ever touch her I'll kill you.'

He laughed, and so did his men. 'You? You will kill me? Of course you will.'

She scowled. He enjoyed getting a reaction off her, she knew that, but it wasn't easy for her to hold back. Her daughters didn't deserve this. She would do anything if it meant they would leave her daughters alone.

'They say witchcraft is passed down the female line. Perhaps both of your daughters are witches, just like you.'

Her voice cracked as she said, 'Please. Don't hurt them.'

'No matter—it's you Lady Witham wants the confession from.' The side of his mouth curved up into a wicked smile. 'Saying that, if you were to confess, we would have cause to arrest both of your daughters too. I am certainly excited at the prospect of having those young, pretty girls in here instead of you.'

Mary tried to regulate her breathing, to calm down. As long as she stuck out this day, her daughters would be safe. If they couldn't make her confess, Bess and Agnes would be safe. A thought flashed through her mind—if they arrested her again, would she be able to hold out for another three days? She shook it off. There was no time to think of that now. She was so tired it felt like they could make her say anything. But no. It was her daughters' safety at stake. She would have to hold out.

Sir Henry waited for her to respond, then shrugged. 'I'm afraid you leave me no choice then. Let's see what we have here for you.'

His two men had sick smiles plastered on their faces. They were both large men with bald heads and ears that jutted out. Mary thought they were probably brothers. One of them had a sliver of dribble down his chin. He was so excited at the prospect of torturing Mary that he hadn't noticed.

'It's illegal,' Mary muttered.

'What did you say?' Sir Henry shouted at her. In her tired state the shock of him shouting was as bad as if he had slapped her.

'Torture. Using any of these devices is illegal.'

He motioned to the others, 'did you hear that? It's illegal, she says.'

They paused and laughed, unsure if he was serious.

He went on, 'what are you planning to do about it? Report us? Who's going to believe you over us?'

A flicker of recognition passed over the brothers' faces—they understood now that he was being sarcastic.

Mary had heard that this sort of thing went on around the country, but she never thought it would happen to her.

'Where were we? Ah, yes. See here, these two are great. First, we have the Duke of Exeter's Daughter, and next to it the Scavenger's Daughter.'

Mary looked at the wooden racks in front of her. Cobwebs covered them, as if they hadn't been used in a long time. She had never heard of anyone being tortured on these devices, so it must have been a long time ago. News in Kippax spread fast.

'I don't think we'll be using these today either. Too much obvious damage.' He waved dismissively at them. 'The first one stretches you, the second compresses you. In the end you can't really use your hands or legs for anything. It makes it difficult to hide what we've done.'

Mary was relieved. She couldn't imagine the pain if they were to stretch or compress her body. How would she live if she couldn't walk? She wouldn't be able to work, and she doubted Elizabeth could support them both. Her heart dropped as the thought of Elizabeth crossed her mind. Would she ever be able to tell Elizabeth what they had done to her in here? No. She didn't want to. She didn't need pity, and she knew Elizabeth would feel guilty if anyone had hurt her. She always wanted to protect Mary, so knowing that she had been tortured would be too much to handle.

'Here.' Sir Henry walked over to the corner of the barn and gestured to a pair of small metal devices.

Mary hoped they wouldn't be as painful as the iron chair and the rack. As they were so much smaller, maybe the injuries would be easier to hide from Elizabeth. It also meant that they might hurt less, and make her less likely to confess. That was the most important thing. She blinked hard and told herself firmly. Do not confess. Whatever happens today, do not confess. The lives of Bess and Agnes depend on it.

'Don't worry, I'll talk you through it before we use anything on you—we're not monsters!' Again, he laughed. He sat down on a hay bale so that he was on the same level as Mary, now kneeling on the ground. He picked up a pronged instrument. 'Have you ever seen one of these?' His voice was gentle, as if he were trying to soothe a baby.

The thought was preposterous. Even in her current state, Mary knew what he was doing. He wanted her to trust him, to feel as though she could share things with him. He was trying to make it seem like Mary was the driving force here. Like she was the one forcing his hand, because if she only confessed, it would all be over. Mary shook her head hard. She was determined not to let him break her. She could handle whatever he would do to her, as long as her girls were safe.

'They call this the Breast Ripper.'

Mary's eyes widened, but she tried not to respond, not to give away how terrified she was feeling. Her teeth were chattering, so she opened her mouth slightly—that way he wouldn't hear, and hopefully wouldn't notice. The iron instrument had two large pointed prongs on each side, which he held over the fire while Mary tried not to think of what was about to happen.

'Hold her,' he commanded the brothers suddenly.

It was as if they had rehearsed this. One of them ran at her and pushed her back against the wall of the barn, keeping his body pressed against hers. He was kneeling down so that his head pressed her belly against the wall. His brother had also run at her, but he was holding one hand around her neck and the other on her arm. They were pressing her whole body firmly against the wall of the barn, except her right arm.

Sir Henry smirked, glad to have surprised her.

She tried to speak, but the hand on her throat meant she could barely breathe. Speaking was out of the question.

'Before I show you how this works, have you anything to confess?'

Although she couldn't answer him, she stared at him, defiant, and he understood her meaning. He spun around, holding the instrument with both hands, and used the force of the turn to dig the prongs into her right arm.

Mary screamed. Then she berated herself. She wasn't supposed to react. Calm down, she told herself. Calm down, calm down. Don't let them see you're scared.

Blood spurted from her veins but she couldn't apply any pressure to the wound. The men still pressed her body against the wall, one of them keeping his face so close to hers she could smell his stale breath.

The pain was intense. She wanted to scream again. Her heart was racing. She bit down hard on her lip to stifle her groans.

'I think I've proved my point.'

Her blood covered his face, but he smirked and his white teeth shone through, his teeth and eyes the only parts of his face that weren't bright red.

Mary repeated to herself again and again: calm down, calm down, calm down. She had to get through this. For her daughters' sake.

'Do you confess?'

Again she stared at the whites of his eyes but made no effort to speak.

He nodded to the man holding her throat, and he moved this hand to Mary's right arm. Sir Henry then ripped open her underdress to expose her breasts. Mary felt like she was going to be sick.

He pushed the device into her chest. She screamed again, but this time it came out as a groan, as her teeth were dug into her lip so much that it was bleeding. So much blood. There was that metallic smell you get around large quantities of blood that made Mary gag. Surely they would let her go soon? She lowered her eyes to see how much damage there was. The wounds on her chest looked shallow, but they could dig in deeper at any moment. Mary held her breath.

He nodded to the brothers, and she let out a sigh of relief. Finally, the day was over. As quickly as she could she ripped some lengths off her dress. It was easy enough as there were so many rips in it already. She wrapped one piece around the gash in her arm. It was difficult to do one-handed, especially with her left hand, but she managed to knot it tightly. She took another two pieces and wrapped them around her, where the prongs had ripped into her breasts.

Sir Henry took a handkerchief from his pocket and wiped the instrument clean. The men stared at him eagerly. A knot formed in Mary's throat. They weren't finished. Worse than that, this was only the beginning. They were excited because the next instrument was what they had been waiting for. They whispered into Sir Henry's ears, one from either side. If the situation were different, it would have been almost comic. Sir Henry was the tall, slim master of the house, and the two bald, fat men were his ignorant but cruel servants, unable to come up with any ideas themselves, but both eager to do as they were commanded. Mary steeled herself, repeating another mantra: I'm ready, I'm ready, I'm ready.

But she couldn't have prepared herself for this.

Sir Henry pushed the men aside and picked up another metal device. 'The Pear of Anguish,' he announced, unable to wipe the grin off his face.

Mary was no longer restrained, but she backed away into the wall again. She looked at the shape of the Pear of Anguish and a thought crossed her mind. No, it couldn't be. Nobody would do that. She shook off the thought.

'Lucky you're too old to want any more children,' he smirked.

Mary swallowed and pressed her palms firmly on the wall behind her, as if she thought she could press hard enough to make the wall fall down and allow her to escape. Her underdress had been completely ripped off the upper part of Mary's body, and it now hung around her waist. The makeshift bandages covered her breasts, so she had at least a degree of modesty, but Sir Henry nodded at one of the men, who rushed at her and ripped the last piece of her dress from her body. They laughed. Mary had no modesty left. She stood against the wall, naked but for the bandages.

The other brother pushed her onto the ground and for a moment Mary thought he was going to lie with her; maybe they all were. He straddled her and looked her in the eye. As stupid as he was, he could see what she was afraid would happen. He winked at her. 'Not today. You're too old for my taste.'

Mary gulped. What were they going to do to her?

He shuffled his sweaty, heavy body upwards so that he was sitting on her chest. It was sore, having him press on her wounds, but she knew medicine. She knew that really, this was a good thing. Pressure on the wound meant the blood would clot, and she might not bleed to death. Again, she repeated a mantra to herself: I'll be fine, I'll be fine, I'll be fine.

Sir Henry stood directly over her, holding the Pear of Anguish. 'This is the last instrument for today. Do you want me to show you how it works? You won't be able to see while it's in action, after all.'

Mary's heart felt like it was going to beat out of her chest. Despite feeling faint, tired, and in pain, she was sure that she would get through this. She stared at him, that look that was understood between them to mean she was not going to confess.

He pointed at the four petal-shaped segments of the long metal instrument. 'You see these? When I turn the corkscrew lever at the other end, these petals open up inside you. It will destroy your insides, but you will live to feel the pain.'

Her breaths were quick and shallow. She repeated her last mantra of the day in her mind: it's nearly over, nearly over, nearly over.

He raised his eyebrows. 'Let us know if you want to confess at any time.'

Kneeling down at her feet, he prised her legs apart and pushed the device into her.

13

DEATH – ELIZABETH

E lizabeth lined up to report to William. She took a deep breath. Now that she had seen where they were keeping her, all she could think about was Mary. She could see it in his eyes too. He was worried for his sister. She longed to ask him if he had heard anything, but with the other servants around it was not possible. He half-heartedly inspected the uniforms of the footmen, pacing and looking them up and down. Elizabeth had roughly tucked her mouse-brown hair into her collar, not hiding her gender very well. William had no comments and simply nodded to them to collect the breakfast trays from the kitchen.

The Head Cook ignored them, focusing instead on the kitchen maids. Elizabeth had never taken to the art of cooking. She could bake soggy, heavy bread and not much else. She was happy to clean and scrub if she had to, but as a footman, conveying dishes and laying tables was less strenuous and better paid.

She climbed the stairs, today tasked with taking the food to the children. The eldest boy, Henry, named for his grandfather, was only twelve. He was nothing like his father and just as arrogant as if he were the man of the house. Elizabeth shivered at the thought that now, technically, he was. She knocked three times.

'Yes?'

Pushing open the door, she saw the young boy dressed in a

sharp, clean jacket and pressed trousers. He was standing at the edge of his bed admiring himself in a handheld looking glass.

'Your breakfast, sir.' She bowed her head, and he gestured to the bed to signal that she should place the tray there.

He was attempting, without success, to fasten his tie. 'Help me with this. It's important that I look my best today.'

Elizabeth tied it for him slowly, so that he might learn how to do it himself. He did not trouble himself to watch. 'Such a shame about Father.'

Elizabeth nodded.

'I suppose I am your employer now.' There was no sign that he had been crying, no sign of sadness at the loss of his father.

'Yes, sir.'

'What do you suppose my father used to do in the mornings?'

'Sir, as I understand, your father used the mornings to catch up on his correspondence.'

'Yes, of course. Have someone fetch it for me, I shall have to take care of it myself.'

'Sir, I believe it has been taken care of.'

'Excuse me?'

'An associate of your father was sent for last night. He arrived in the early hours and has been sorting through your father's things.'

'Oh. Well then. Send him to me.'

'Yes, sir.'

Next, Elizabeth delivered breakfast to eleven-year-old Gertrude, eight-year-old Edward and seven-year-old Thomas. All three of them were still asleep, so she left their trays in their rooms. Their fires had been lit so they would wake up warm. Without Mary here, Elizabeth didn't know who was in charge of lighting the fires anymore. She held back tears. It wasn't right, Mary being arrested, and Elizabeth would do whatever it took to save her.

The youngest children squealed from the nursery. Five-year-old William and three-year-old Ellen were named after their mother and father. It was as if they had known these would be their last children. The nursery maid, Alice, was trying to calm down Ellen, who seemed content running in circles around the room. It wasn't exactly a run, but the waddle of a toddler who hadn't yet mastered walking. William, in contrast, lay in his bed, his chesty cough somehow much too loud for his tiny body. Elizabeth poked her head round the door, and the sight saddened her. He was pale and very skinny. He had not been eating. Mary had been worried about him for a long time. Elizabeth had no knowledge of illnesses so could not help. She brought the breakfast trays inside and put Ellen's on the table next to the door.

Alice nodded at Elizabeth but said nothing. She was now combing Ellen's hair as she sat in front of her on the floor. 'Ouch!'

'Shh, Miss Witham.'

'Stop it! It hurts.'

She continued to comb her hair, even more roughly, it seemed to Elizabeth. 'Be brave. A girl should have tidy hair.'

Elizabeth turned away and as subtly as she could, licked a finger and scraped back the strands of her own hair that had become loose.

Ellen continued to moan and groan, fidgeting and trying to push away the comb.

In the meantime, Elizabeth walked over to William and sat on the edge of his bed, the breakfast tray on her lap. 'Good morning, Master Witham.' She wasn't much good with children, but he was a sweet boy and needed to eat.

He looked up at her in response with his wide, blue eyes and let out a wet, chesty cough.

'I hope you slept well last night?'

He gave a slight shake of his head.

'Oh dear. Well, what I want from you is to eat up your breakfast. Can you do that?'

No response this time. She tore off a piece of bread and placed it in his mouth. He chewed gently, so she gave him another piece.

'Well done, Master Witham. You will be better in no time.' He coughed again.

Alice addressed Elizabeth. 'I'll be taking Miss Witham for a walk in the grounds. You're to stay with the boy until I return.'

With that, she took Ellen's hand, grabbed the plate of bread and cheese Elizabeth had brought for the girl, and walked out.

Elizabeth was glad of the rest. She hummed a tune that Mother Pannell used to sing to her as a girl, and it seemed to soothe William. She exhaled in relief, for there was not much she could do for him.

'What is that racket?' Lady Witham, dressed all in black from head to toe, entered the room. She held a small bottle.

Elizabeth stood, hands behind her back and looking down. 'Sorry, Lady Witham. He can't stop coughing.'

'Yes. I can hear him. Where is Alice?' Her voice was hoarse. She had been drinking again.

'Taking Miss Witham for a walk. They just went to the gardens, but I'm sure they'll be back shortly.'

'How is my William today?' She shoved Elizabeth aside and lowered herself onto the same spot of the bed Elizabeth had occupied moments ago.

'Better. He took some bread just now, ma'am.' He coughed, looking at the two women, aware they were talking about him.

'Good.' She stroked his cheek. 'We need you to get better, don't we, William?' He let out a gentle moan in response.

Lady Witham took the cork from the glass bottle in her hand and gave it to Elizabeth to hold. 'Eli, is it?'

'Yes, ma'am.'

'Hold that for me.' With one hand, she angled the bottle and with the other she opened her son's mouth, so that the viscous liquid ran down the back of his throat. He coughed violently and his mother rolled him onto his side. 'There, there.' She rubbed his back until his coughs subsided.

Elizabeth was pleased Lady Witham had obtained medicine for the boy.

'Eli, I have some things to attend to about the house. When Alice returns, you may leave.'

With that, she swept out of the room, taking the stale alcoholic odour with her. Despite her mourning attire, she did not seem like a sorrowful widow. In fact, she seemed no different from usual. Had she even cried over her husband's death?

Elizabeth sat back down on the bed and stroked the boy's hair. He smiled weakly but began coughing again. She rolled him onto his side once more. These coughs were louder than before. Elizabeth grabbed a piece of cloth and held it at the boy's mouth while he coughed. It was marked with bright red blood, being ejected from the boy at an alarming rate. She had seen this before. A woman who had come to Mother Pannell's. The woman had not survived. Mary would know what to do, but she wasn't here.

'You'll be fine.' To keep her voice steady, she tried to breathe deeply. She didn't want to scare Master Witham.

He was silent. Elizabeth's heart was racing. What should she do? Her breathing was becoming uncontrollable. Breathing! That's it. She held a hand over his mouth to check his breathing. Nothing. She screamed. Grabbing his shoulders, she shook him hard.

'Master Witham? William? Wake up!' Nothing.

Footsteps sounded in the corridor behind her, and she jumped up, hurrying out of the room. Alice told Ellen to wait behind her as she went to investigate. She had heard Elizabeth's scream.

Elizabeth spoke quickly. 'It's Master Witham. He's not breathing. It's the sickness, it's taken him.' She had never felt the small, lifeless body of a child before. She hoped she never would again. Lady Witham would be devastated. Elizabeth shook her head. No, she would be angry and looking for someone to blame.

14

TORTURE – ELIZABETH

Elizabeth's feet squelched in the wet mud as she hurried to Mother Pannell's house—in her hurry she had left behind her pattens.

Mother Pannell called to her. 'Elizabeth! Get in here.'

She did as she was told. Mother Pannell must have been outside too—her long white plait dripped water down her back and her dress was damp. But she only concerned herself with her daughter.

'You are shivering, my child!' She touched her cheek with the back of her hand. 'Off with your wet things. Here, put these on.' She handed her a pile of clean clothes. 'Oh, Elizabeth, you've ruined your boots!'

'Yes, Mother. Sorry, Mother.' She stood next to the fire to undress. Elizabeth pulled off her cap and leaned forward, tipping her head upside down. She shook her head, her hair flowing free and spraying water all over the hut. The drumming of the rain from outside still meant that her mother had to raise her voice to be heard.

'Will you stop that?' Mother Pannell tutted. She was on her hands and knees, spreading out the muddy straw among the clean straw instead of replacing it. 'How was work today?'

Elizabeth didn't answer. She threw her waistcoat and shirt on the floor and pulled a clean, cotton underdress over her head.

Mother Pannell narrowed her eyes but busied herself rear-ranging her bottles of herbs. 'Has something happened?'

Elizabeth kicked off her boots one at a time and peeled her soaked trousers off her legs. She ran her hands up each leg, against the direction of the hair growth, trying to dry herself off. Her feet were all wrinkled from the damp that had seeped into her shoes. It felt good to be inside, finally. 'Yes.'

'Is it about Sir William?'

'No.' Elizabeth shook her head, confused. 'What about him? He's dead.'

Mother Pannell looked away quickly. She scribbled something on a label and tied it around the neck of a bottle, before putting it back on the shelf. 'Nothing. Tell me what's wrong.'

Elizabeth sighed. 'Yes, Mother.' She pulled a cloak around her shoulders and gestured to Mother Pannell to comb her hair. 'Before I do, may I ask you a question?'

'Of course. Here, sit down.' She pulled the wooden bench away from the wall.

Elizabeth sat down. 'What if they find Mary guilty?'

'Look, talk of witches has been growing for a long time. Especially around here. If Mary gets convicted, she should get out of Kippax at the first opportunity.'

'But where could we go?'

'We?'

Elizabeth nodded. 'I won't leave her.' She stared at her mother, determined.

'If it did ever come to that, I wouldn't want you running off without a plan.' She took a deep breath. 'My family left me, once. It almost killed me. I want you to promise me if you leave town with Mary that she'll love you like family.'

'She will. She does.'

Mother Pannell hesitated before adding, 'you have a relative in London—a cousin of your father.'

She frowned. If this were true, why didn't she already know about it? Elizabeth knew very well how she had come to be adopted by Mother Pannell—a young pregnant woman had come to her, alone, and died in childbirth. She hadn't been accompanied by any husband, and no man had ever come looking for her. She repeated the words, 'my father?'

'Please don't ask me anything else. All I know is that your father was related to James Chapman, some sort of gentleman living in London.'

'He was a Chapman? But then—' Elizabeth's mind raced. Mary used to work for the Chapmans—she knew the family well. Could it be that she had family right here, in Kippax?

'That's enough.' She continued to comb her hair, standing behind the bench, with more force than before. 'Besides, you don't need to be thinking about any of this. They might not convict Mary.'

'What if they do?'

Mother Pannell shrugged. 'It's unlikely. These accusations get thrown around, but I haven't heard of anyone being found guilty of witchcraft in a long time.'

'But you have heard of it happening?'

She put down the hairbrush and sat next to her daughter. 'Do you really want to know about this?'

Elizabeth nodded.

'I don't know much—I've never seen it happen in England, and what I saw was a long time ago.' Mother Pannell sat down on a pile of rushes next to the fire. She motioned for Elizabeth to join her. Just like in her own hut, Elizabeth liked it here, as long as the fire was lit. When the fire went out, it became the coldest part of the hut, right under the gap in the thatched roof. 'My child, I love you. You know that, don't you?'

'Yes, Mother.'

'If they find Mary guilty of murder by witchcraft, they will hang her and burn her body.'

Elizabeth gulped. Nobody around here had been hanged in a long time, but the penalty for sorcery was well known.

'But as you know, that is not the worst part. The worst part is the questioning, when they try to extract a confession and get the names of any accomplices.'

Elizabeth's eyes widened. 'That's where she is now.'

'Well, this is only the first time they've arrested her. They will go through the standard questions, see if she breaks easily.' Mother Pannell reached for a dish of nuts, took a handful and offered them to Elizabeth.

'I'm not hungry. How do you mean?'

'Well, one of the best ways to break someone's spirit is to deprive them of sleep. They probably aren't letting her sleep while she's in the lock-up.'

Elizabeth thought of Mary, locked in that place for three days, unable even to sleep. 'How could they stop her from sleeping?'

'There are various methods. Let's not go through them all now.' She sighed, wearied by this conversation. She chewed the nuts with her mouth open.

'What else?' Elizabeth knew she could not stop this, but felt it was her duty at least to find out what Mary was going through. She pulled her legs into a cross-legged position, keeping them close to the fire to stay warm.

'Well at this stage, probably not much. There may be some minor physical violence. The worst comes later. The second, third time they arrest her.' She reached for a cup and took a large gulp. 'Once they have more evidence that she is a witch, they are much more comfortable doing what they like to her. They bring out all their instruments.'

'Instruments?'

'Yes.' She took another sip.

'They need to use instruments to extract a confession. Witches are not just anyone; they say they are in league with the devil. They will not confess without a push.'

Elizabeth scoffed. 'Mary is not in league with the devil! None of this sounds true. How could you possibly know all this, anyway?' She knew her mother had travelled a lot before her family had left her in England, but it wasn't something they talked about.

She reached over to her bed of rushes and pulled out an old leather-bound book from underneath. It was bursting at the seams and filled with loose sheets of paper. 'I want you to have this. It was my mother's.'

Elizabeth turned it over in her hands and squinted at the first page. 'Is this English?'

Mother Pannell nodded. 'Excuse her handwriting—English wasn't her first language. She begins with some simple recipes, herbal remedies and her drawings of plants have been very useful over the years.' She flicked through the pages, pointed at the flowers, leaves and roots that filled the middle of the book.

'This is your hand,' Elizabeth said.

'Yes, since she gave it to me on my wedding day, I've added bits and pieces.' She pointed to a drawing of a root that resembled a fat, naked man. 'This is mandrake root. It's a powerful anaesthetist and fertility symbol, but it doesn't grow here. I've added a note as a warning that the English bryony root which resembles it is no substitute for the real thing.'

Elizabeth was grateful for the gift, but truthfully Mary was the one who could make use of it. 'Thank you,' she muttered.

'Here is what I wanted to show you.' She flicked to the end of the book and ran her finger down some of the loose pages. 'These are my mother's diary entries for those times we came across witches on our travels.'

Elizabeth eagerly scanned the page. 'Why did she keep this?'

Mother Pannell raised her eyebrows. 'We were a foreign family known for our use of medicines. She wanted to warn me exactly what could happen if I were ever arrested.'

'Were you ever arrested?'

'Let's not talk about me. Do you want to know what we saw?'

Elizabeth widened her eyes.

The crackling of the fire seemed ominous in a way it hadn't before. She held a loose piece of paper up to the window so that she could read it properly. 'They say that witches have sexual relations with the devil. A witch will let him, or a familiar, lick some private part of their body. Not just anywhere—they do it underneath the hair, to hide the mark it leaves.'

Elizabeth felt a lump form in the back of her throat. Who could think Mary would lie with the devil? Would they inspect her for these marks?

'To find the marks, a witch pricker stabs them all over until they find them. One girl from our village had some of these marks, but when they pricked her, she felt pain, and so they let her go.' Mother Pannell continued.

Elizabeth stared, willing her to go on.

Mother Pannell skimmed over the next sheet of paper and gestured to her fingertips. 'There was a man who refused to cry or scream for days, no matter what they did. They put him in the boot—blocks of wood are pulled in to crush the feet, one by one. He even had to endure the rack—even I remember the sound of his joints cracking apart—but still he made no sound. Until one day they stuck a knife under his fingernails and prised every single one off his fingers.' She bit into a large nut but the sound did not distract Elizabeth in the slightest.

Elizabeth's hand covered her mouth.

Her mother nodded grimly. She took the next sheet, widened her eyes and put it back. She discarded another couple before reading from another. 'There's the iron chair which they used on this woman's daughter. She was only twelve years old.'

Elizabeth spoke quietly, 'What is it?'

'They tied her to a chair covered in spikes. Then they laid out coals on her lap to weigh her down into the spikes. It was to get her mother to confess—they weren't looking to kill her. The mother cried out, insisting that she would confess, but they ignored her.'

Elizabeth grabbed the piece of paper in disbelief—but Mother Pannell hadn't explained half of the gruesome detail that her mother had written, and it made her feel sick. Tears wet Elizabeth's cheeks, hot with anger. 'Shut up!'

Mother Pannell blinked in shock. 'My child, have I upset you?'

'How can you talk like this? Even if any of this is true, it was years ago. There's no way they still treat people like that. Not in England!' She shouted at her mother and threw the papers up in the air.

'Don't go asking questions when you can't handle the answers! I only set out to tell you the truth.' She collected the papers, stuffed them into the book and put it into Elizabeth's pocket. 'Don't lose this.'

'There is something seriously wrong with you.' Elizabeth muttered under her breath before storming out.

15

PLANNING – BESS

Bess addressed Elizabeth, 'are you sure this is a good idea?'
Elizabeth nodded. 'Molly will help us, I'm sure of it. But I don't like putting you in danger.'

'I can handle myself. If Agnes is right, this is our best chance at finding out Sir Henry's plan and stopping him.'

When they got to Ledston Hall, Bess crouched behind the short stone wall and waited for Elizabeth to bring over Molly. Molly's face was red and blotchy like she had been crying.

'Miss Witham, I hope you don't mind me coming over unannounced,' Elizabeth began, gesturing for her to sit next to her at the edge of the fountain.

'Of course not, Eli. What did you want to talk about?' Her dark curls encircled her face, bouncing in the wind as she walked.

'I had your letter to Mr Thomas Jobson of Cudworth delivered.'

Molly's face lit up.

'And then, when the boy handed him the letter, he had him wait there while he read it so that he could reply right away.'

'Oh!' She squealed, showing all her teeth, and joined Elizabeth on the stone wall.

'Here you go, Miss.' She handed Molly an envelope.

She tore open the letter and her eyes darted from left to right as she surveyed its contents.

'Oh, Eli, thank you!' She bit her lip, her face falling. 'I will have to give him the news of Father and young William.'

'I suppose so.'

'I will think over what to send.' She held the letter close to her chest and let out a deep breath.

Elizabeth hesitated. 'There was actually something else.'

'About Mr Jobson?' She replied quickly.

'No, not about him. I have a favour to ask of you.' She looked down. She hated asking people for favours.

'Yes?' Molly turned her face to the side, curious.

'Is Sir Henry here today?'

Molly nodded. 'He's meeting Mother in the drawing room shortly. Why?'

Elizabeth sighed. 'It's all this talk of witches. I'm worried he's going to do something.'

The sun shone on the two women but a sudden, harsh gust of wind made them both pull their cloaks around themselves. Bess tried to stop her teeth from chattering.

'There's a lot of pressure on him to convict somebody. There's a food shortage right now, and with Father's death, and then poor William... I think you're right.'

'Is that why he wants to see your mother?'

'Yes. I have to warn you, she blames Mary.'

Bess caught Elizabeth's eye. She didn't know Molly was aware of their relationship, and she didn't like it. Not everyone was comfortable with the idea of women being together—it was safest to keep it quiet.

'She's in trouble, isn't she?'

'I'm sorry, Eli. I know you love her. What can I do to help?'

Elizabeth sighed. 'I hate to ask, but I need money.'

'Don't you earn money working here?'

Bess rolled her eyes. Molly didn't understand what it was like to live as a normal person.

'Not enough.' She paused before adding, 'I'm going to ask Mary to run away with me.'

She gasped in delight. 'How romantic! The two of you, stealing off into the middle of the night...'

Bess clapped her hands to her mouth. Surely Molly wouldn't accept that two women were in a relationship with each other?

'Shh! We can't let anybody hear us.'

In fact, Bess thought, maybe Molly really believed that Elizabeth—Eli—was a man. It would explain why she didn't have a problem with her romantic attachment to Mary.

'Yes, yes. Of course. I'll get you the money you need and you can have some of my jewels too. Where will you go? How will you get there? Do you have somewhere to stay?'

'Oh, thank you so much, Miss Witham.' Elizabeth didn't mention Bess or Agnes, but Bess could see why. They were nothing to Molly, and if they wanted her help, it was easier to get her to sympathise with a love story than the tragic affair of an entire family having to flee their home. 'I think we should go to London. Sir Henry might send someone to look for us, and London seems big enough that he won't find us.'

'Yes, good idea! Do you have a map?'

'No, but I can read. Mother Pannell taught me.'

'Good, I'll get you a couple of maps, and you can always ask for directions along the way. How will you be travelling?'

'Well, that's one reason we need money—to hire a carriage.'

'Oh no, you cannot travel all the way to London in a coach! You will be travelling over bumpy paths and through wet marshes. It could take weeks, and Sir Henry would find you in a day. Can you both ride?'

Bess bit her lip. Agnes couldn't ride—in fact, she was terrified of horses, but Elizabeth might not know that.

Molly went on, 'you will buy some horses. Then you will need to stop every few miles to let the horses rest. But to get to London it shouldn't take much more than a week.'

'A week? Is it that far away?'

Bess hadn't realised it would take that long. Even on horseback, that was a significant distance, let alone on foot.

Molly nodded. 'I've never been, but that's how long it takes Father.' She corrected herself. 'That's how long it used to take Father.'

'Thank you for your help, really, I appreciate it.'

Molly grinned. 'Of course. I'm happy to help—just come and see me one day so I know you made it! I'll give you some money to get you started, but do you have somewhere to stay in London when you get there?'

Elizabeth nodded. 'I have some relatives there, but I don't know their address.'

Molly stood up. 'Let's go to the library—we might have a record of them. What's the name?'

Elizabeth followed her and gestured for Bess to follow them back to the house once Molly's back was turned.

Bess found her way to the window Elizabeth was pointing at and peeked into the room. There was nobody there, so she slid open the dusty old window and waited.

Eventually, the creak of the large door to the drawing room sounded, and Lady Witham invited in Sir Henry.

'I know it was her,' Lady Witham said. 'That woman has always been odd. She has no sons of her own and after her husband died, she never remarried. She's bitter and jealous and I want her punished.'

Sir Henry croaked back in a voice that made Bess's skin crawl. 'Don't worry about that, we'll get her.'

'Has she confessed?' Lady Witham replied without hesitation.

'Not yet. We have to release her tomorrow but as soon as we do, we'll arrest her daughters.'

Bess shivered. Sir Henry had been lying to Agnes.

'Go on.'

'She'll know exactly what we're capable of, so as soon as they're in custody she'll confess to anything we want.'

Lady Witham let out a deep, throaty laugh. 'After what she's done, she and her whole family deserve to be punished.'

Bess crawled away from the window, and once she got to the path, ran all the way to the Middletons' farm where Matthew was tending to the horses in a field—fortunately, there was nobody else around.

'What's wrong?'

Bess burst into tears. 'It's happening. They're going to arrest

Agnes and me. Mother will confess so they don't hurt us, but even then they won't let us go. Lady Witham means for us all to hang.'

Matthew patted the horse on its side and it galloped off. 'Come here.'

He pulled her into a warm hug and kissed the top of her head. 'You're strong. You'll be fine. Did you think about what I said?'

She nodded, still leaning against his chest. 'We have a plan to leave.'

'Good,' he said, though his voice wasn't completely stable. 'It's good that you're leaving.'

Bess nodded, holding him tighter.

'Where are you going? Do you have enough money to get there?'

'Yes, I think so. London. Elizabeth knows someone there who can help us settle in, find somewhere to live, somewhere to work.'

'Good.' He stroked her back and eventually added, 'I'll miss you.'

Bess pulled away and looked into his eyes. They had never held each other like this before, and it felt like something had changed between them. 'Me too. I don't want to leave.'

He blinked away his tears. 'You have to leave. But once you're settled, have someone write to me, give me your address. I'll come to you.'

16

HOME – MARY

Mary had lost track of time. Without being allowed to sleep for more than an hour before being woken up, her mind had gone foggy. Had she only been here for three days? Maybe they had kept her for longer than they said they would. She lay on her stomach, the wooden planks pressing into her ribs. Her long black hair was uncombed, matted and wet with a mixture of water, sweat and blood. It fell through the spaces between the planks of wood and touched the ground. She stared at the strands, trying to make out where one ended and the next began. The smell coming from the chamber pot filled the small room. Her lips were dry and cracked. What she would do for a drink. Mary was aware of people walking along outside, whispering and trying to peer in through the cracks in the wooden door. They would not be able to see anything. Mary had tried to look out but the cracks barely allowed in any daylight, let alone a glimpse at the outside world. Dried blood stuck to her skin and ripped cotton slip. They had taken the rest of her clothes. There was a pool of blood on the ground but by now her blood had clotted and no longer flowed from her wounds.

A familiar voice sounded. A woman's voice. It was loud and confident, but angry. It made Mary's heart jump.

'Let her out!' Elizabeth's voice brought tears to Mary's eyes. A part of Mary had thought nobody was coming for her. Finally, she could leave. Elizabeth would make them let her go.

A reply came by way of a grumble. A man's voice—Mary did not recognise it.

'Let her out immediately. If she hasn't confessed, she's free to go.' Her voice was firm. Elizabeth would know what to do. She could make it all better.

Another grumble, but this time Mary could make out the words. 'You just wait. More evidence will come. We'll get her locked up again.'

This made her shiver. She hadn't meant for anything to happen to Sir William. She would never hurt him. But they hadn't even asked her about him. All their questions had been about the devil. About Mary's faithfulness and her obedience to God. Didn't they want to collect evidence specific to the murder?

A loud metallic clunk interrupted her thoughts. The bolts of the door. Mary squinted as the daylight shone into the small prison. Rain poured down outside and yet she wanted to feel it. The whoosh of the wind only made her want to feel it on her cold skin. Before she could blink, Elizabeth was next to her, inspecting her arms.

'What have you done to her?' She shouted at the man again.

He grumbled again and his footsteps became quieter as he walked away.

'Mary? Mary, can you hear me?'

She wanted to say yes, to tell Elizabeth how glad she was to see her, but the words didn't come.

'Can you stand?' She pulled her arm over her shoulder and helped her to her feet. A bruise under her arm made her squeal in pain.

'I'm sorry, Mary. I'm so sorry.' She was able to stand her up, but as soon as she let go, her knees buckled and she fell towards the ground. Elizabeth caught her. Despite Mary's full figure, she still stood a foot shorter than Elizabeth, so she was just about able to swing her over her shoulder. 'You will be fine. I'll take you home.'

The raindrops fell on Mary's bare legs, covered in goosebumps. Her head swung back and forth on Elizabeth's back but her legs were held in place by Elizabeth's arms. Time passed in a blur. Did they stop somewhere or was that her imagination? She knew they were walking, but the ground was unfamiliar. The stones on the ground turned to grass, which became mud. The nosy voices from the villagers quietened and the bellowing of the cows became clearer but she couldn't help but doze off. When she came to, she was lying on the rushes inside the hut she shared with Elizabeth.

'Are you hungry?' Elizabeth tore off a piece of rye bread and placed it on Mary's tongue. Her mouth watered and she swallowed. She continued to let Elizabeth feed her, while she gradually took in more of the surroundings. The chickens were clucking away, ignorant of all that had happened over the last few days. Mary sat up straight and tucked her icy cold legs into a kneeling position. Elizabeth wrapped a blanket around her shoulders and rubbed her arms dry. Her tangled black hair was still wet and covered the side of her face. Mary reached to pull a strand of hair out of her mouth and tucked it behind her ear. Elizabeth passed her a cup of water. She drank. What else was there to do?

After what seemed like hours of staring into the crackling embers of the fire, Elizabeth came over and pulled a blanket around them both. 'Are you feeling better today?'

Bess and Agnes lay sleeping in their bed next to the window. No light shone through, so it must be night-time.

Mary laid her head on Elizabeth's shoulder. 'Did you carry me all the way home?' She asked, after a while.

'Only to William's. He carried you back here.' Elizabeth handed her some bread. 'Here, eat.'

'Thanks.'

Elizabeth bit her lip. 'I'm so sorry, Mary. I have to tell you something.'

Mary sat up straight. 'What is it?' She croaked. Her voice wasn't back to normal yet.

She leaned in and whispered, 'it's the Witham boy.'

Mary felt a lump in the back of her throat. 'Oh no. Don't tell me the sickness got him?'

Elizabeth broke eye contact. 'He was only a young boy. And so sweet, right to the end.' She kept her eyes on the straw-covered ground of the hut. 'I held him as he died.'

'Oh.' Mary dropped the blanket. She let out a sob.

Elizabeth pulled Mary into a hug and rubbed her back. 'He was so small.'

'I really thought the salve would heal him.'

Elizabeth tucked a loose strand of long black hair behind Mary's ear.

Her sobs punctuated her breaths. She dug her fingernails into her scalp, grabbing handfuls of her hair.

'He was not alone.' She ran her fingertips down Mary's arm. 'He went quickly. There was very little pain. I promise.'

She sobbed some more.

'We did everything we could. Even when Lady Witham fed him the medicine, it didn't help. It was too late.'

Mary froze. 'What do you mean, she fed him his medicine?'

'There was no time for it to work. Not long afterwards the poor boy was coughing up blood. Even I know what that means.'

Mary sat up straight and pushed Elizabeth away. 'Please, tell me exactly what happened. She fed Master Witham the medicine? The salve, in the small glass bottle?'

'Yes, that was it. He couldn't even sit up by himself so she had to pour it straight down his throat.'

'No. Oh no. Please, dear God, no.' Mary muttered under her breath. Sweat formed on her brow.

'Whatever is the matter?'

She let out a whisper. 'It's me.'

'Mary? What are you talking about?'

'It was all down to me.' Her voice was trembling.

'You weren't even there.'

Mary pushed Elizabeth away and fell to her knees. 'It's my fault.'

'Come on, you didn't do anything.'

'It's my fault.' The fire lit up her face. Her eyes were wide and unblinking. Her fists were clenched, held at her side. 'It's my fault.'

Elizabeth frowned. 'Stop saying that. Mary, please. You know that boy's illness could not be your doing.'

She shook her head violently, and kept muttering, 'It's my fault.'

Elizabeth knelt down next to her and put a hand on Mary's fist. 'Talk to me.'

Mary looked into the flames and blinked. She opened her mouth as if to say something but shut it again.

'You can tell me anything.' Elizabeth tried.

Mary blinked again and brought her gaze to Elizabeth. She stared at her, still trembling, and kept her voice to a whisper.

'It's all my fault. Mother Pannell made up the salve for the boy. I gave it to Sir William and made it absolutely clear that it was to be spread on his chest. Mother Pannell should have written out specific instructions on the label.'

Elizabeth brought a hand to her mouth.

Mary continued, 'He assured me he would administer the cure himself. Otherwise, I would have spoken to Lady Witham; you know I would have.' Her sobs returned.

'Mary, this wasn't your fault. I mean it, this is nothing to do with you. Lady Witham killed her husband, then fed her sick child a bottle of something she had never seen before? Nobody in their right mind would do that.'

She nodded. 'You're right.'

Elizabeth tried to hug Mary, but she pushed her away.

'You're right,' she repeated. 'It's not my fault. It's hers.'

Elizabeth's eyes widened.

Mary stood up. 'This is all Lady Witham's fault.'

'Be careful. We'll leave as soon as Bess and Agnes wake up and then we'll get some horses. I have some money and the address of a relative in London—'

Mary interrupted, 'she won't get away with this,' before storming out of the door. Blood spots dotted her dress, although Elizabeth had done her best to bandage up her wounds.

'Don't leave like this. Please, she's dangerous. Besides, it's the middle of the night.'

She ignored her and marched along the wet path in the dark towards Ledston Hall. 'Someone has to stand up to that woman, for once.'

Elizabeth ran after her the whole way there, shouting for her to come home, but she ignored her.

Mary pushed open the front door, not even bothering to go through the servants' entrance. 'Lady Witham?'

Elizabeth urged her to be quiet, 'please, let's just leave right now.'

'Lady Witham?' Mary called again.

Several servants came running to the hall, including Matthew, holding a box of something he had come to deliver. William put an arm around his sister and tried to lead her back outside. Mary shook him off.

Lady Witham pushed open her door and made her way downstairs, with an evil grin plastered over her face. She gave Elizabeth an odd look—she only knew her as 'Eli'—but Mary didn't have time to care about that.

Lady Witham began, 'how dare you? First you come after my husband, then my child, and now me? With all these witnesses! You stupid woman.'

Every servant of Ledston Hall crowded around them.

Mary shook her head, determined, and raised her voice. 'No one here believes I hurt either of them. We all know it was you. You even pulled your boy into your mess—and you call yourself a mother?'

Elizabeth pulled Mary's arm again. 'Please, let's go,' she said under her breath.

Lady Witham gestured to Alice and whispered something. Alice hurried through the front door and out into the night.

'Tell them!' Mary demanded. 'Tell them what you did.'

Molly and her siblings had gathered in a group at the top of the stairs, watching to see what was going to happen.

Mary went on. 'Tell your children, your servants. Explain how you murdered your husband, then managed to kill your own son along with him.'

'You really are a witch, aren't you?' Lady Witham walked up to Mary and grabbed her shoulders. 'Only someone like you could ever think I would hurt my own child.'

Mary slapped Lady Witham across the face and the servants let out a gasp.

Molly screamed from the upstairs window. 'It's Sir Henry! He's marching here with his men right now!'

Mary's eyes widened in fear.

'Shut up, girl!' Lady Witham shouted at her daughter.

'I'll hold them off for as long as I can,' promised William.

Matthew whispered to Mary, 'I'll tell Bess and Agnes. Go.'

Elizabeth grabbed her again and this time Mary let her. They ran to the stables. Elizabeth threw Mary a saddle. 'Do you know how to put this on?'

Mary nodded. 'I'm sorry. I'm so sorry. I didn't really think she would—'

'We don't have time for that now. Here, let's take two horses and release the rest. It will slow them down.'

17

LEAVE – BESS

Bess jerked awake when Matthew shook her by the shoulders. 'What is it?'

'You've got to leave—now.'

'Agnes, wake up,' she called.

Agnes groaned.

Bess threw the blankets off them both and pulled a cloak around her. 'I just need to get some things ready.' She threw some clothes into a cloth bag.

'There's no time. It's Sir Henry—'

Agnes let out a louder moan. 'I hate him.'

Bess nodded. 'We know. They're coming to arrest us. I overheard him yesterday. As soon as Elizabeth brings Mother home—'

'No, you don't understand. Your mother just woke up Lady Witham to confront her about everything.'

Bess's eyes widened.

'I was there, I saw it. Lots of us did.'

'What happened?'

Matthew put a hand on her shoulder. 'She sent for Sir Henry and his men. Your mother and Elizabeth stole some horses so they have a chance at escaping them, but they'll be coming for you too.'

Bess shook her head. 'I don't understand. Are Mother and Elizabeth coming here first, to get us? We're all going to London together.'

'Of course they are, they wouldn't leave us here,' Agnes said.

'I'm sorry Bess,' said Matthew. 'They won't have time to come here first. The men will ride faster than them. Their only chance is to lose them somewhere on the way to London.'

Agnes let out a sigh of disbelief. 'You don't know them. They would never leave us.'

Bess looked into Matthew's eyes and knew he was right. But she didn't want to scare her sister. 'Don't worry. We'll follow them, meet up with them in London.'

Matthew squeezed her hand. 'Be careful. You'll be heading down the same path as Sir Henry and his men. Don't let them find you.'

Bess shook her head. 'We don't have any horses—and Agnes can't ride, anyway. That means we'll be slow but we don't have to take the main path. It will be easier for us to hide along the way.' She didn't know if this was strictly true, but Matthew and Agnes's silence gave her confidence.

Matthew pressed a bag of coins into her hand. 'Here, it's all I have. I'm sorry it's not much. It should be enough for you to find somewhere to stay on the way down to London.'

The sound of horses outside the hut made Bess freeze. She whispered, 'what do we do?'

Matthew put a finger to his lips and looked through the gap in the door. He gestured to the window at the back of the hut, just behind their bed, and Bess and Agnes climbed out, one by one. Bess blew a silent kiss to him, took her sister by the wrist, and they slipped away.

18

DEPARTURE – MARY

Mary groaned in pain.

'Shh,' Elizabeth whispered. She pointed ahead to what looked like a small outbuilding—it was difficult to tell in the dark. 'You see those stables? We can stop as soon as we get there.'

It was unpleasant, her legs stretched wider than was comfortable, and Mary hadn't ridden a horse in years.

Elizabeth helped her to dismount. 'How are you feeling?'

Mary pressed a hand against a cut on her upper thigh. It was drenched in thick blood. 'The saddle, it was rubbing against my leg—' She didn't want to explain to Elizabeth the full extent of her injuries from her time in the lock-up.

'What do you need? We don't have anything here, will you manage?'

'Yes, I'll be fine. I've dressed a wound before.'

Elizabeth nodded. 'Of course. Just tell me what you need.'

'I could do with some marigold—the sunshine-coloured flower —I think I saw some a while back. It's for the cuts and sores.' Mary groaned and lowered herself to the grass. 'But first, I need to clean my wounds.'

Elizabeth led the horses into the stable and called out, 'go and wash in the river and I'll find you some marigolds.' She pulled an old book out of a pocket and squinted at it in the moonlight before heading back the way they came.

Mary crawled to the riverbank and let her feet dangle in the water. When Elizabeth returned, she rested a hand on Mary's shoulder, but her touch brought out a sob. Mary's thoughts came pouring out. 'What is happening? Why is this happening to us? How will we ever find Bess and Agnes?'

'I'm sorry, Mary. We'll sort this out, I promise.' She held out the marigolds. 'Is this what you need?'

She nodded. 'We need to light a fire, and then—'

Elizabeth interrupted, 'and then soak them in water, boil them until infused, and then strain the mixture.'

Mary blinked. 'How did you know that?'

Elizabeth held out the book she had taken out earlier. 'Mother Pannell gave me this. It's got all of her remedies and cures in it.'

'She wrote everything down?'

'It was actually her mother's. She has some diary entries at the end as well.'

'You'll have to read some of it to me later.' Mary didn't know how to read, but this book could help her continue to learn about medicine without Mother Pannell.

'Of course. Let me find some firewood.'

Mary made her way into the stables, as a shelter from the wind. She grabbed some hay and fashioned it into a bed for them both, where she lay down and rested her eyes. It wasn't until Elizabeth jerked her awake that she heard the horses' hooves heading towards them.

'Quick, get up.'

Mary jumped up and spread out the pile of hay so that there was no trace of them there. She followed Elizabeth back down to the river, and they both sank down so that only their eyes and noses were out of the water. Daylight was creeping up on them and they would be easy to spot in such a flat landscape.

'Have they found us?' Mary asked.

'Shh,' said Elizabeth. She whispered into her ear, desperate not to make too much sound. 'I know as much as you do, only their horses woke me up before you. If they find us, we're dead.'

Mary shivered. The water was icy cold. It wasn't too bad last night; in fact, it had soothed her cuts well. But now that her whole body was submerged, she was sure they would both fall ill and be unable to continue their journey.

'Over here!' Sir Henry's voice shouted, not far from them.

Mary held her breath.

Sir Henry's horse galloped past the stables, followed by a group of the same men who had arrested Mary.

'There's nobody around,' one man said.

'I'll check these stables. Otherwise, we turn back. It could be that they circled right back to Kippax.'

Mary gasped. Elizabeth held a hand to her mouth to keep her quiet.

Sir Henry jumped down from his horse and pushed open the stable door. Mary prayed that he wouldn't recognise the Withams' horses. She held her breath, convinced she was about to be arrested again. But when he came out, he dismissed his men with a wave of his hand. 'No one's in there, only horses. Let's go.'

'Can't we stop for a quick drink?' One man pointed to the river and Mary's heart beat faster. Surely they were about to be found out.

'I said, let's go,' Sir Henry repeated.

When they finally left, Mary let out a sigh. 'I was sure they'd find us.'

'Well, they didn't. Come on, let's make this tincture. We don't have any time to waste.'

'It will need time to infuse.'

Elizabeth sighed. 'As soon as it's ready, we're leaving.'

'Leave it to me.'

When it was ready, Elizabeth applied the paste to Mary's wounds and ripped off pieces of her underskirt to bandage her up. 'Can you ride?'

Mary held her face in her hands. 'I don't know if I can do this. They're going to keep coming after me.'

'At least we got you away from them today.'

'But who knows how long this is going to last? I'm so sorry for dragging you into this.'

Elizabeth wrapped her arms around Mary. 'Don't apologise. You have done nothing wrong. Besides, once I found out what they were doing to you...' She tried to catch her eye but Mary looked away. She hadn't told Elizabeth what happened, and she did not intend to. 'I knew I had to get you out of there. They were going to arrest you again, and this time question you until they got a confession.'

'They almost did.' Mary admitted.

Elizabeth gripped her hand. 'I don't know how you stayed so strong. I'm so sorry I wasn't there. Thank you for coming back to me.'

Mary sniffed.

'If riding is too difficult for now, we can walk with the horses.'

'Won't that be too slow?'

'We've got time. Sir Henry and his men have turned back—the important thing is to keep moving.'

'I don't know if I have the energy anymore.'

Elizabeth led Mary back into the stables and untied their horses. 'Here, take her by the reins.'

They each led their horse down the path with their outside hand, and with the other, they held each other's.

19

JOURNEY – BESS

Agnes groaned yet again. 'How am I supposed to get around this tree?'

Bess turned back and held the mass of branches aside so that her sister could climb through. 'Just step exactly where I step. You're shorter than me anyway, you'll be fine.'

'I still don't know why we don't just walk along the main path.'

Bess sighed. 'Sir Henry will go that way.'

'I can handle him,' Agnes insisted.

'Like you handled him at the house?'

'That was different, you didn't give me time to figure out what to do.'

Bess rolled her eyes.

'Let's just walk back to the path and if it's clear, we can go that way, just until we hear them coming.'

'No. It's too dangerous.'

Agnes threw her arms up in the air. 'And this isn't? We'll die out here before we ever reach London—we're completely out of food and drink. Not to mention we'll never find Mother this way.'

Bess had to admit, her sister had a point. 'Look, how about this: we'll make our way towards the main path, I'll climb a tree to look for Sir Henry and then we'll decide what to do?'

'Fine.'

Bess had missed her mother's warm bowls of broth more than

she was willing to admit. She kept wondering if they had made a mistake in leaving Kippax. Were they really in danger of being arrested or even hanged? When they found the path, Bess easily climbed a large oak tree and saw the men straight away. She glanced at Agnes and held a finger to her lips to urge her to be quiet. The men were riding away from them, back to Kippax. She climbed back down and told Agnes.

'So we can walk along the path?'

'For now,' she agreed.

After a while, they came across a collection of derelict buildings, one of which had a pole above the door, covered with foliage. Bess recognised this as the entrance to an inn. The greenery meant they sold wine, and the pole stood for beer, after the implement used to stir it. She stepped into the alehouse and blinked. There was an unpleasant smell in the air from the tallow candles and the tobacco smoke made it difficult to see much in the dark. Once her eyes had become used to it, she could just about make out a figure sitting on a bench, near the hearth. Opposite him sat a man shuffling a deck of cards. Two barrels, with a plank of wood balanced on top, formed a makeshift table between them, and various coins were placed on top.

'Excuse me,' Bess called.

An old man came stumbling round the corner and gave Bess an odd, one-sided smile. He was missing so many teeth that his voice was difficult to understand. He frowned at Bess.

Agnes pushed past her older sister, evidently not intimidated by the men, drunk as they were. 'We need some food and water, please.'

He raised an eyebrow. 'Coming up.'

They sat on a bench and he brought them each a large cup of beer.

Bess whispered to her sister, 'don't drink that.'

Agnes ignored her and gulped it down. 'I have had nothing to eat or drink in days. I'm not saying no to anything right now.'

Bess paused but then drank too. She was just as thirsty.

They listened to the men sitting and drinking behind them.

'It's killing them all.' A croaky voice said.

A deeper voice replied, 'Oh come on. You're always saying this.'

'I know! It's been spreading for a year or two now.'

His friend cleared his throat. 'You better stop spreading this rubbish around. You'll scare people off going to London.'

A boy came over, holding three bowls in his arms. He served each of them a rounded piece of pastry stuffed with a vegetable stew. The pastry was too hard to eat, so it functioned like a bowl. There was bread on the table, softer than the bread they had been eating, but made of barley rather than wheat. It soaked up the stew and enabled them to have their first warm supper in days.

Bess sat up straight and leaned backwards towards the group of men, trying to hear the rest of their conversation.

The man with the deep voice said, 'It's true! I heard it from my wife.'

'No way. I don't believe it.' He croaked back.

'It was over in The Fens. Warboys. Witches of Warboys, they're calling them.' The deep-voiced man insisted.

'I don't think so. It's women that deal in witchcraft.'

'Oh yes, it was a woman who they first found. What was her name?' He paused. 'Mother Samuel, they called her.'

'But it's not right, is it? To hang the husband and daughter as well?'

Bess gasped but Agnes said nothing. She wasn't listening to the men; she was too busy gulping down her food.

'Oh, but they were in on it. They were as bad as her, don't worry about that. They held a trial, there was evidence presented, lots of witnesses turned up.'

'What was their crime?'

He lowered his voice but Bess could still make out the deep sound, 'Murder. Murder of a Lady, at that. Lady Cromwell. You don't get away with something like that.'

'You're quiet,' Agnes said to her sister with her mouth full.

Bess jumped in surprise.

'Eat, before your food gets cold.'

'Yes, I will. I'm just tired.'

Agnes kicked her foot. 'Are you thinking about Matthew?'

'Can we not talk about him right now?' Bess gulped down her soup.

'Why not? Do you miss him?'

Bess rolled her eyes.

'I know you do. But you shouldn't waste your time—you'll never see him again.'

'You don't know that.'

Agnes shrugged. 'I can't see Lady Witham letting this go. She'll keep looking for us and it will always be too dangerous for us to return to Kippax. Besides, we're still young. It won't be long until we're both married to a couple of London gentlemen.'

'Is that what you want? What about Sir Henry? You are technically still engaged.'

'Oh, please. We were just using each other. He won't hold me to our engagement.'

Bess sighed. 'Anyway, if he found us, he'd arrest us without hesitation.'

When they finished their food, the landlord agreed to rent them a room for the night. They paid half upfront, with the rest due in the morning. The room they slept in was just off the main part of the inn, with damp, muddy rushes covering the floor. There were already a few men asleep on the ground, so they spread their cloaks out in the far corner and slept right next to each other.

Bess whispered, 'do you think it's a good idea for us to stay here?'

'Stop worrying so much,' Agnes said. 'We'll be fine.'

In the morning, the rest of the men in the room had gone, and so had Bess's small coin purse.

20

ARRIVAL – MARY

Southwark, South London, 1593

They rode alongside the river Thames, towards the cathedral that towered over the city. St Paul's Cathedral. It was a structure made from a mixture of timber and lead, much grander than St Mary's Church back home. There had once been a spire, 489 feet tall, but lightning had destroyed it years earlier. The building was impressive and could be seen from a distance. Elizabeth slowed down and Mary sped up so that they rode side by side. The magnificent nave, St Paul's Walk, was 586 feet in length. It struck Mary that this should be a sacred place—it was a religious building, built for the glory of God. But the crowds within the nave were hardly churchgoers. Many others were like themselves—travellers or tourists—looking around, lost. Some women were offering to do all sorts of scandalous things to the men passing by. There was shouting from every part of the nave, and pickpockets ran through the crowds, unnoticed but for those on horseback with a much better view.

Mary was glad to have arrived in London, finally, but she didn't feel safe here. 'Elizabeth, we need to leave.'

She nodded in agreement.

'Look to your purses!' A young boy shouted. On seeing a

woman on her own grab something inside her jacket, he ran to her, took it, and ran off with it. Elizabeth gasped.

What sort of place was this? Mary sighed. She would have to learn to live here.

The tall arches of the nave somehow seemed out of place in this world of thieves and prostitutes. Mary hoped there would be more to London than this. They rode on, stopping now and then so that Elizabeth could check the map. The alleys they travelled along became narrow and dark. Rats scurried along the ground at every turn and Mary longed to be back in the countryside. She tried to push the thought from her mind. It was too late to go back. They would press forward with their plan. As they walked along, various wooden doors had a red cross painted on them.

A man screamed.

Mary jumped. 'What was that?' The man let out another, longer scream.

The other people walking along the street did not hesitate. Nobody went to help. People seemed to be in a hurry to leave the street, pulling their cloaks around them and keeping their eyes down.

'It's the sickness, isn't it?' Mary spoke in a low voice. 'Plague.'

Elizabeth nodded and grimaced. 'I heard it came to London last year, but I thought it would have gone by now.'

Mary shivered.

Behind another crossed front door, there came the cry of a girl. Mary envisioned a child. In horror, she pictured her own young daughters. She didn't know what symptoms the Plague presented, but imagining her own children in this much pain brought tears to her eyes. This was not a good place.

Elizabeth dismounted her horse and entered a nearby tavern.

'Are you sure we should get off here?' Mary asked. But Elizabeth ignored her. Maybe she hadn't heard her. There was a lot of noise around them.

'Let's stop here for some food and something to drink.' She helped Mary to tie their horses to a post around the back of the inn before going inside. They entered through a door so low that Elizabeth had to crouch to get in. The dark room had low, timber beams holding up the ceiling that looked like they could give way at any moment. The front of the inn was full of men and women, eating and drinking, but the room at the back was empty of people. It comprised heaps of straw, where they were to sleep. Various piles of rags around the room indicated that they would be joined by others.

'I don't like this.' Mary frowned. If the Plague was going around, why would they stay inside in a room full of potentially infected people?

'Please Mary, stop worrying for once. I'm exhausted and you must be too. We finally made it to London so let's just eat before we have to go looking for James Chapman.'

Mary didn't want to start an argument, so said nothing else.

Elizabeth ordered and paid for some drinks and a pie for each of them. A sort of brown slime spilled out of them, full of chunks of what looked like meat. It didn't taste like any meat Mary had ever eaten, but she did not complain. They ate in silence.

When they had finished eating, a man pushed open the door of the inn with a shout. Mary span around and dropped her cup on the floor. It spilt on the cold ground. Elizabeth whipped her head around to look towards the door. The man had a large sore on the side of his face. Mary gagged. She grabbed Elizabeth.

'Help me,' he groaned. The people inside the tavern stood up and backed away.

'You can't come in here!' One man shouted at him.

The innkeeper agreed, 'Out! Out right now or I'll have you arrested!'

The man groaned in agony. Tears were strewn down his face and he walked with a limp. He seemed to realise nobody was going to help him so he turned and staggered away as fast as he could. A crowd of people from the inn hurried out to see where he was going. He ran to the end of the nearby pier and jumped straight into the river Thames.

Mary and Elizabeth did not stay to look at his body, as many other patrons did, but hurried back into the inn. They stayed silent, listening in on the conversation of two men sitting behind them.

'The Plague is causing madness.' One man said to another.

'Only for us. The working class are the only ones affected, of course,' he replied.

'I know. The rich leave us to die in this filthy, poisonous air while they run off to their safe homes in the country.'

Mary whispered to Elizabeth, 'Is that true? Is it safer in the country, away from the Plague? Have we made a terrible mistake?'

Elizabeth looked blankly at her, but a man in front of her turned around.

'No, no.' He addressed Mary. 'Did you hear about Newcastle?' The girls shook their heads. 'That's countryside, if ever I saw it. Thousands died there a couple of years ago, when the Plague hit.'

'But what are we supposed to do?' Mary blurted out.

'Not much we can do. Wait it out. When the rich return, that's when you know it's safe again. Until then, stay away from the sick, even burials. The dead can still pass on the disease.'

'What else?' Mary was itching to get more information.

'Those foreigners, they keep dirty houses. Stay away from them too. Cleanliness will keep it away. And don't go about in crowds, either. That's why they shut the theatres. They say the poisonous air spreads faster in crowds.' The man turned back around to continue the conversation with his friend.

Elizabeth whispered, 'It's not a good idea for us to stay here. There are too many people.'

Mary nodded, relieved. 'Let's go.'

They found the large town house right near the river, and to Mary's relief, the area was much cleaner and quieter than the area by St Paul's Cathedral. The man who answered the door was wearing a pair of striped red and black trousers tucked into his white socks. His too-tight jacket was grey, with puffed sleeves, and his grey hair was frizzy, untamed by any sort of cap. Altogether, he looked rather eccentric.

Elizabeth cleared her throat. 'Hello. We're looking for a James Chapman?'

'Who's asking?'

'My name is Elizabeth Pannell, and I believe he's a relative of mine.'

His eyes widened. 'You'd better come in.'

Mary followed Elizabeth into the grand hallway and gazed up at the high ceilings. A servant brought them drinks and something to eat and gestured for them to sit.

'My name is George—James was my father. He passed away a long time ago. So you're Sir William's...'

'No,' Elizabeth interrupted. 'This is Mary, and I'm Mother Pannell's daughter.'

At the mention of Mother Pannell, George smirked. 'Of course.'

'You know her?'

Mary gulped down her wine and bit into a large juicy apple. It had been too long since she had eaten.

'I do. Is there something I can help you with?' He didn't touch his food or drink, instead choosing to stare at his guests.

Elizabeth fidgeted in her seat. 'Actually, we were hoping we could stay here for a while.'

George stood up and headed for the door. 'I'm sorry, but times are tough for us all at the moment.'

'Please, wait—we have money.'

He span back around. 'Why don't the two of you stay for dinner?'

Over dinner, they explained their situation, and he seemed unusually sympathetic. 'The law is a mess. Created to benefit a very select few, it does nothing for the vast majority of us. The Queen has no interest in the people.'

Mary gasped.

'What's wrong?' George asked, biting into his last piece of meat.

Her cheeks flushed red. 'I'm sorry, it's nothing.'

'No, please go on.'

'I just... isn't that treason?'

George smirked. 'Let me worry about that. Anyway, I would be delighted to rent you a room in my house. It's always a delight to help family.'

Elizabeth nodded eagerly, 'thank you so much, George.'

Mary asked what George did for a living, so he explained that he was a writer, a poet and a thinker. In fact, his masterpiece was soon to be published.

Elizabeth seemed impressed by this. 'What's it about?'

He grinned with pleasure and gave them some context. 'The Shadow of Night concerns melancholy. That state which allows for the deepest of thought and understanding, where one might observe the world in a new light, with an open mind.'

Mary nodded but didn't understand. She looked to Elizabeth, who seemed utterly fascinated by George's thoughts and stared with wide, unblinking eyes, as he continued.

'During the day, we find ourselves overwhelmed by the distractions of work, money and the politics with which people inevitably find themselves involved.' He swallowed, and sensing he was losing his audience, raised his voice. 'But! Night time. Night time is when the brain comes to life. Without the worries that take up the daytime, it can concentrate on the search for meaning, for truth. The truth they will tell you to look for in God.'

Mary felt a knot forming in the pit of her stomach. This sort of talk, against God, was dangerous.

'The first part of my work, Hymnus in Noctem, in the spirit of the hymns of Orpheus, appeals to Night as a primordial goddess.'

'The second part gives the portrait of the moon goddess Cynthia. She is representative of power, in particular, Queen Elizabeth.'

Mary interrupted him, desperate to change the subject, 'that was a lovely meal, George, thank you!'

George grinned. 'You both enjoyed it, I hope?'

Elizabeth nodded. She hadn't quite finished but scooped up the last bit of bread before George had the plates whisked away.

Elizabeth addressed George, 'thank you for all of this, but there is something else we need.'

Mary kicked her under the table and whispered under her breath, 'be careful.'

She ignored her. 'Mary has two daughters, just eighteen and twenty-four years old, who are also on their way to London, and we are eager to find them.'

Mary hoped they could trust George.

'I can certainly make some enquiries—what are their names?'

'Bess—that is, Elizabeth—and Agnes,' Elizabeth said.

'Please only ask people you trust,' Mary added. 'We don't want word to get back to Kippax of where we are.'

He raised his eyebrows. 'Who exactly are you hiding from?'

Mary took a deep breath. 'The Withams. They're looking for us. Please promise me you won't let them find us or my daughters.'

He stroked his chin before answering. 'I promise. But if I am to keep your secrets, you must keep mine as well.'

Elizabeth patted Mary's shoulder and ran her fingers through her long black hair before whispering, 'don't worry so much. They'll be fine, why wouldn't they be?'

21

LONDON – BESS

Whitechapel, East London, 1593

Agnes frowned. 'What is this place?'

Bess could just about see the outline of a wooden building, the only light coming from a candle in the window. She edged towards it, back against the wall, trying to see inside. 'Shh,' she whispered, though they wouldn't be heard above the murmur of voices in what seemed to be a tavern. There were benches filled with men, laughing and slamming mugs of beer onto tables.

'Wait here,' Bess told Agnes. 'I'm going to find some food.' She made her way around the back and, as quietly as she could, sifted through the contents of the bins.

Agnes shivered and groaned behind her. 'It's so cold.'

After weeks of wading through the wet, miserable countryside, they were starving. At least here, they might be able to scrounge up scraps of food. But the bins were bare. She went through them one by one, finding a mixture of empty vegetable crates and animal bones, all picked clean. Bess ran her fingers through her hair, thinking about their options. They had no money, no idea where to go and if they didn't eat soon—she looked behind her, where her sister was crouched on the wet ground, leaning on a metal bin. Pale and so thin that her cheekbones seemed to be poking out of her face, she wouldn't survive for long. 'Stay here,' she said. 'I won't be long.'

She pushed open the door a fraction to reveal a grimy kitchen area. Her eyes were immediately drawn to a loaf of bread on the table in the middle of the room. It was covered in mould but Bess's mouth watered all the same. She stood completely still, anxious not to catch the attention of the man in front of her. Short and stout, he stood in front of a large barrel of liquid, stirring it with a wooden implement. Bess wrinkled her nose at the stink of stale beer and waited until he went into the main part of the tavern. Finally he left. She rushed in, grabbed the bread and ran out to give it to Agnes.

'Here, eat.'

Agnes didn't move.

'Agnes!' Bess hissed. She tore off a piece of bread and held it up to her.

She opened her mouth and chewed weakly.

'That's it. Keep going, you need to build up your strength.'

Agnes cleared her throat before leaning in and whispering, 'you too, have the rest.'

Bess ignored the grumble of her stomach and lied, 'I already had some—this is for you.'

She nodded and fell backwards, accidentally knocking over the bin. It crashed into the side of the building and landed on the cobbled stones.

'Agnes! Quick, let's get out of here.'

But it was too late—the landlord pushed open the back door and glared at them. He was a middle-aged man with a large, round belly, accentuated by his too-tight shirt, and spoke with a lisp. 'Who's there? Thieving bastards, I'll have you arrested!'

'I'm sorry, sir. We were just leaving—' Bess gave her sister a look, praying she would have the energy to follow her. She tried to pull her up by the shoulder.

He narrowed his eyes at Agnes and surveyed Bess once more. 'What are two young girls like you doing out here on your own?'

'Please, let us go. We're looking for our mother. We didn't mean any harm.' She tugged on Agnes's arm again but she just groaned.

'Look, she's not going anywhere.' He stepped onto the wet ground and pulled Agnes over his shoulder. 'You'll stay here tonight.'

Bess bit her lip. She couldn't imagine that this man would have any reason to help them, but what choice did they have? She picked up the filthy lump of bread, shook off the dirt and took a bite out of it, then followed them inside. The tavern smelled of damp and those tallow candles made of animal fat, but there was still quite a crowd inside.

'Sit down, both of you. You look like you've been through hell. Let me get you something to eat and drink.'

Agnes offered him a half smile and as he left she croaked, 'thank you, sir.' She took some more bread from her sister and the colour returned slowly to her face.

He smiled. 'Please, call me Thomas.'

Bess made a face. 'What are you doing? We have no reason to trust this man. Besides, our best chance of survival is Mother. We've already wasted too much time getting to this wretched city —we need to find her.'

'Look at us! We'll die of thirst or hunger before we get the chance. Anyway, nobody is going to take us seriously while we look like this. We need to clean ourselves up and then we can start asking around.'

Bess looked down at their dirty, ripped clothing. They had a bag of clothes they had brought from home, but it all needed washing. At the moment they looked like vagabonds, and there were laws against that. If someone reported them, they could be whipped and sent back to Kippax. 'Fine,' Bess said, 'But we're not staying here for long.'

When the man returned, he introduced himself as Thomas and handed them each a bowl of lukewarm lumpy soup, locking eyes with Agnes. 'What brings you here, then? You don't sound like Londoners.' He smiled an odd, toothless smile.

Agnes gulped it down without a second thought, but Bess frowned. There could be anything in this. 'No, sir. We come from up north,' she said.

He addressed Agnes rather than Bess, 'expecting to stay here long?'

'No. We have family here,' Bess said quickly. She slurped down the soup, trying as hard as she could not to make a face. It had an odd, sour taste to it, but Agnes was looking better already, so it couldn't be that bad.

'Of course you do.'

Agnes caught her sister's eye and added, 'thank you for this. We appreciate it. But I wonder if you could help us find our mother?'

He wiped the beads of sweat from his forehead. 'I suppose I can ask around. What's her name?'

Bess shook her head at Agnes. It was not a good idea to tell this man who they were.

Thomas sighed. 'You don't have to tell me, but how do you expect to find her? The city's a big place.'

They were in such a rush to get away from Kippax that they hadn't thought about how they would actually find their mother.

'We know that, but...' Bess bit her lip.

Agnes blurted out, 'we think she's staying with the Chapman family.'

He cleared his throat. 'Well, I'll see what I can find out. And in the meantime if you decide to stay, I could use some help here at the tavern.'

Bess shook her head. 'I appreciate the offer, but we'll be fine. We'll be out of your way tomorrow.'

'We would offer you money, but we were robbed at the last inn we stayed at,' added Agnes, her voice shaking.

Bess widened her eyes in frustration. She didn't want this man to know how desperate their situation was.

'I see, yes. Well, unfortunate as it is, that does happen.' He looked from Agnes to Bess and hesitated. 'I'll leave you to eat, and then I can show you to the back room where you can sleep.'

When he left, Bess kicked her sister under the table. 'Why did you tell him about Mother?'

She rolled her eyes. 'How else are we going to find her? We'll have to trust someone.'

'Didn't you think he was staring at you a bit too much?'

Agnes shrugged. 'It's what men do.'

Bess scoffed. Matthew would never gawk at her with his mouth open like that. He was a respectable man. She felt a lump at the back of her throat at the thought of him. Her plan had been to write to him as soon as they arrived in London. But looking down at herself, she knew she couldn't face him. After weeks spent trawling through the countryside, she was ashamed at the state of her ripped clothes. She could even smell herself. Desperate for a proper wash and the time to pull herself together, she resolved to wait a few days to write to him—just long enough for her to get herself sorted. She couldn't face him yet.

22

LOST – ELIZABETH

E lizabeth led the way down the narrow cobbled street. She knew the way to Tyburn, and Mary was following her. The riverbank was busy. Men hurrying off to work, children running around. It was mostly men, but Elizabeth supposed that going to see a hanging wasn't something many women and children would be interested in. However, once she got to the point where Tyburn Road met Tyburn Lane, she realised how wrong she was. There were thousands of people, including whole families with infant children. It seemed like everyone in London wanted to see Anne Karke hanged.

She turned and tried to find Mary, now lost in the crowd. When she caught her eye she pushed through and took her hand. 'There you are,' Elizabeth said.

Mary sighed. 'We shouldn't have come here.'

'We had to come.' Elizabeth thought they would never be able to resolve this argument. In fact, they had barely spoken in weeks.

'You don't understand.'

Elizabeth spoke through clenched teeth, 'you need to see exactly what will happen to you if we go back to Kippax.'

'How many times do I have to tell you? My girls might need me. In all this time we've heard nothing of them. All I can think is that they have been arrested, or worse. Nothing we see today is going to change my mind.' Mary pursed her lips.

Elizabeth led them to a small gap, next to a mound of earth which Mary could stand on. They could then both clearly see the famous triangular wooden structure that served as the gallows: the Tyburn Tree.

It wasn't long until they heard the procession coming from the city. Anne Karke wasn't from a wealthy family, so she hadn't been able to afford a covered coach. This meant the spectators were throwing rotten fruit, mud and stones at her. She had her hands tied behind her back and swayed as she walked, as if she had had too much to drink. The executioner gestured for the coachman to come right up to the gallows, where he tied the noose around her neck. She screamed and sobbed but all the crowd did was cheer. Elizabeth squeezed Mary's hand.

A man stepped up onto the gallows and spoke for a while, but he was far away and difficult to understand. He gestured to Anne Karke, who also said something that Elizabeth couldn't make out.

Mary pushed Elizabeth away, held her hands to her face and forced herself to look at the spectacle through her fingers.

The executioner gestured to the coachman to drive off, and Anne was left swinging from the rope.

Elizabeth reached for Mary's hand but again she pushed her away.

Anne didn't die immediately. Instead, her body swayed from side to side and her legs flailed about in all directions. The crowd watched, shouted and cheered as if they were enjoying watching this slow, agonising death. Elizabeth couldn't tear her eyes away. It seemed horrible that they were stood here, unable to do anything but watch. Finally, a woman in the crowd ran up to her and pulled on her legs, hard. She stopped moving then.

Elizabeth wrapped her arms around Mary, whose face was wet with tears and angled downwards, unable to watch the spectacle anymore. She whispered into her ear so that she could hear her over the cheers, 'it's done.'

Mary sobbed. 'I'm sorry. I'm not being reckless, I promise. But I'm a mother—I cannot let them do that to my girls.'

Elizabeth stroked her back. 'I know.'

'You don't understand. How could you? Only a mother knows the pain I'm going through right now. How am I supposed to go on without knowing where they are? I don't even know if they're alive or dead.'

People were pushing past them now, to get a closer look at the dead body. The executioner was now permitted to sell off pieces of Anne Karke's hair or clothing, and there were plenty of offers being shouted out.

'Come over here,' Elizabeth said, leading them to a quieter area behind a row of now empty wooden benches. 'I know it's difficult, but you've got to think of yourself too. You putting yourself in harm's way is no use to them or you.'

Mary sobbed. 'I miss Mother Pannell. She would know what to say.'

Elizabeth scoffed. 'What would my mother say that I haven't already said?'

'Don't get so defensive, I just think that she would know what to do.' Mary pulled away and stood up straight, looking over at the corpse hanging from the gallows.

'Why would she know any more than me?' Elizabeth cleared her throat. 'I've brought us all the way to London and found us a safe place to stay. With my carpentry and your work as a seamstress, we've made enough of a living to keep George happy. All I want is for you not to get yourself arrested. It won't help us and it won't help the girls either.'

'Will you stop being so naïve?' Mary pushed Elizabeth away and sat down on the bench. The surrounding crowds were pushing past, not interested in their conversation, so she raised her voice. 'We can't do this alone.'

'We're not alone—we have each other. We have a good life here, with George. He's been good enough to involve us in his readings and take us to the theatre—there's no need for us to leave.'

'Elizabeth, you don't know what the real world is like. My daughters could be in danger right now. Even if they're fine—our life here with George won't last. He has no obligation to look after us, and eventually we'll be on our own again. Without Mother Pannell, we don't have a chance.'

'What are you talking about? I can take care of us. I've got us this far, haven't I?'

Mary sighed. 'Of course. All I mean is that Mother Pannell always kept you in this bubble. She never imagined you'd have to restart your life in a new city and she didn't prepare you for it.'

'Mother didn't keep me from anything. She taught me to take care of myself.' It was true—it was Mother Pannell who had taught her how to find work as a footman. That was how she had always supported herself, without ever needing to rely on a husband.

'She's always stretched the truth.'

'When? Give me an example.'

'She told me never to tell you what happened to my husband.'

'That's irrelevant, it wasn't her secret to tell. It was yours.'

'That's not all. She lies to you.'

Elizabeth shook her head. 'Don't say that. She wouldn't do that.'

'Didn't you ever wonder why she took you in? Who your real parents were?'

Elizabeth shook her head. 'I trust her. There's nothing else to say.'

Mary raised her voice. 'Do you really not know who your parents were?'

'Stop it. My mother was a servant who died in childbirth, and Mother Pannell never knew my father.'

Mary groaned in frustration before blurting out, 'it's Sir William Witham!'

Elizabeth span around to face her. 'What did you say?'

Mary bit her lip. 'Look, I'm sorry. But his affairs were no secret. He used to take the younger servants to bed, and well, eventually one of them fell pregnant.'

'What?' Elizabeth's voice wobbled.

'Didn't you ever wonder how it was so easy for her to find jobs there? For both of us?'

Elizabeth blinked, trying to organise her thoughts.

'Sir William sent the servant girl to Mother Pannell. To take care of it. She tried to cut you out of that wretched woman, thinking you weren't fully formed yet, but she'd lied—said she wasn't as far along as she was. In the end, there was too much blood. She died, but you survived. Mother Pannell vowed to protect you from that day on.'

She shook her head. 'You're unbelievable. There's no way. She would have told me. Mother Pannell doesn't lie. She loves me.'

'Mother Pannell shields you from everything. She doesn't want you to know anything that might upset you. She treats you like a child.'

Elizabeth scoffed and pushed past a crowd of people, but stopped dead in her tracks.

'Don't be like that, I'm just being honest with you,' Mary said, following her.

Elizabeth's eyes locked onto a group of men standing by the gallows. Their faces were familiar, and with a sense of dread she recognised the man at the front. 'Please, God, no,' she muttered under her breath. She jumped down and grabbed Mary's arm.

'What is it?'

'They're here.'

Mary wiped her tears with her sleeve, trying to shake off Elizabeth's hold. 'Who's here?'

'It's them. Sir Henry and his men.'

23

LATE – BESS

When Agnes finally pushed open the door, Bess was sitting on their bed waiting for her. 'Do you know what time it is?' Bess asked.

'Leave me alone,' Agnes slurred. She threw her bag on the ground and set about undressing for bed.

Bess shook her head at her sister. 'And you're drunk, again.'

Agnes ignored her. She pulled the pins out of her hair and grabbed a cloth to wipe the rouge from her cheeks.

'Where have you been?'

Agnes groaned. 'What's with all the questions? Can't I do anything without your approval?'

Bess stood up and grabbed her sister by the shoulders. 'Listen to me. Have you been with a man? Are you seeing someone?'

Agnes pushed her off. 'No, no. Nothing like that. I was just out.'

'Where?' This wasn't the first time Agnes had been out late, and it was worrying her.

She pushed Bess aside and got into bed, pulling the blankets over herself. 'Gl—The Globe,' she muttered.

This meant nothing to Bess, but that was even worse—if anything happened to her, she wouldn't even know where to look. 'I can't believe how irresponsible you're being.'

'Stop trying to act like Mother.' Agnes rolled over and scrunched her eyes shut.

'Someone has to! We do not know where she is, and we're stuck in this city with no money and no family. If we don't find her soon, we'll be stuck here forever.' Bess walked from one end of their small room to the other and threw her hands up in the air. 'Is that what you want? To have to live in this place for the rest of our lives?'

Agnes shrugged. 'Will you relax? Just go to sleep.'

Bess knew if she wanted to find out anything, now was her chance. Agnes was much more likely to tell her the truth while she was drunk. 'Were you with a man tonight?'

Agnes mumbled something unintelligible.

Bess's heart sank. 'You were, weren't you? What was his name?' Bess tried again.

'George.'

'George?'

'George Chapman.'

Bess's eyes widened. So Agnes had been seeing a man at this place—The Globe. Wherever that was. She could only imagine what they had been doing together at this time of night. Especially while Agnes was this intoxicated.

24

STORIES – ELIZABETH

George's voice spread all around the house, smaller now than the house they had first moved into with him. 'Hurry, we need to leave soon!' George had continued to write—his most recent play was called The Blind Beggar of Alexandria. Since moving into George's house, Elizabeth had fancied herself an intellectual. She listened as he told them stories. She pictured the characters and wondered at their relationships.

'We have a while yet, don't we?' Elizabeth opened the door and saw George standing by the window in the front room of the house. 'Mary!' She called up the stairs.

George winked. 'I have a quick reading for you first. You'll love it.'

Elizabeth liked her nephew. She grinned. 'What is it?'

'It's about Hippocrates.'

She shrugged, not recognising the name.

'Some call him the father of modern medicine. In fact, there's an old myth that says he saved his village from the Plague, back in the day.'

Elizabeth frowned. 'What are you talking about? Hippocrates? That's not possible.'

'What do you mean?'

'That story—about saving the town from the Plague. I've heard it before. It's not about Hippocrates, it's about Mother Pannell.'

George shook his head. 'Elizabeth, this myth has been around for thousands of years.'

'But my mother always said—'

He smirked. 'I don't know what to tell you. Except that people love to tell stories.'

It was uncomfortable, the thought that her mother had lied to her about something as simple as her own life. 'Mary!' Elizabeth called.

This time Mary replied, 'Yes, I heard you the first time—I'll be down in a minute!' She would still be in their room, getting ready. Mary didn't appreciate how lucky they were to be in this position —they were luckier than Elizabeth had ever thought possible, so why wasn't she happy?

'Anyway, it sounds like you really like my stories.'

Elizabeth nodded, 'I do.'

George accepted a cup from Mary and took a gulp. 'Well then, you should learn Greek. It really is the most beautiful language, and Homer's is the most fascinating poetry I've ever read.'

Elizabeth grinned. 'I don't know if I could ever learn Greek. English is hard enough.'

'Everyone starts somewhere!' He insisted.

'I suppose.' Elizabeth said. 'No. Only one way around it—you'll have to translate everything into English in the form of poetry and read that to me.'

'Maybe I will!' George grinned.

Mary came into the room. 'Ready?' She called.

'Nearly,' Elizabeth smiled. 'George is just trying to convince me to study Greek.'

Mary sighed. 'I'll never understand why you two care about any of this. What good will Greek do you in the real world?'

'Not everything is about money,' Elizabeth said.

Mary continued, 'There was a time where money was everything to us. We both worked every day of the week, all day, so that we could afford food for our family.'

Elizabeth crossed her arms. 'We still work! Just not to the point of exhaustion. And why not enjoy it here while we can?'

Mary sighed. 'Fine—are we leaving now?'

'Hold on, my friend is just outside. I'll see what he wants.'

'Is that a member of his club?' Mary asked.

'Yes, I think so. And it's called the School of Night,' Elizabeth sighed.

'Whatever it's called, it's dangerous.' Mary insisted. Their discussions of philosophy, theology, astronomy and even atheism, worried Mary. Elizabeth did not like to think about it, but Mary was right. If the authorities found out what they were talking about, they would be in serious trouble.

As Elizabeth gathered her things and led Mary out of the large wooden door, she thought of the play they were going to see. 'What is it called again, George? The play that's on today?'

George waved off his friend and gestured for Mary and Elizabeth to follow him. 'As You Like It. Come on, or we'll be stuck at the back!'

Mary, trailing behind the others, quickened her pace. 'What's it about?'

George quickly explained, 'two young duchesses flee to the Forest of Arden. That's supposed to represent the Ardennes, in France. There they meet some young men who have also fled, and lots of the characters end up falling in love with each other.'

Elizabeth was hanging onto every word. 'Who wrote this one?'

'Ah.' George sighed again. 'This was created by William Shakespeare.'

They followed the sizeable crowds walking in the same direction.

'Shakespeare—he's a rival playwright of yours, isn't he?'

George laughed. 'It's true, we don't get along, but I enjoy his plays. He's acting today—look out for Adam, the servant of Orlando. Orlando is the main man—he falls in love with one of the duchesses.'

The theatre they normally headed to was boarded up. The crowds were all heading into the building next door. 'Hold on, nobody is going to The Rose Theatre.' Elizabeth frowned.

'Ah, today we are going to The Globe.' George said. The theatres stood next to each other, on the south side of the river

Thames. The Globe was a hexagonal structure, three storeys high with no roof.

Elizabeth and Mary had never been to The Globe, although they knew William went often.

'The Globe? I recognise the name…' Mary wondered.

Elizabeth whispered to her, 'Shh, that's where George spends all his money. It's a gambling house.' She paused and lowered her voice further. 'And a brothel.'

Mary gasped.

George cleared his throat, pretending not to have heard.

When they got nearer the theatre, a flagpole emerged above the crowds. Today the flag was white, showing the play would be a comedy. Along the riverside there were stalls selling merchandise and refreshments. Some people haggled with the sellers. Others flitted between the market stalls to steal items for sale or reach into the pockets of the playgoers to see what they could find.

Elizabeth followed George into The Globe and dropped her penny into the box. Now that there were people pushing her from all sides, she grabbed Mary's hand and led her to the pit. Surrounding them were the galleries, where the richer individuals sat to watch. Some had brought cushions to sit on, and some were wearing masks so that you couldn't tell who they were. Not that Elizabeth would have recognised anyone important, anyway. Unless they were George's friends, she supposed. A couple of men actually sat on chairs right on the stage. Probably noblemen, Elizabeth thought. There must have been thousands of people in the audience altogether.

They were lucky to not have any rain, as there was no roof over the stage. Two men walked onto the stage. The character of Adam wore loose trousers tucked into his boots and a shirt of the same fabric. It was not unlike what William was wearing today, Elizabeth noted.

The playgoers around them were discussing the play as it was acted out. They were loud, and it was difficult to make out the actors' words. A balding, fat old man was selling rotten tomatoes out of a small bag for the onlookers to throw onstage. Luckily, nobody had accurate enough aim to hit the actors.

'Come on, Mary. This way.' Elizabeth dragged Mary towards the front. 'We'll be able to hear better if we get closer to the stage.'

Mary whispered back, 'Where did George go?'

'I haven't seen him—he probably went off with some friends.' Elizabeth added.

'Oh, yes. Probably.' They got closer to the stage. As women, most people let them push past. 'I can hear much better now. Thank you.' Mary whispered.

Elizabeth looked back at the stage. They hadn't missed much —both men still stood talking on the stage. Orlando was young and attractive. Tall, broad shouldered, dark hair. He had donned a brown leather vest. It was tight across his chest and all eyes were on him.

Elizabeth nudged Mary. 'Do you see him? Adam?'

Mary rolled her eyes. 'Yes, of course I see him, he's right there.'

'That's him. That's Shakespeare.' Elizabeth said, triumphant.

'Oh! Are you sure?' Mary asked.

She nodded.

'He's not as handsome as George, is he?' Mary remarked.

Elizabeth shook her head. 'He's not a very good actor either. Not very expressive.'

Mary agreed, 'It must be his writing which distinguishes him.'

When the men went off the stage, two boys entered, this time wearing dresses. Mary smirked. She was not the only one. The audience seemed to find this funny and there was a general low laughter that sounded throughout the theatre. 'Mary!' Elizabeth whispered. 'Stop it, that's how they do it. You know that!'

Mary put a hand over her mouth to hide her laughter.

The play continued, with the two women, Celia and Rosalind, realising their only choice was to flee their home. It was eerily similar to their own lives.

'Doesn't it sound perfect? The rhythm of their lines?' Elizabeth whispered. 'It's like George, reciting his poetry.'

Mary nodded but Elizabeth wasn't sure she had heard. She had lost interest, almost dozing off.

'As if country life could ever be better than life in a busy town,' Elizabeth mumbled, echoing the thoughts of the characters.

'Oh no, I prefer country life. Who would choose town life over what we had back home?' Mary sighed.

Elizabeth whispered, 'You don't get to go to plays like this back in Kippax!'

One actor broke into song.

'I'm glad of a break from all the talking!' Mary exclaimed.

Elizabeth grinned. 'See? It's good! I wish we could come and see more plays together.'

Mary, Elizabeth, and most of the people around them let out a laugh, as Celia read out a terrible love poem about Rosalind.

'Please, never compose something like this about me!'

Elizabeth smirked.

Mary giggled again. Her rounded cheeks were now delightfully rosy. Elizabeth loved seeing her happy. She squeezed Mary's hand and pulled her closer. Mary's eyes widened. 'Elizabeth!' She whispered.

'It's fine, nobody's looking at us.' Elizabeth insisted. Mary stayed there, pressed up against her body.

The play was coming to a close, with all the mistaken identities being found out and all the relationships ending in marriage. Ganymede then promised Orlando that he could marry Rosalind, just as Phebe and Silvius could marry and Oliver would marry Aliena. The next scene was a song and dance with all the actors onstage.

'This is much more upbeat than the last song.' Mary pointed out, swaying to the music.

Elizabeth grinned and let herself move to it as well.

When the play finished, the audience applauded and cheered. It was a sudden end and before they could talk about anything, people pushed past them to get to the exit.

Elizabeth took Mary by the wrist. 'This way,' she shouted. 'There, see George?' She gestured over to where he stood, chatting with a group of men.

'Where? I don't see him.' Mary was shorter than Elizabeth, shorter than most of the members of the audience.

'Wait—look! Is that—' Elizabeth was cut off. It was so loud in here.

'What did you say?' Mary shouted.

'It is! It's her! Molly!' Elizabeth called. It was no use; she couldn't hear her.

'This way.' Elizabeth pulled Mary by the arm but a man bumped into her and she let go of her. 'Mary?' She called. 'Mary!' She couldn't see or hear Mary anymore. She would find them eventually. Elizabeth pushed past the crowds in the direction that Molly had been walking. She didn't want to miss her.

'Molly! Molly, it's Eli! Molly Witham!'

A man whose arms were linked with Molly's turned at the sound of her name. He whispered something to her, and she turned around.

Her face lit up when she saw Elizabeth. She had the same bouncing brown curls as she had always had. She waited for Elizabeth to run up to her.

'How lovely it is to bump into you! I didn't expect to see you at the theatre!' Molly held out her arms for Elizabeth to embrace her. 'Thomas, I would like you to meet Eli. Oh! I apologise. I would like you to meet Elizabeth. Elizabeth, meet my husband Thomas, Lord of Cudworth.'

Elizabeth widened her eyes. This meant Molly had always known her true identity. It made sense. If anyone was going to figure it out, Elizabeth thought, it would be Molly. She was a perceptive young woman. Elizabeth thought back to all those whispered conversations, the walks through the grounds. Molly would never have behaved that way with a man. And since her family would never have let a woman work a man's job, Molly must have kept her secret for years.

'How are you? I'm afraid I don't have long. We need to get back.' She looked to her husband who was almost dragging her away.

'Good. Mary is good too, it all worked out.' Elizabeth tried to look around for Mary, but couldn't see her. 'We found a home here in London and it's all going great. How's Thomas? Are you happy together? Do you have children?'

Molly grinned. 'I'm so glad—we are perfectly happy. He is a wonderful husband. No children yet but it won't be long, I'm sure.'

Her husband tugged on her arm again.

'I wish I could stay and have a proper conversation with you, but we need to go. You should come to visit us! We live in Cudworth, on the estate up there. It's near Kippax, but not close enough that anyone would recognise you.'

'Thank you, I'm sure we will. Please, come and meet Mary, I know she would love to see you—' Elizabeth stood on her toes, trying to see over people's heads, but still couldn't see Mary.

'I'm sorry Elizabeth, I have to go.'

'Of course, of course.' A thought occurred to Elizabeth. 'We haven't heard from Mary's daughters since we left—would it be too much to ask you to let them know we are safe? Have someone check on them?'

Molly's face fell.

'What is it?' Elizabeth said. 'Are they well? Have they married? How are their husbands? Oh, please tell me.'

'Elizabeth, I'm sorry. I thought you would know.'

'What? Know what?' Mary should be here. Elizabeth was getting anxious now; where had she gone?

Molly's husband muttered something under his breath to her.

'Yes, I'll be one moment.' Molly addressed Elizabeth. 'They had to leave Kippax. It wasn't safe for them anymore. Only days after you left.'

Elizabeth held a hand to her mouth. 'But that was years ago!'

'I would have helped them; you know I would. Only I didn't know they were leaving until it was too late.'

'Why did they leave?'

'It was my wretched mother. She still has Sir Henry out looking for Mary, and her daughters too. She knows she might not find Mary, but she wants to use them to draw Mary out from hiding and shift the blame onto her. I'm so sorry.'

Elizabeth shook her head. No. This couldn't be true. 'Where are they now?'

'I wish I could help you. I don't know how they travelled. Do they know where you are?'

'We told them London, but that's all.' Elizabeth scrunched up her eyes, chastising herself. 'I didn't even tell them about George. I didn't know about George when I last saw them. Oh, what have I done?'

Molly's husband pulled her arm once more.

'I really have to go. I hope you find the girls. If they are anything like you, they're strong enough to look after themselves. Anyway, I believe you'll find them. And I mean it, do come to visit me one day.'

Elizabeth nodded absent-mindedly. How was she going to break the news to Mary? She caught George's eye in the crowd and made her way towards him. Now there were fewer people here, it was easy enough to find him, towering over most of the theatregoers, but there was still no sign of Mary.

'Elizabeth,' George slurred. He smiled at her then went back to talking to his friends. One or two of them had been to the house before, she was sure of it. They were a part of his group of thinkers.

Elizabeth ignored him. She stood on her toes once more and tried to find Mary, but couldn't see her. Where did she go? Suddenly Elizabeth recognised her long black hair.

'Come on George, let's go.' Elizabeth said.

George said his goodbyes but Elizabeth dragged him away before he could finish. 'Ah, what's going on? What's got you all worked up?'

Elizabeth replied with a sigh, 'Nothing, I want to get to the other exit, catch up with Mary.'

George patted her on the back. 'Yes, yes, of course. Time to go.'

25

THE GLOBE – BESS

Bess kept her eyes closed, pretending to be asleep, while her sister got dressed and ready to leave. As soon as the slam of the door sounded, she jumped up and pulled on a cloak before running out of the door to follow her sister. The tavern was quiet—it was still early. The landlord, busy wiping down tables, caught Bess's eye. 'Shift starts soon,' he called.

Before leaving out of the front door, she shouted back, 'Don't worry, I won't be long.'

He rolled his eyes.

It was dark out. By this time of year it was getting darker and colder earlier by the day. Bess shivered. Up ahead, Agnes made her way towards the river. Bess kept her head down and pulled her cap over her forehead, so as not to be seen.

Agnes stopped at a tall, wooden building, with at least two, maybe three floors, as far as Bess could see. It was a hexagonal structure, and coming from it was a cacophony of music, singing and chatter. She slipped in and Bess followed. There was no roof, so although it felt like they were inside a building, it was still cold, and if it rained, they would be soaked. Bess frowned at the people around her. The women wore dresses hitched up above their ankles or pulled down to expose their bosom. Scattered about the place were tables set up for card games, where groups of men sat gambling away their money. Agnes made her way to a staircase at the side of the building, going straight up past the first floor onto the second. Bess tried to look into the rooms they walked past, which encircled the space below like it was a sort of stage. The doors were all closed.

She stopped outside the room Agnes had entered and took a deep breath. What she expected to find in there she couldn't say. But either way, she had come here for answers. Bess wanted to know what her sister was doing, and if she was putting herself in danger. She closed her eyes and pushed open the door.

When she opened her eyes, she let out a yelp. 'Agnes! What is this?'

A bed was the only item of furniture in the room, only just large enough to fit it inside. Agnes poked her head out from under the blankets and widened her eyes. 'What are you doing here? Get out!'

In the next moment, a man, not much older than Agnes herself, also emerged from under the bedsheets.

Bess raised her voice. 'Who are you?'

He looked back to Agnes. 'Should I leave, or—?'

'I said, tell me your name.' She crossed her arms and stood in the open doorway.

With a wide grin, he addressed Bess. 'I apologise. Chapman. My name is George Chapman.'

Agnes pointed to the doorway behind her sister. 'Get out, right now. I'll talk to you in a minute.'

'I'm not going anywhere. I'll give you a minute to get dressed, but only a minute.' Bess slammed the door shut.

Nobody else in the Globe seemed to bat an eyelid at the raised voices. It seemed this was not out of the ordinary here.

George pushed past her, still buttoning up his shirt. 'So sorry about this,' he said as he hurried off.

Bess pushed open the door to find Agnes glaring at her. There wasn't enough space in the room along each side the bed, so she climbed over the bed to get off.

'How did you find me here?'

'I'll be asking the questions! How did you even find out about this place?'

Agnes shrugged. 'The landlord told me about it. I give him a cut of my earnings.'

Bess shook her head. 'I knew we couldn't trust him! Do you have any idea what you're risking, by coming here?'

'I'm an adult—you can't tell me what to do anymore.' Agnes wrapped her cloak around her and pushed past her sister.

'Even if we ignore the moral complications completely, what about disease? Have you stopped to think about that?'

Agnes span around and put her face right in front of Bess's before saying in a whisper, 'do not come here, to my place of work, and tell me how to behave. You don't know what you're talking about. I know all about the risks. In fact, I've taken steps to treat the symptoms I've had so far and I'm responding well. The rector says I should feel better in a matter of weeks.'

Bess grabbed her by the shoulders. 'You've caught something? Why didn't you tell me? I could have helped you!'

'Helped me?' Agnes scoffed. 'Look at you! You don't know what it's like for me.'

'And what do you mean, the rector? You've told the rector what you do here?'

Agnes shrugged. 'Like I said, you don't know how any of this works.'

26

SCHOOL OF NIGHT – MARY

Mary held Elizabeth's hand as she crept along the corridor. Tonight was one of the secret meetings of the School of Night.

'I'm going in,' Elizabeth whispered.

'Are you sure about this?' Mary tucked some loose strands of hair under her cap and pulled her shirt down to cover the top of her trousers. 'What if they suspect something?'

'I'll be fine.' Elizabeth pushed open the door and Mary pressed her ear up against it.

'Who would like a drink?' Elizabeth offered.

Christopher Marlowe, a poet whose voice Mary recognised from previous visits to the house, replied, 'With pleasure, thank you.' The clink of glasses sounded as drinks were poured. 'You are—?'

'Eli. I'm a friend of George. Good to meet you.'

Thomas Harriot cleared his throat. 'Good evening, all. Please take a seat.'

The scraping of wooden chairs against the hard ground as the others obeyed. Thomas Harriot was a prominent mathematician and astronomer and led these meetings.

'I know George isn't here yet, but we all know his sense of timing, so I think we should get started.'

A round of suppressed laughter moved about the room.

'We are here to discuss George's recent publication, Shadow of Night.' He spoke in a husky voice, the result of a lifelong tobacco habit. 'Before I go on, it's worth reminding you all of the danger we face, just by discussing these matters.'

Mary took a deep breath. She always worried for George, and certainly didn't want Elizabeth to get caught up in all this.

'You worry too much,' replied Henry Percy. 'Anyone ignorant enough to consider George's work dangerous would never understand it in the first place!'

The room erupted with laughter.

Henry went on, 'you should consider publishing some of your own work.' Henry was the ninth Earl of Northumberland, who lived with Thomas in Syon House.

'I am simply being careful. Discussing these sorts of topics was safe, back in Oxford. Nobody expected anything treacherous. But these are dark times.' Thomas paused to take a sip. 'People everywhere are on the lookout for treasonous activities.'

The word treason made Mary shiver. She pressed her face against the crack of the door so that she could see into the room with one eye.

'But you mustn't let them scare you,' Henry said. 'We must continue to discuss, to research and to write. Our work is important to the world.' Henry said.

'Hear hear!' added Sir Walter Raleigh. 'Thomas, do you remember America?' Not long after he was knighted, Sir Walter had been granted a royal patent to explore the recently colonised Virginia. In fact, he had named it after Queen Elizabeth, the Virgin Queen. George's friends all seemed incredibly important.

Thomas, who had started out as Sir Walter's mathematics tutor, had accompanied him to America and assisted with navigation. 'Of course! Your ships would never have arrived if not for me.'

Sir Walter laughed. 'Yes, I'm sure you are right. Now that we have started to explore the new world, it's more important than ever to always be learning. We should question anyone who seems to speak with authority and seek to understand all that we can.'

Elizabeth interrupted, 'I wish you would stop supporting our efforts in the Americas. The natives hate us and this will not end well.'

'Eli! Good to see you again,' Sir Walter said. 'Though as you know, I don't share your views on America. The natives were excited by our visit. I showed them my compasses and maps, and they said they must be the work of gods, not man!'

Mary heard the front door slam and ran upstairs, so George wouldn't find her listening at the door. Once he entered the room, she crept back down to listen again.

Thomas was getting frustrated by this point. 'Please. We are not here for this. Now that George is back, let's get on with our meeting.'

Murmurs of agreement sounded around the room.

He cleared his throat. 'Queen Elizabeth would have us follow the Church of England. She would have us abandon our talks of philosophy and she would order us to not consider the religions of the past.' He paused. 'We cannot do so.'

More sounds of agreement.

Mary's heart beat fast in her chest. They were speaking directly against the Queen. All of George's work goes back to the Queen, and it was putting them all in danger.

'Shadow of Night explores some of our latest discussions, and I would like George to explain this further.' Thomas said.

The others provided a round of applause.

George began, 'Oxford taught us a lot.' He paused and looked around at his fellow alumni. 'My Classics studies showed me a new way to look at the world. It led me to find a valuable group of peers. Our Socratic dialogue allowed me to question my very own train of thought. In the spirit of the hymns of Orpheus, I appeal to Night as a primordial goddess. The serious contemplation that Night allows us can plunge us into a state of melancholy. It builds, and it builds.' He paused to allow for a few moments of contemplation, and handed around pieces of paper. 'I was hoping to discuss a few key passages this evening.'

'Eliz—' he started.

'It's Eli,' she corrected him. 'Thank you for asking me to join you all this evening.'

'Interesting young boy,' Sir Walter added.

George laughed. 'What are you talking about?'

Suddenly Mary was pushed back as Elizabeth and George stepped out of the room. 'What do you think you're doing here?' George asked.

Elizabeth's cheeks flushed red. 'You said—the other day—you said my point of view was interesting and I should join in with your next meeting.'

He sighed. 'I didn't mean it! Elizabeth, I don't like to be rude, but you're a woman! What hope could you have of understanding the likes of us?'

The men stared at her, whispering among themselves.

Elizabeth stormed outside, tears falling down her cheeks.

Before she followed, Mary slapped George's face, hard. 'You know how much she looks up to you. How could you be so awful to her?'

27

ILLNESS – BESS

B ess ran a comb through her hair and smoothed her skirts. Her shoes needed mending, but she didn't have time. What she needed was some of that white powder to cover up the dark circles under her eyes. Barely thirty years old, she looked at least ten years older. She wondered what Matthew was doing now. Was he thinking about her? Probably not. She hadn't even said goodbye to him before she left. He might have his eyes on somebody else already. She sighed.

'Agnes? It's time for work.'

Her sister, in contrast, still had the youthful black curls that surrounded her face. Her unfortunate illness gave her a pallor that made her more popular with men.

She groaned in pain. 'I'm coming. Give me a minute.'

'Do you need help to get dressed?' Bess called.

Agnes didn't reply. Bess poked her head around the corner and looked her up and down. Soon she would be too ill to work in the tavern. How would they afford the rent with only one of them working? She pushed the thought from her mind. Surely Agnes would recover soon.

'Come on, I'll help you. Here, lean on me.' Agnes was unsteady on her feet but managed to stand. She winced.

'I have someone coming today. He's going to look you over, see if there's something to be done about all this.' She bit her lip.

Agnes nodded. She didn't talk much anymore. After throwing a blouse over her head, she tugged it down hard so that it exposed more of her chest than it should. Then she pulled on her skirt and took in a sharp breath.

Bess held out a hand, and the two of them headed to the main area of the inn. The landlord stood waiting.

'I need to get someone. I won't be long. Agnes can serve anyone who comes in while I'm out.' Bess said. It was more of a statement than a question. She had learned it was easier to tell the landlord their plans rather than ask for permission.

'Fine, fine. But don't be long.'

She kissed Agnes on the cheek. 'Back soon.'

Agnes nodded.

Bess headed outside and took a deep breath, then instantly regretted it. That of rotting fish replaced the smell of stale beer from the nearby market. Nobody bothered to take their rubbish away around here, everything got thrown on the ground. She wrinkled her nose.

The early evening light meant she could see her route clearly. It hadn't taken long to get used to the lay of the land around here. The buildings were close together with narrow, dirty alleyways separating them. Luckily for Bess, the streets were different enough that she could tell the way to the church.

It gave Bess a sense of comfort that this church was also called St Mary's, like the one back home. Maybe that was why they had stopped here when they first got to London the previous year. It wasn't as old as St Mary's in Kippax, but it had stood for around three hundred years, if the rector were to be believed. Richard Gardiner was his name, and he had been here for thirty years or more. He had promised to help Agnes. If anyone had a chance of curing her, surely it would be a man of God.

The bright white of the chapel loomed in the distance as Bess got closer. It was the chalk that gave it such a distinctive colour. That was why the area was known as Whitechapel. The main parish church was far away, in Stepney, but this one was perfectly fine. It was near to them, and that was what was important. Both girls worked such long hours that they barely had time to sleep, let alone trudge to a faraway church.

She found the rector walking around the churchyard, surveying the graves.

'Sir? Richard?'

He turned at the sound of her voice. 'Bess. Lovely to see you. Come in.'

'Please. I don't have much time.' She spoke quickly. If she didn't return soon, the landlord would start asking questions. As hateful as the man was, he gave them somewhere to live, and Bess couldn't turn her nose up at that.

'As you wish. I have all I need here.' He patted his cloak. 'We can go straight away.'

'Thank you, sir.' Bess led the way back to the inn.

Nobody would question what a holy man was doing, so they were safe from anybody's questions. Even so, the rector spoke in a low voice so that he would not be heard by anyone else.

'You are certain she suffers from the French disease?'

Bess broke eye contact. She looked at the ground as she walked. Trying to avoid the muck, she stepped on the cleaner bits of the ground where she could.

'I have spoken to other women who have it, and she seems to have the same symptoms. She has been using your treatments, but she's getting worse.'

'Well, all I gave her was a salve to soothe the affected skin. I did not know this was what ailed her.' His voice was kind, but stern. He was under no illusions of what caused this disease. 'What are the symptoms?'

'There is a sore. On her private parts.' She cleared her throat. She found it difficult to speak to a man about this, especially a rector. 'It was not painful when it first appeared a month ago. Then it was only a pimple, small and inoffensive.'

'And now?'

She sighed. She hated speaking about her own sister this way. 'I'm afraid she cannot take the pain much longer. She cries out in her sleep, full of anguish. The pimple has become encircled with a hard callous. She is weak in her joints and tired all the time. Walking is hard for her and she does not speak much anymore.'

'Yes, yes, these are all common symptoms of the great pox, I am sorry to say.'

'She will recover though?'

The two of them were almost at the inn now. Richard stepped to the side of the street and pulled Bess towards him. He lowered his voice to a whisper. 'You know how she caught the disease?'

She squeezed her eyes shut. 'It's not her fault.'

'This is God's punishment for fallen women. Was it both of you?'

'No, sir. It was only Agnes. But don't blame her. She only wanted to protect us both, and she could not find work anywhere else. I would have stopped her if I had known, honestly I would.'

'Hm.' He shook his head.

'Please. We were desperate. We would have been out on the streets, begging.'

'Look, if you both repent and follow the treatments I give you, we can hope God will take the illness from dear Agnes.' He shrugged his shoulders. 'But the final decision to save her is out of my hands. It is up to God to decide what's in store for her.'

She followed him into the inn. The landlord raised his eyebrows on seeing her enter with a rector, but allowed him to go into the rooms with Agnes all the same.

'Now you,' he said to Bess, 'it's time to get on and serve these men some beer.' The landlord gestured to a group of men sitting in a circle in the middle of the inn.

28

FOUND – ELIZABETH

Southwark, South London, 1603

Mary called, 'wait for me.'

Elizabeth stopped walking but didn't turn around.

Mary wrapped her arms around her. 'Are you cold? It's windy today.'

'I'm fine.' She hoped her voice was more stable than it sounded. She didn't want Mary to know she had been crying.

'Don't let George get to you. He doesn't know what he's talking about.' She rubbed Elizabeth's back with one hand. 'Come on, let's go home,' Mary said, leading her back towards the house.

'He's right, though. It's no use arguing with him. I don't have an education like he does—how can I hope to join in with his intellectual conversations?'

Mary screwed up her eyes. 'Don't talk like that. You're allowed to discuss these things, and form your own opinion. These meetings are dangerous and I don't know how I feel about you being involved, but George had no right to treat you like he did.'

Elizabeth locked eyes with Mary.

'You'll be fine. Trust me.'

She nodded.

'Good.' She took her hand, and they walked through the

narrow streets until they got to the house. The meeting was still going on, so they went straight to their room.

'I miss my mother,' Elizabeth said, falling backwards onto the bed.

Mary lay down next to her. 'I miss Mother Pannell, too. She was always good to me.'

'She would stand up to George, wouldn't she?'

Mary grinned. 'She would've stood up to him a long time ago. There's no way she'd let him be rude to you.'

'Do you think she misses us?' Elizabeth squeezed Mary's hand, looking up at the plain white ceiling.

'I know she does.'

'How?'

'Family is everything to her,' Mary said simply.

'I wish I knew more about her family.'

Mary bit her lip.

'Do you know something?' Elizabeth rolled onto her side.

'I—I don't want to break a confidence.'

Elizabeth gasped. 'You know something! Well, she's my mother, if anyone has a right to know about her family, it's me.'

'I suppose.'

'Mary, please.' Elizabeth looked right into her eyes. 'Talk to me.'

'What do you want to know?'

Elizabeth jumped off the bed and rooted around in the cabinet until she found what she was looking for. 'Here, this is her mother's book of recipes, herbal remedies, even those diary entries about the witch trials she came across. How does she have this? Did she write it?'

Mary nodded. 'Her mother wrote some of it, and then she gave it to Mother Pannell on her wedding day, to say goodbye.'

'Goodbye?' Elizabeth sat back on the bed. 'What do you mean?'

'Her family had to leave right after Mother Pannell got married. They were travellers—foreigners, and the King passed a new law sending them all away.'

'When was this?'

Mary bit her lip.

'When?'

'She was only twelve.'

'Twelve?' Elizabeth gasped.

Mary nodded. 'I'm sorry. She asked me not to tell you.'

'Why wouldn't she tell me? I don't understand.'

'How could you understand?' Mary sighed. 'You never got married. You don't know what it's like, having a husband you hate and no family around to help you.' She stood up and paced the room. 'She was alone for years and wasn't even blessed with a child. It's not right!'

Elizabeth hesitated. 'I'm sorry. I forgot—you and she had that in common, didn't you?'

'I don't want to talk about it.'

'Mary, I'm sorry.'

'I'm fine. We both got free of our husbands, eventually.'

'I know.' They hadn't spoken about Mary's husband in years, though Elizabeth would never forget what happened.

'You mean when they died,' Elizabeth said.

Mary went on, 'all I'm saying is that you are everything to Mother Pannell. She wished for a child for so many years but it never happened. So when she ended up with you, her whole life changed. I promise you, she misses you more than anything right now.'

Elizabeth lay down on the bed, and Mary lay with her head on her chest. They dozed off, not moving until they heard the shouting at the front door.

Elizabeth froze. 'Mary, are you awake?'

Mary moaned quietly. 'What's wrong?'

'Shh. Listen. Do you hear that?'

Mary's face went white. 'Is that—'

Elizabeth nodded. 'Sir Henry.'

Sir Henry was arguing with George, claiming that he could send him to prison. He said he knew what George was up to with his group, but all he was interested in was Mary and Elizabeth. He claimed he had a witness tell him they were staying with him.

'He wouldn't tell them anything, would he?' Mary whispered.

'No. He can't afford to be questioned, with all he's involved in—they'd arrest him straight away,' Elizabeth said.

'What if they look around the house?'

Elizabeth put a finger to Mary's lips. 'Shh. Listen, they're leaving.'

Their door swung open and George shouted at them, red-faced and sweating, 'they've found you.'

'Are they here?' Mary's voice quivered.

'No, I sent them away, but they'll be back. I can't hold them off forever.'

Elizabeth narrowed her eyes at him. 'There must be something you can do. You've kept them from us for all these years.'

He sighed. 'Elizabeth, I don't know what's got into you lately, but use your head. London is a big place, but the family searching for you has enough money to keep looking until they find you. This was bound to happen one day.'

'Mary, I'm sorry. I thought we'd have more time. I thought—'

Mary held her hand. 'We'll figure something out.'

'There's something else I've been meaning to tell you,' George said. 'It's about your daughters.'

Mary gasped and put her hands to her mouth. 'You've found them?'

'I think so.'

29

TREATMENT – BESS

Whitechapel, East London, 1603

Bess lay in bed, unable to sleep. Agnes's screams were becoming unbearable. She thought of her life back home. She had a good job, a happy family and even had a man in the picture. Matthew. He might have married since Bess left Kippax. He probably had; they were in their thirties by now. If she had married Matthew, she and Agnes might never have had to leave. Agnes might still be healthy and everything might be well. She shook her head. It wasn't worth going through these scenarios in her head. Her sister lay there screaming, and she didn't want anyone to hear them from the tavern. She had to do something. It seemed to Bess that the treatments were only making things worse, but what else was there to do? At least she didn't cry out all day. It seemed to be worse when she was sleeping.

The screaming was high-pitched and pierced the afternoon air. Bess shook Agnes awake.

'Agnes? Be quiet! Agnes, wake up.'

She shook her sister awake, who threw her head from side to side in confusion. The pain made her burst into tears. She reached for Bess to comfort her, but Bess stood up. It was best not to get too close. After all this time, Bess hadn't caught the disease from Agnes, but she had also been very careful not to touch any of the sores. The rector had told her this was how the disease spread. Every inch of Agnes's skin was covered in a rash and she was in constant pain. All Bess could do for now was talk to her, try to keep her calm. She couldn't even give her sister a hug.

'Shh. Don't worry, we can figure this out.'

Agnes didn't work anymore, thank goodness. The landlord had not asked Bess to cover Agnes's share of the rent, and she hoped he wouldn't. She could never do the sort of work Agnes had been doing. What if she were to catch the same thing? Who would look after her? No. Bess would keep serving food and drinks and make sure that was all.

'I want Mother.' Agnes managed to say.

'I know. I do too. She's in London somewhere, we know that. We will find her, I promise. But first, we need to treat you.' It wasn't a lie exactly. Bess believed Mary was in London, but she didn't even know where to start looking for her.

Agnes nodded.

Bess pulled her hand away from her sister and lay her head on a pillow.

'I'm going to light the fire now.'

Agnes whimpered. She knew what was coming next. 'Please. I don't want to.'

'Be brave now. This is how we are going to get you well again.' She pulled together the smaller pieces of kindling. Once the spark had caught alight, she blew gently to get the fire going. 'There.'

Agnes stared at the fire and shook her head. She repeated, 'I don't want to.' The mercury had already caused most of Agnes's teeth to fall out, so her words came out as a mumble. Bess still understood her though. Of course she did; they were sisters.

'Come on, it's not so bad.' She reached onto a shelf to get the mercurial ointment. Bess rearranged the pieces of wood in the fire to make sure it would burn hot and then placed a chair right in front of it.

'Sit.' She kept her voice stern. There was no time for arguments —she had to get on with this so that she could go to work afterwards.

Agnes winced as she pushed herself off the bed. She walked

slowly to the chair. She had lost her former beauty. Her tight black curls had long gone and most of her hair had fallen out. The few strands that remained hung limply on her head. Now that she had lost her teeth, her lips caved in and they had no colour at all. She had even lost her full figure, and now, like Bess, was far too thin.

Bess sighed. 'That's it. Lift your nightdress. There.'

Bess had next to her a bucket of water and a cloth. She handed Agnes another cloth, this one rolled up. 'Bite down.'

Agnes nodded, tears in her eyes as she knew what was coming. Bess rolled up her sleeves and pulled on her gloves. The rector had given these to her, to keep her from getting infected when she applied the cure to the sores. She reached her head and shoulders under her sister's nightdress and inspected the main wound. It was by far the largest, and the first one that Agnes had found. It was getting worse. To stop her sister from writhing as she cleaned the wound, she placed one arm across her waist and held her firmly on the chair. She cleaned the wound as best she could with the wet cloth. Agnes let out a low groan.

'That's it, well done. Now for the inunction. This might sting.' Agnes's legs tensed up. Bess scooped up the ointment and pressed it onto the abscess. There was a foul smell coming from it that she had not noticed before. That couldn't be a good sign.

'Almost done,' she called.

Agnes held her hands in tight fists and screamed into the cloth she was biting into. Bess hoped they wouldn't be heard from the tavern.

'There.' Bess came out from under Agnes's nightdress and motioned for her to stand briefly. She adjusted the nightdress and repositioned the chair to be right in front of the fire. Both of them were sweating by this point, so Bess wiped the sweat from her own brow with the sleeve of her dress.

She replaced the lid on the ointment and put another couple of logs on the fire.

'Now you need to stay there.'

Agnes rolled her eyes, and for a moment Bess saw her sister's old personality poking through. 'It's too hot.'

'It's good for you!' She ignored her. Bess tried again. 'Please. It's good for you. You know what they say—a night with Venus, a lifetime with mercury.'

Agnes managed a weak smile.

'That's it. Your sweat is good, it purges the body of all the syphilitic poisons.'

She nodded. 'Bess?'

'What is it?' Bess was trying to dress quickly, before the landlord came in looking for her. Where had she left her cap?

'Am I going to die before we find Mother?'

Bess froze. How was she supposed to answer that? But she couldn't lie to her sister. She went back to the fire and held Agnes's hand.

'I don't know.' She said simply.

'I know you'll find her one day, even if it's after I'm gone.'

Bess nodded and saw the tears in Agnes's eyes. She must have been thinking about this for a while.

'Tell her it wasn't her fault, won't you? I don't want her to blame herself.'

Bess kissed Agnes on the back of her hand. 'You can tell her yourself. We'll find her once you're recovered. Don't worry about anything. I'll fix this, I promise.'

30

WHITECHAPEL – MARY

Mary's mind was buzzing with thoughts of her daughters. She hoped they were safe. George had told her to walk north, across the river, and towards a small church in the East—in an area called Whitechapel. Elizabeth had insisted on coming, too, but Mary walked a few steps ahead. She had no desire for small talk.

London Bridge was a stone masterpiece eight hundred feet long. It was propped up by arches and square piers along the river which gave extra support to the buildings on each side.

From a distance the bridge was magnificent, but when Mary approached the Southwark gatehouse, she kept her eyes down and held her breath. This was where they displayed the heads of traitors. They executed them and stuck their heads on long iron spikes attached to the roof. More than thirty heads were on show, right at the entrance of the busy bridge, to warn others against breaking the law. Birds came to peck at the rotting flesh and pieces would sometimes fall to the ground. Mary wrinkled her nose at the smell. Elizabeth groaned from behind her.

The next part of the bridge had two enormous water wheels, one on either side. They had been installed not long after Mary and Elizabeth had moved to London. They took their power from the water and used it to grind corn. The idea was copied from the original water wheels which still stood at the north end of the bridge. Elizabeth always said the design was ingenious, but today she didn't comment on it.

Once on the main part of the bridge, it was easy to forget you were standing on a bridge at all. It was solid, thanks to the stone arches holding it in place, full of crowds of people and the entire length of the bridge was covered on each side by houses. There must have been a hundred houses altogether, all of them four or five storeys high. The ground floor would house a shop, most of which were haberdashers.

Mary looked in the windows as she walked past. In the first shop, a woman was arguing about the price of a length of linen. In the next, some women were walking around, surveying the fabrics on offer. Mary had done some work as a seamstress in London, but she had worked from home, and her customers had always come to the house, thanks to George who organised it all. If things had been different, she might have worked in a shop on this very street. She wouldn't have minded. Further along, the shops sold kitchen-ware—glasses, spoons and knives. These also seemed to be full of women. A few small grocers had set up stalls in the spaces between houses, but Mary didn't stop—she continued on towards Whitechapel. Towards the north end of the bridge, the shoppers were men. These traders sold daggers and swords. Mary pulled her cloak around her and quickened her pace.

The interior of each house was almost identical. Mary had never been upstairs in any of them, but you could see in through most of the windows. There could be chambers on any floor, but the kitchen and waterhouse were always on the second floor. At that moment, a young girl reached out of a window on the second floor and hauled up a bucket of water from the river. It was clever, having a house right here. Like the water tower, it would mean never having to walk far to fetch water. At Ledston Hall she had spent countless hours going back and forth with heavy water buckets.

When she got to the far end, Mary watched as the water wheel at the northernmost arch collected river water at its base. This drove a pump that raised it to the top of a tower. From there, pipes conveyed it into the rest of the city. It was fascinating. Water was being brought right to people's homes. It meant the people in the city might never have to go to collect water from the river again.

Once she came off the bridge, the crowds dispersed, everyone going their own way. Mary didn't come north of the river very often, but she knew roughly where to go. She turned right when she could and followed the road when it veered off to the left.

A scream interrupted Mary's thoughts.

High-pitched. It came from a child.

Mary blinked. She stopped dead in her tracks and looked around. 'Where is everyone?'

Elizabeth shrugged.

The usual crowds were nowhere to be seen. Instead, the wooden doors were all shut. Some featured a red painted 'X'. She hadn't seen one of those since ten years ago. The Plague. The only person around was a child. It was a toddler, lying on the cold ground, staring at her. She could not tell if it was a boy or a girl, but their blanket had been kicked aside. Her heart dropped. She wanted to scoop up the child in her arms, rock them to sleep. But one look was enough for her to keep her distance. Bloody boils covered the child. Mary wrinkled her nose. The smell of blood. Old blood or new blood—she couldn't tell. One wound covered the child's right cheek, and there was one on each shoulder. Tears welled up in her eyes. She cleared her throat. Her mouth opened, but no words came out. What would she even say?

She ran. Drops of sweat formed on her face. Elizabeth called after her but she didn't care. A knot in her stomach made it harder to run, but she pushed through. She kept running in the same direction until she could run no longer. Finally, Mary bent over and rested her hands on her knees. Panting to get her breath back, she looked up and spotted it: the small white church. She stood up straight and sniffed. With the back of her hand, she wiped the tears from her face. It was completely white, like George had said.

'Is this it?' Elizabeth asked, panting behind her. 'White Chapel? So this tiny church made of chalk gave its name to the entire area?'

Mary shrugged. It didn't matter. The church had a four-bay nave, connected to a tower at one end with an enormous clock halfway up. A small church like this must have a small congregation, she thought.

It was quiet; there was no service on. The rector was inside, pacing in thought.

Mary sniffed and wiped the tears from her cheeks with her sleeve. 'Wait here.' She cleared her throat and stepped inside. 'Hello?' She tucked the loose strands of black hair behind her ears.

'Hello there.' The rector had a kind face with lots of laughter lines. 'Richard Gardiner. I'm the rector here. Is there something I can help with?'

Mary sniffed. 'Yes, please. I—' She couldn't help it. She broke down crying.

'Oh dear. Come over here.' He gestured for her to advance. 'There, there. Have a seat.' They sat next to each other in a pew at the back.

'I'm—my name is—' the words wouldn't come out. She was desperate to see her girls, but terrified. Something was wrong, she could feel it.

He rubbed her back. 'That's fine. You speak to me when you are ready.'

A few seconds passed, the echo of her sobbing off the high walls the only sound.

'Is it the Plague? Have you lost someone?'

Mary thought of the child she saw outside. So it was true—it was back. She shook her head. 'It's not that.' She took a deep breath. 'My name is Mary. Mary Pannell. I believe you know my daughters. They are twenty-eight and thirty-four years old. Bess and Agnes.'

The rector's eyes widened. He was younger than Mary, but he wasn't young. He looked kind but then he was a holy man. Of course he was a good man. Perhaps he had helped to look after her girls when they had come to London.

'I miss them so much. I haven't seen them for ten years.' She sobbed again but there were no tears left to cry. 'Please, do you know where they are? I don't even know what they are doing now.

Did they marry? Do they have children of their own? There is so much I do not know. I should never have left Kippax without them.'

'Don't worry about that now,' he said. 'Thank God for bringing you here. I can tell you where they live.'

31

REUNION – MARY

Mary and Elizabeth held hands as they walked. Over the years they had discovered that people wouldn't notice this, as long as their cloaks were at least arm-length. Mary did not mind—the evenings were cold at this time of year.

'Do you remember the last time?' Mary asked. 'The last Plague outbreak?' She didn't want to talk about her daughters at the moment.

Elizabeth hesitated. 'Yes. We missed most of it, luckily. But I remember the fallout. Most families lost people.'

'At least it felt as though it was coming to an end. This time, we don't know how long it will last.'

Elizabeth cleared her throat. 'It's not just that. We're ten years older now. It feels riskier.'

'I know. And the girls—' Mary took a deep breath. 'Well, to have my daughters here... I don't want them mixed up in this.'

'Neither do I.'

'So we're agreed? We have to leave?' Mary's voice was more high-pitched than before. She tried to gauge what Elizabeth was thinking. Going back to Kippax would be dangerous.

'Yes.' Elizabeth's voice was firm.

'We will have to face Sir Henry. I will have to face him.' Mary's voice wobbled.

Elizabeth bit her lip and watched her footsteps as they walked. 'We'll have to make a plan. But first, are you sure about this?' Elizabeth always sounded so confident, like she knew everything.

'Yes.' She paused. 'What's going to happen?'

Elizabeth cleared her throat. 'You shouldn't worry. Lady Witham might go easy on you.'

She shook her head vigorously. 'He was her baby. She will never forget.'

'But you were not to blame!' Elizabeth raised her voice.

'It was I who brought the remedy into the household!' Mary pulled her hand away.

'You explained everything to Sir William. It's Lady Witham's fault. If she hadn't done away with her husband none of this would have happened.'

'Even more reason for her to blame me. Lady Witham will not allow anyone to see her as a criminal. She is an important woman.'

'Still. I will not allow them to imprison you. There must be something we can do.'

They walked in silence until they arrived at the tavern.

Was this it? This was where Richard Gardiner had told her to go. The small door on the corner was almost identical to the others on the block. There were lots of houses along here. They were tiny. There were gaps in the walls, in the doors. It must be so cold inside. Even their hut back in Kippax was built better than these. The streets around here were awful. There were rats running about the place, and the ground was covered in dirt and muck. It was a far cry from the life of luxury she had been living with Elizabeth. A pang of guilt hit her in the gut. She took a deep breath and knocked.

A thirty-four-year-old dishevelled Bess opened the short wooden door. She gasped and squealed.

'Mother! Elizabeth!' She pulled them into a tight hug.

Mary's heart jumped as she held her daughter close. It had been ten years since she had said goodbye to her daughters. 'My girl.' Her eyes watered.

Elizabeth joined in the hug. 'It's wonderful to see you, Bess.'

'Please, come in. I'm working but it's quiet today. Would you like a drink?'

They followed her and accepted a cup of beer each. Mary couldn't stop staring at her daughter. 'Bess...' She muttered. She reached out her arm and stroked her shoulder. She frowned. 'You're too thin, what have you been—'

Elizabeth interrupted her. 'Your mother and I have been so worried about you. How are you? Have you been living here for a long time? Is Agnes with you?'

Bess spoke quickly and poured a drink for another customer as she spoke. 'It's great to see you.'

Mary's eyes widened. Something was wrong. 'Come here, give your mother a kiss.'

Bess went on without stopping, 'How did you find this place?! We have been looking for you for years. I thought we would never meet again, but Agnes knew you would come.'

Mary's smile fell from her face. 'I'm so sorry we left you. If I could go back—' Her breaths quickened. Had they lived like this all this time, when only a few miles down the road, Mary and Elizabeth had been living a life of luxury?

Bess took a breath. 'It's not your fault. But staying in Kippax wasn't an option.'

Mary cleared her throat. 'Please, I'm so sorry. I thought we'd have time to come back for you. You know I wanted us to all travel down together.'

Her daughter nodded grimly. 'Sir Henry planned to arrest us both to force you to confess.'

Mary stole a guilty glance at Elizabeth. She couldn't look Bess in the eye. 'It's not fair that they dragged you into this. I'm so sorry. It's all my fault.' She reached over to hold Bess's hand and squeezed it tight. 'This is all my doing. I should never have left you.' She sniffed, trying to stop herself from crying.

'Please, no. Agnes wanted me to tell you that none of this is your fault.' Bess pulled her hand away and tidied away some mugs, stacking them on a shelf behind her.

'Oh, Agnes. When will she be back? Are you two living together? Did either of you get married? I have missed so much of your lives. Come over and give me another hug, I'm sure you can take a break.'

Bess changed the subject. 'How did you find me here?'

'George—George Chapman, that is—'

Bess flinched at the name.

'Is something wrong?' Mary asked.

Bess shook her head, her eyes wide.

Mary explained how George had found the rector who had given them the address. 'I am so sorry. Bess, I hope you will forgive me. I never dreamed we would lose touch for so many years. All I ever wanted was for the two of you to be safe.'

She nodded. 'I know. You would never do anything to hurt us. Don't worry about me.'

'How did the two of you manage to find work and lodgings here?'

Bess murmured, 'the landlord was kind to take us in. He took pity on us.' Then she shook her head and raised her voice. 'We don't need to speak about that. You are finally here! What do we do now? Where are you living? Can I come and live with you?'

Mary told her daughter that they had been living with George, but she didn't go into detail about how Sir Henry had found them and she didn't say they were planning to return to Kippax.

'That's great. I'm pleased for you both.' Bess looked at her mother, wide-eyed. Tears were forming in her eyes. But she shook her head, trying to hide her sadness. 'It's great to hear how you have both settled in. Truly great.'

Mary's heart beat faster. Why was Bess being so strange? Her words sounded unnatural. Tears had started to fall down her cheeks. She still hadn't mentioned Agnes. Mary whispered, 'where is Agnes?'

Bess sniffed. 'Oh, Mother.'

'What is it? What's happened to my Agnes?' Mary stood up. Her chair fell to the ground. 'Take me to Agnes!' She commanded her daughter.

'Mother, please. She is not the same girl you once knew.' Bess spoke in a whisper. 'It might be better not to see her. Not yet. You have to remember her as she was, not as she is.'

'Bess, you listen to me. Take me to my daughter.'

'Elizabeth?' Bess pleaded.

'You had better tell us what's going on. Has the Plague taken her?' Elizabeth asked.

Mary interrupted. 'Please, God, no. I had a bad feeling. I knew something was terribly wrong.' She sobbed and the men in the tavern all turned to face her.

'Please, you must calm down. It's not the Plague—it's worse.'

Elizabeth cut in once again. 'Out with it, Bess. What could be worse than the Plague? She hasn't died, has she?'

Bess shook her head. 'Death would be a mercy at this stage. It won't be long. Death will come for her any day.'

'Look at your mother! Tell us what has happened at once!'

Bess sniffed and wiped her eyes with her sleeve. She whispered, so quietly that Mary and Elizabeth could barely hear her. 'It's the French disease.'

Mary looked blankly at her daughter.

Elizabeth shook her head. 'No. It cannot be. The French disease?'

'What is it, Elizabeth? How can this disease be worse than the Plague?'

Elizabeth shook her head. 'Bess, no. You must be mistaken. The only people who catch it are—well. It's the women who —who—'

Mary's eyes widened.

'I'm so sorry. We struggled when we came to London. I thought we were going to die. We had no food and no lodgings. The only person who offered us a place to stay was the landlord, and when we couldn't afford to pay, he got Agnes some extra work.'

Mary's hand flew to her mouth. 'Please, God, forgive me. It's all my fault.'

'It wasn't long before I found out what was happening. But it was long enough for her to catch something from a man.'

Mary and Elizabeth looked at each other but said nothing. Bess went on, 'I have been treating her. The rector talked me through the mercurial treatment, and all the money I earn goes towards paying for the medical supplies I need. I have been nursing her all these years, but he keeps saying if it's not God's will, she may not survive. I would do anything to be in her place.'

The men in the tavern were now staring at them. It was strange enough to see three women alone there, let alone in such a state.

'Bess, take us to see her. Now.' Elizabeth spoke in a voice that told her she would not be denied.

'This way. She's through here.'

The room where Bess and Agnes slept was hot, stuffy and small. Mary had forgotten what it was like to live in such cramped quarters. Even back in Kippax, they had not lived in such squalor. She wrinkled her nose. What was the smell?

Bess called over to a lump of blankets huddled in the corner. 'Agnes?'

Mary gasped. 'She's in here? Agnes? Agnes, my girl? It's me, it's Mother.'

She ran over and pulled back the blankets. Lying there was a tiny mass of bones and skin, covered with a thin cotton nightdress. She was curled up in a ball, her chin tucked into her chest. Mary rolled her over and gasped. Large red sores on Agnes's forehead and cheekbones completely covered her eyes. Her breathing was loud and laboured, restricted by smaller sores along her jaw. Her collarbone protruded awkwardly from the nightdress. Mary screamed.

'She's dead!'

Elizabeth pulled Mary backwards. 'Come on, we shouldn't be here. Let's go. Now. Out.'

They backed up to the door but Bess shook her head. 'She's not dead. She can't see, she has no teeth and her memory is gone. Her personality has long faded away and her body is failing her. But she is quite alive.'

Mary wept. She wailed and screamed and fell to her knees. Poor Agnes was covered in foul-smelling abscesses and ulcers. How did she get here? What had Mary ever done that God would do this to her daughter?

'Who are you? What are you doing here? Don't touch me! Get out!' Agnes's words were difficult to understand now that she had lost her teeth.

Mary jumped. Her daughter's voice was unfamiliar. Sharp and piercing. It was nothing like the warm, flirty, playful voice of eighteen-year-old Agnes from Kippax. This was the harsh voice of a city woman whose family had abandoned her.

'Oh, Agnes, it's your mother. This is all my fault. I have killed you. Because of me you were driven here, and because of me you are here now. Oh, what have I done?'

She tried again to hug Agnes, but she pulled away.

'You were always such a beautiful young girl.'

Agnes addressed Bess with the croaky voice of an old woman. 'What is she doing here? Take her away. I want her gone. Why isn't she gone?'

Bess led Mary and Elizabeth back into the main area of the tavern. The landlord glared at them, angry they had been making a noise. Mary didn't notice. She was busy thinking about her daughter. Bess refilled their cups and sat down. They drank without speaking. The landlord could see something was going on, so left them to it. He served the men of the tavern for the time being.

Elizabeth broke the silence. 'Bess, you must come and stay with us. This is no place for you.'

'But what do we do about Agnes?'

Mary stifled a sob at the mention of her daughter's name.

'Mother, please. What will we do? Agnes doesn't know anything anymore. She doesn't even recognise me. It's exhausting.' Bess's words ran together as she sped up, overwhelmed at the thoughts going through her mind.

'I have no time for anything. I barely earn enough money here to feed myself, and that's before I've paid the rector for the mercurial cures. Agnes won't eat for days and she hardly drinks anything. I'm worried she's shrinking away to nothing. She can't see, she can't walk. She never has energy to speak because she spends every night screaming in agony.'

Mary stared at Bess. 'My girl,' she whispered. 'What have I done to my girl?' She knew she had to be quiet, everyone was looking at them already.

'It's not your fault, Mother. It's mine.' She took her hands. 'I thought I could take care of us both. I never knew she was doing that kind of work. Not until it was too late. Trust me, I would never have let her. I would do it myself before I wished it on her. We should never have come to this hateful place.' Bess was squeezing Mary's hands so tightly it was hurting. But she wasn't crying. Mary's sobs were relentless, but Bess sat there, shoulders hunched, nails digging into her mother's palms.

Elizabeth pulled Bess and Mary into a hug. 'Shh. We can figure this out. At least the three of us are together.' She kissed each of them on the top of their head.

'What will we do?' Bess asked.

'We will take things one step at a time.' Elizabeth tried to keep her voice steady. 'Agnes is ill, so we will consult a physician. Then we'll bring you home.'

'What about Kippax? The Plague?' Mary's voice was soft, almost silent.

'Later. We can discuss all of that later.'

The others nodded, grateful Elizabeth was there to take charge.

'Bess, you need to pack up your things and anything Agnes needs and then tell your landlord you will be leaving.'

She looked over towards him and scoffed. 'He won't care.'

'Good. We'll help you pack up. Let's go.' Elizabeth and Bess headed back into the room where Agnes rested, but Mary couldn't bring herself to go back in there.

32

TRAGEDY – BESS

Mary rolled Agnes onto her side and pulled off the old bedsheets.

'Mother, is that necessary?' Bess rolled her eyes. 'I have been looking after her for ten years. The sheets are fine!'

'The sheets need changing weekly. I should have taught you this kind of thing, like Mother Pannell taught me,' Mary muttered.

'What did you say?' Bess called.

'Just get over here and help me!'

'Yes, Mother.' She had not missed this. She grabbed the clean sheets and threw one end to Mary.

'You've only ever worked on a farm.' Mary shook her head.

'Just because I wasn't a housemaid all my life doesn't mean I don't know how to change a couple of bedsheets.'

'You need to learn these things. One day you will make a brilliant wife, and you will need to know how to look after your house.' Mary said.

Bess rolled her eyes. She thought of Matthew and the wife he probably now had. Someone younger than Bess. Younger, prettier and all too eager to give him lots of children. 'Mother, I am thirty-four years old. Who do you suppose wants to marry me? No. I shall be a spinster. That's if the Plague doesn't get me first. Or the great pox. Maybe I'll go like poor Agnes.' Bess groaned at the thought. 'Actually no. If I ever find one of those sores on me, I'll kill myself.'

'Stop that!' Mary shouted at her daughter. 'You mustn't talk like that. It's not Godly.'

'Godly!' Bess shouted back. 'Where is God in all this? What has God ever done for Agnes? God has abandoned us, Mother.'

'Stop this right now.' Mary stepped back from the bedsheets and pointed a finger at Bess. 'You listen to me. We will figure out all of this. I promise. We will figure out what to do and where to go. You are a beautiful young woman. We will find you a husband. And you will be a good wife, and a good mother. Do you understand?'

Bess groaned but did not respond.

Mary was insistent. 'Anyway, this girl needs proper care. I need to look after her, and the best place for that is here, at home. Our home.'

Bess raised her voice. 'I have done everything for Agnes! She has had nothing but the best.'

'Please see sense!' Mary shook the bloody sheets in the air.

Bess wrinkled her nose at the smell. It wasn't a smell she had ever got used to.

'Agnes needs to be kept as clean as possible. She is covered in wounds and we must keep out infection.'

'Keep out infection? Look at her! Too late on the lecture, Mother.'

'My herbs aren't enough for her. Your ointment is too weak to be doing anything. Keeping her clean is all we can do right now. Clean and warm.' Mary motioned to the fire. 'Add some more logs. That's it. She must continue to sweat.'

'I do have a basic understanding of medicine, you know.' Bess said.

'Of course you do. Now fetch her some water.'

Mary rolled Agnes back onto the clean sheets as Bess left the room. Since bringing her back to George's lodgings, the state of Agnes's skin appeared to have improved. The sores were less swollen, and they didn't bleed as much. But those on her face still obscured her eyes and pressed on her throat. She still screamed out every night, and she was thinner and paler than ever.

There was a knock at the door so Bess went to get it once she had filled up the bucket. It was a man—tall, bald and dressed in an expensive-looking overcoat. He held in his hand a large bag, made of a brown leather, as far as she could tell. One of George's friends, perhaps? He addressed Bess with a nod. He did not offer his hand.

'Good day to you. I'm here to see the girl. George has filled me in on her... condition.'

'Oh, thank you for coming. Are you a healer?'

He cleared his throat, suppressing a laugh. 'A healer? No. I am a physician, my dear.'

Bess rolled her eyes and led him upstairs. He was one of those men—convinced he knew better than any woman.

'Of course, sir. I apologise.'

He followed her inside and frowned at the bed next to the fire.

'It's a physician,' Bess told Mary.

'Oh, thank you—and please, what can we do for my daughter?' She motioned for him to follow her to the bed.

'Under whose care has the girl been?' Pushing past Mary, he stared into Agnes's face. He placed his bag on the floor next to him and flipped it open.

'Mine, sir.' Bess put down the heavy bucket of water and stumbled into the room. She wasn't very strong these days. 'I have been looking after her since she became ill.'

'Yes?'

'Sir?' What was he getting at?

He tutted. 'When did she become ill?'

'Ten years ago, sir. Though she wasn't this bad at first. For the first year she was still eating, she had no problems with her memory and her vision was fine. In fact, the sores on her face are relatively new.'

He scoffed. 'Well, yes. I can see that.' He poked them with a small metal stick and Agnes let out a groan. Was she asleep or awake? Bess couldn't always tell these days.

'Yes, sir?' Bess phrased it like a question. How could he know?

'She won't survive for long with this. It's almost completely restricting her throat. Once her throat is blocked, she's gone, I'm afraid.'

Mary nodded and opened her mouth to speak, but no words came out. Bess walked over to her mother and put a hand on her shoulder.

The physician added, 'That is not to say there is nothing to be done, of course.'

Bess didn't like this man.

'What can we do?' Bess asked.

He now held a metal implement in each hand and stuck both of them down Agnes's throat. 'Yes, I see. Right.' He pulled them out and put them back in his bag, before closing the leather flap once more. 'It's simple enough. Continue what you are doing. Keep her clean and warm. But her only hope of survival now is to inhale a solution of mercury.'

Bess interrupted, 'Yes, I have been giving her mercury, an ointment. There is a mercurial ointment the rector mixed for me that goes on her sores.'

Mary nudged her. 'Shh.'

'The rector? You have been taking medical advice from a rector instead a physician?' He stood up from Agnes and raised his voice.

Feeling Mary's eyes on her, Bess changed tact. 'Oh, not much, sir. Once, in fact. He suggested something but I don't think it worked.'

Mary nodded. 'I checked, and I'm not convinced it had any mercury in it at all. The girl hasn't received treatment yet, I'm sure of it.'

The physician nodded. 'Fine. These men of God, they mean well, but their cures can do more harm than good. You'll do well to listen to my advice, and my advice only.'

'Yes, sir.' Mary and Bess both nodded.

'First, I would like a nice cup of ale. Then we can begin the mercury inhalation. You two will remain downstairs for your own safety. This is complicated to administer.'

He led them out of the bedroom, and Mary gave him his cup of ale. He drank it silently then went back upstairs to see to Agnes.

Mary and Bess sat opposite each other. 'When will Elizabeth get back?' Bess asked.

'I'm not sure. Not for a while. She had to go to the market. I didn't want to go, not with Agnes like this.'

'Yes. Of course.'

Agnes's groans grew louder but did not reach a scream, so neither Mary nor Bess thought it necessary to check on her. When the physician returned, he poked his head round the door briefly. 'That's it for today.'

'As for payment—' Mary started. She didn't want him to think she wouldn't pay him.

'Not to worry, I can sort out that kind of thing with George. I'll be back daily from now on.' With that, he swung his bag behind him and out of the front door. Mary and Bess went into Agnes's room where she lay, just as before. There was no reason to think the physician's medicine wouldn't work. After all, he seemed to know what he was talking about.

Within two weeks, Agnes was dead.

For those two weeks, Mary spent every minute dedicated to her daughter's care. She made sure she had all the luxuries possible. She changed the sheets every day, washed her every other day and made sure her hair was always combed. The physician administered the mercury inunctions every day and commented on how well Agnes was responding to the treatment. But all Mary saw was her already ill daughter becoming thinner, paler and less responsive. With her limited amount of knowledge, she thought the physician was making things worse, but she said nothing. After all, who was she compared to an actual physician? All for nothing. The day Agnes died Mary wept. She cried solidly for days. Bess and Elizabeth brought her food and drink which she barely touched. They tried speaking to her, to no avail. Mary cried and sobbed and screamed throughout the day and night.

They buried Agnes at St Mary's in Whitechapel. An unmarked grave, but right next to the church. People of her class would not normally be awarded such an honour, but Richard Gardiner had agreed this was a special situation. The money George had donated to his chapel surely helped him to make his decision.

It was a brief service. Richard read some passages from the Bible and they all prayed over Agnes's grave. Bess did not cry at the graveside. She had been crying over her sister for years. Her death seemed almost a blessing at this point. Her terrible pains were finally over, no matter how they had come about. She was tired of blaming herself and had no desire to blame the rector or the physician.

'Is that it?' Bess asked.

She looked to the rector, and he nodded in return.

'We can go now,' Elizabeth said.

Bess looked over to her mother, on her knees next to the mound of earth that marked the spot where Agnes lay. She was leaning all the way forwards, pressing her forehead into the ground.

'What about Mother?'

Elizabeth walked over to Mary, leaned down to whisper something in her ear and kissed her cheek. 'She'll be fine, but will need to stay here for a while. Let's go.'

33

GOODBYE – BESS

B ess walked with her mother and they chatted like they had never spent any time apart. Mary did not mention the extra lines on Bess's face or the dark circles under her eyes, but she ran her concerned eyes over her all the same. Back at the farm with Matthew, she was always happy and healthy, but now her cheeks were hollow and her collar bone protruded from her dress. It was helping to take her mind off Agnes, being with Mary. They could share their grief by not talking about their grief —together.

When they got back to the house, Elizabeth took the bags from them.

'George?' Mary called. He had been away, so they hadn't told him about Agnes yet.

Footsteps sounded, and he came in to join them. 'Good afternoon. Lovely to see you.'

'George, I would like you to meet my daughter. This is Bess. Bess, this is George Chapman, your cousin. He has been kind enough to offer us a place to stay since we arrived in London.'

Bess wanted to scream at George.

'Thank you for helping us,' Mary said.

Bess gritted her teeth and glared at him.

'Bess!'

'Mother, look. Whatever George's reason for reuniting us, it wasn't for our benefit.' She wanted to explain what happened, to tell her mother that this man, who they thought had been so kind to them, was, in fact, to blame for everything that happened to Agnes. But she was exhausted. She knew telling them wouldn't fix anything.

Mary frowned. 'You know nothing about George or the sacrifices he has made for us.'

'I know enough.' She scowled.

George fiddled with his jacket, pulling it down and brushing out the creases. 'It's fine, Mary.' He cleared his throat. 'Who would like something to drink?' He made drinks for everyone while Mary set about making some food.

'Here you are.' He handed everyone a cup.

Bess looked George up and down. She frowned at his neat hair and brightly coloured clothes. He didn't look like anyone they had known in Kippax. He was a different class of person than she was used to. 'What is it you do?'

Mary shot her a glance. 'Manners, girl.' She set out some bread, meat and cheese, then sat next to Elizabeth.

George laughed. 'I am a scholar foremost, and a poet second.'

Bess frowned. What kind of job was that?

'George, I need to tell you something.' Elizabeth took a deep breath. 'Agnes has died.'

'Really? What happened?' His voice was higher than before. He already knew.

'Agnes...' Mary hesitated. She didn't like to talk about how her daughter died.

'The Plague took her,' Elizabeth mumbled. She cleared her throat. 'George, we are so grateful to you for helping us find her and Bess, but Agnes was already sick. It was too late.'

'I'm so sorry to hear that.' George walked over to Mary and pulled her into a hug.

'I finally found her. After all this time.' Mary sobbed.

'I know. At least you have Bess now.'

'Here it comes,' Bess muttered.

Mary sniffed. 'Is something wrong?'

Bess didn't reply. It would be best to stay quiet and not upset her mother any more than she already was.

'Have you considered going back?' George asked Mary.

'Back? To Kippax?'

He nodded. 'Unless you want Bess to have to spend her life on the run. She'd never be able to marry, and having children of her own would be difficult.'

Mary bit her lip and kept her eyes on the floor.

'Mother, don't listen to him. I'll be fine,' Bess snapped.

'But they'd arrest me.'

'Perhaps,' George said. 'But actually, you have a good chance of being able to clear your name.'

Mary caught his eye. 'Is that possible?'

Bess glared at George. What was he trying to achieve?

'It's more than possible. I've been looking into it for weeks now, and I believe if you turn yourself in, they will have no choice but to give you a fair trial.'

'What exactly would that mean?' Elizabeth asked.

'Evidence would be presented, witnesses called. Mary could make a statement herself, if she wanted.'

'But I didn't commit any crime, so what evidence could there be?'

George grinned. 'Exactly. That's why I think you have a good chance of being acquitted.'

'And if I am, I'll be free to live my life? Bess and Elizabeth, too?'

'Of course.'

'It won't be that easy,' Bess said.

'But if it means you'll be able to live without the threat of arrest, I'm willing to try.'

'Mother, please. Don't listen to him.'

'Bess, stop it. This is my decision.'

Elizabeth took a deep breath. 'What exactly would happen? Would they put Mary back in gaol?'

Mary's face fell.

'Not for long. Only until the trial.'

'But they'll treat me as they did last time? Try to force a confession out of me?'

George sighed. 'I'm sorry. But it's only a matter of time until they find you in London. Don't you want Bess to have the life she deserves?'

'Don't trust him, Mother. I'll be happy anywhere. There's no reason for us to risk going home.' Bess raised her voice.

Mary took Bess's hand in hers and pressed it to her lips. 'Bess, please try to understand what it's like to be a mother. I would die for you. If I need to do this to ensure your safety, I'll do it. Anyway, like George said, it won't be long until the trial and after that I'll be free.'

'I think that's the right decision,' George said.

Anger rose from within Bess. She pulled away from Mary and smashed the plate of meat on the floor. 'Tell them the truth!'

'Bess!' Elizabeth shouted. 'Apologise to George, now.'

'I won't. He's not telling you everything.'

'I'm sorry, George,' Mary said.

'I understand. It must be difficult for her, now that she's lost Agnes.'

'Don't say her name,' Bess said through gritted teeth.

'Bess, if you have a problem with George, just say it.'

'He killed her!'

Elizabeth frowned. 'Bess, you know Agnes wasn't killed. She died from—'

'If you say the Plague, I'm going to scream,' Bess said.

Mary glared at her daughter.

'Fine,' Elizabeth said, avoiding George's gaze. 'She died from a disease.'

'A disease George gave her!'

George said nothing.

'He couldn't have,' Elizabeth muttered.

'Tell them! Tell them how you used to meet her in that tiny, sordid room at The Globe.'

Elizabeth's eyes widened. 'You've been going there for years.'

Mary put a hand to her mouth. 'Please, George. Tell me it's not true.'

'Believe me, I didn't give Agnes any disease. If I did, I would be ill myself. But as you can see, I'm in perfect health.'

'But you've known Agnes for years,' Bess said.

'No.' He kept his voice calm. 'Mary, Elizabeth, listen. I met her once, but she was already ill. As soon as I found out who she was, I told you where to find her.'

Mary sighed. 'Please, stop talking about her. I don't want to hear it.'

'He's lying. I know he was seeing her for years.'

'Please. I know I've made mistakes, but I'm doing my best to make amends.'

'You can't really expect us to believe that?'

'That's enough, Bess,' Elizabeth said.

Bess groaned and went to leave the room.

'Wait.' George shifted uncomfortably in his seat. 'There actually is something I have been meaning to tell you for a while.'

She span around. 'Of course there is.'

'No, no. It's a good thing. But it means I need to move house.'

Mary sat up straight.

'I have been offered the patronage of Prince Henry. He has granted me a position in his household.'

Prince? How were they related to George, anyway? What sort of person gets a position in a royal household?

'Why would you want to live with Prince Henry?' Bess asked. 'Is this about money?'

Elizabeth shot Bess a glare.

'Yes, it is a paid position.'

'But you never do things for the money.' Elizabeth said.

'He's not who we thought he was,' Mary muttered.

'It's not just about money. If I can retain this position, I'll be safe from arrest.'

'Why would you be arrested?' Bess immediately asked.

'The School of Night.' Mary sighed.

'Exactly. I don't particularly relish the idea of going back to gaol.'

'Of course you don't.' Out of all of them, only Mary and George had ever been arrested, so she knew how bad it could get. 'Well, if that's your decision, I suppose we must part ways. It's probably best, given what we've just found out.'

Since Agnes's death, Mary was different. Her voice croaked whenever she spoke and she was always tired.

'Thank you. I was nervous to tell you, actually. I didn't want you to be left with nowhere to live.' George replied.

Elizabeth sighed. 'Well, we have talked about going back to get Mary acquitted. Especially now that Sir Henry has been here. It won't be long before he comes back.' She looked from Mary to Bess. 'Besides, I think we've been in London for as long as we can manage. We could all do with getting out of the city. Especially now that the Plague has returned. It will be good for us. All of us.'

'If you're sure, then I'm happy for you. I know you have been missing home. You must be eager to return to Mother Pannell.'

Mary took a deep breath. She walked over to George, reached up and slapped him across his cheek.

Bess jumped at the sound. Nobody said anything.

'How dare you hurt my daughter?'

George was speechless.

'Get out. I don't want to see you again.'

He stuttered at first, unsure of how to respond. 'O-of course. I need to meet someone, anyway. I'll be back late this evening.' He pulled the door shut behind him.

Mary leaned against the door and exhaled loudly.

Elizabeth walked over and pulled Mary's head onto her chest, grinning. 'I can't believe you slapped him.'

Mary let out a faint giggle. 'Me neither. But he deserved it.'

'I know.'

'Mother, are you serious about leaving?'

She retrieved her wine and took a sip. 'We'll talk about it, but I would like to go home. I've never felt at home in London, and you deserve to live your life without fear.'

'Mother, I'll be fine. George was only saying that to get rid of us.'

'This isn't about George. It's our decision. Do you really want to stay?'

Bess thought of her sister and how strange it was that she would never see her again. Even when Bess was unsure about coming to London, Agnes insisted they would be able to make a life here. But she was wrong. They should never have come. 'No.'

'Because if you want to stay, we'll find a way.'

'I want to go home. But I don't want them to arrest you again,' Bess said.

'Me neither,' Elizabeth said.

Mary pulled them both into a hug. 'Don't worry about me. We'll figure out all the details later, but I know this is the right decision. I can feel it.'

'When will we leave?'

Elizabeth answered. 'If we're leaving, it should be soon. The streets are empty these days and I don't want to stay here for any longer than we have to. A lot of the taverns have closed for good, and people everywhere are fleeing London. Now that the Plague is back, nobody wants to be around when people start dying again.'

Bess sighed and finished her wine in a few large gulps. She was ready to leave.

34

CUDWORTH – ELIZABETH

The Cudworth Estate, South Yorkshire, 1603

After days of riding and sleeping outside, Elizabeth could see the others were losing hope. Conversations were shorter and more to the point. She was doing her best with Sir Walter's map and compass, but she wasn't very experienced in navigation. One morning Mary, fed up of asking for Elizabeth's help to mount her horse, had tried to do it alone. She had fallen and twisted her ankle on a rock and so now had to ride sidesaddle. She was not a skilled rider, but this meant they were travelling slowly. Bess caught up with her and spoke under her breath, but Elizabeth could still hear.

'We haven't been travelling along roads or even paths, but through fields and forests. I thought we would be able to stop at inns and taverns. Even have a proper, home-cooked meal.'

'I'm sorry. I thought so too, but we can trust Elizabeth. It's a hard journey but I promise she'll get us home.' Mary said.

Bess nodded and sighed, then held back so she rode behind the others.

When it darkened that evening, Bess called out to Mary, 'What's that? Up ahead, do you see that? Is that Kippax?' Elizabeth felt a wave of guilt wash over her. She hadn't told them she wasn't actually heading there first. It had seemed simpler to keep this to herself. Even now, she decided not to tell the others that she wanted to visit somebody on the way home. After all, what if Mary wanted to ride on by and go straight back to Kippax? No, this was too important and Mary might not understand.

'Elizabeth! Do you see?' Mary shouted. 'It's not Kippax. Are we lost?'

It was raining for the first time in days. As they got closer to the building up ahead, it became clearer. It appeared to be a large manor house.

'Leave it to me. I will ask where we are and see if they can offer us shelter.' Elizabeth said.

She kicked her horse and sped up ahead at twice the speed of Mary and Bess. She did not look back. Her heart rate quickened. This must be it. This must be where Molly lived. Her horse rapidly sped up when the tall, damp grass turned into a stone path leading up to the entrance to the Cudworth Manor and Estate. She jumped off her horse, gave him a quick stroke and headed up the steps to knock on the door.

A servant answered the door.

Elizabeth curtsied. 'I wonder if I might ask for your help.' She gestured to the others who had just pulled up behind her. 'We have travelled a long way, from London. Might we trouble you for directions? Perhaps a place to rest?'

She nodded. 'Wait here.'

The others joined Elizabeth at the top of the steps.

'What did they say?' Bess asked.

'It was a servant. She has gone to speak to the family.'

Bess stayed with the horses, stroking and feeding them. A few minutes later a different woman came to the door. A twenty-four-year-old woman. Elizabeth gasped. She put a hand to her mouth.

'It's you! Miss Witham!' She corrected herself. 'Mrs Jobson!'

Molly gave her a warm smile. 'Please call me Molly. What a wonderful surprise. I'm so glad you have come.'

They had made it! 'How are you?' Elizabeth laughed. 'So we have reached Cudworth? I wasn't sure my navigation skills would get us here. It's lovely to see you. I hope this is a good time. I'm sorry to bother you!'

Molly held out her arms. 'Not at all. Come here.' She gave Elizabeth a hug. 'You have arrived in South Yorkshire. Kippax is not far from here at all.' She glanced at the others. 'Mary! It's lovely to see you too.' Elizabeth pulled away and ran to her bag. She rummaged through it until she found what she was looking for.

Mary bowed her head. 'Good evening, Mrs Jobson. Molly. It's a pleasure. Please meet my daughter Bess.' She gestured to the horses.

'Bess! Get up here.' She did as she was told. 'Here she is.'

'How lovely to make your acquaintance. I'm so glad you found your mother and Elizabeth in the end.' Molly glanced to Elizabeth who gave a slight shake of the head. She wouldn't ask about Agnes. Not right now, anyway. 'Do come in.' She held out her arm, and they followed her inside. She spoke to her servants. 'Please feed our guests. Give them something to drink, bathe them and tend to their horses. They will all stay here tonight at least.'

Elizabeth took her hand. 'Thank you, Molly. You don't have to do this. You are too kind.' She reached into the small bag of jewels she had retrieved and handed it to Molly.

'Nonsense. I am fascinated to hear your story. Ten years later and you are once again fleeing your home. Other than our very brief meeting a few years ago! You must relax tonight as my guests. Then tomorrow I shall hear all about you.' Molly opened the bag and gasped. 'Oh, Elizabeth! You kept them, all this time?'

She smiled. 'I hope you are not offended. I always wanted to give them back to you one day. To thank you for everything you did. I don't know what I would have done without you.'

'I'm afraid I don't have too many of my old things here, everything is back home.' It struck Elizabeth as odd that Molly still called her childhood home 'home', rather than the home she shared with her husband. Maybe she did not love Thomas as much as she said. 'Thank you, Elizabeth.' She held the jewels close to her chest and took a deep breath in and out.

'You're welcome.' Elizabeth followed her into the house, pleased that she could finally keep her promise.

As she had commanded, the servants whisked each of them away. They were all given warm baths and that evening they sat at a long mahogany table where more servants waited on them, refilling their cups and offering more plates of food until they couldn't eat any more. That night Elizabeth and Mary slept on a bed so soft they didn't even wake up until a servant girl came to help them get dressed. They had all been given dresses and corsets to replace the muddy clothes they had arrived in.

Elizabeth closed her eyes, raised her shoulders and took a deep breath. They had finally made it to somebody who might actually help them. Molly had influence. They were so close to what they had wanted for all these years.

'Is Molly awake yet?'

'Yes, Miss. She is reading in the morning room.' The servant replied, pulling on Elizabeth's corset.

'Not so tight. I will be leaving here on horseback.'

'Of course, Miss.' She tied it as it was, without pulling it any tighter.

The servant pulled up numerous skirts and over her corset she put her in a soft, cotton blouse.

'Thank you.' Elizabeth said.

Once Elizabeth's hair had been combed and tied into an uncomfortable spiral shape, she asked, 'Now may I please see Mrs Jobson?' Elizabeth asked.

She nodded and gestured for Elizabeth to follow her. 'This way.' Elizabeth glanced back at Mary before she left. Best to let her sleep. She had a lot to face up to once they got back home.

Molly sat up straight on an armchair next to a large bookcase. Elizabeth had got used to books when she had stayed with George Chapman, but this was another level. Surely nobody could read this many books. The walls were covered in shelves, which were so filled with books that some had to be piled up on the floor, waiting for a home of their own.

Elizabeth curtsied on entering the room. She wasn't sure of the protocol but figured it was best to be as polite as possible.

'Eli!' Molly replaced her bookmark, handed her book over to a servant who stood near her and smiled at Elizabeth.

She fidgeted with her hands, not sure what to say. She hadn't heard that name in a long time.

'Oh, do forgive me. Elizabeth. Come in and have a seat.' It felt strange when Molly called her Elizabeth.

'Thank you, Miss. Thank you for your hospitality to all of us. We appreciate it. Before we leave today is there anything at all we can do for you?' Elizabeth asked. She was keen to help Molly if she could, but she had little to offer.

Molly's eyes seemed to twinkle in the morning light, coming in through the large windows next to her. She still had those bouncing curls she had as a girl, but now her hair was tied into an elegant knot, with a few ringlets falling down at the sides of her face. 'Not at all. I hope you like the clothes. You will be given food and directions back to Kippax of course.'

'Thank you. I am so grateful.'

Molly held out her hand to stop Elizabeth. 'First, I wish to thank you.'

Elizabeth raised her eyebrows. 'Thank me?'

'Do you remember the last time I saw you—not in London, I mean in Kippax?' Molly asked.

'Yes, Miss. We were in the gardens at Ledston Hall.' Elizabeth remembered Molly well. She had been one of her only friends back in Kippax, although she was her employer. They had got on well.

Molly smiled at the memory of her childhood home. 'If not for you delivering my letter that day, I am sure I would never have married my husband, Thomas.' Elizabeth remembered how Molly was so excited to write to him after the first time he had visited. She was glad it had turned out well for her.

'You're welcome, Miss. I was happy to do it.' Elizabeth replied.

'I am sure you remember what my mother was like.' Molly scowled at the thought of her.

Elizabeth, not wanting to offend, nodded.

'The last time Thomas had visited, she had expressly forbidden him from coming to see me again. It was her opinion that it was too early for me to marry, and that I was too infatuated with him. She said that passion had no place in a marriage.' Molly explained.

Elizabeth said nothing.

'So I thank you, sincerely. Thomas has been a wonderful husband to me and I am looking forward to starting a family of our own.' She smiled again, and this time put a hand on her stomach. Elizabeth was happy for her. It seemed to be what she wanted.

'Pleased to hear it, Miss.' Elizabeth said. 'Actually, there is something I wanted to tell you.'

'Yes?'

'I apologise for my candour, and I don't know how much of this you know already—'

Molly caught her eye. 'What is it?'

'I found out who my father was.' Elizabeth took a deep breath. 'I found out that my father was Sir William Witham. We are sisters.'

Molly gasped.

'I'm sorry if you didn't know. I didn't want to tell you like this—'

'Oh, Elizabeth!' Molly pulled her into a tight embrace. 'I had heard talk. I always knew it was possible, but I didn't know for sure. To have you for a sister—what a blessing! If there is ever anything you need, please ask.'

'I must admit, there is something I would like from you.'

'Bring us some wine.' Molly commanded a servant, who scurried out of the room.

'Mary and I are going back home, with Bess. Sir Henry chased us all the way to London, and we just want to be free. We are hoping to clear Mary's name, and therefore Bess's name too.'

The servant girl returned with a tray, containing a ceramic jug and two cups. She poured them each a cup of wine.

'I think we can help each other.' Molly gulped down her wine. 'It is no secret what my mother thought of my father.' Molly paused. 'Of our father, I should say. Forgive me if I seem unaffected, but I have struggled with this for years. Nobody seems willing to admit what happened.'

Elizabeth's eyes widened.

'She killed him.' The tone of her voice was unchanged. The calmness of it brought a chill to Elizabeth's spine. She had told Elizabeth this back then, but she had been only a teenager. Elizabeth wasn't sure if Molly had believed it at the time, but she certainly did now.

'It's time. What I would like to do is to bring his murderer to justice.' Molly added.

'I see.'

'Would you help me?' She took another sip and this time, so did Elizabeth.

Elizabeth wanted to help her, but spoke slowly so as not to seem too keen. 'Of course, Mrs Jobson. But how can I help?'

'Since the harvest failure of 1596, the population of Kippax has fallen dramatically. More recently, the sweating sickness has come upon our dear town and unfortunately many of our population has fallen ill, or even died. I was lucky to have met Thomas and to have left there when I did.'

'I'm glad things seem to have worked out for you both?'

Molly smiled. 'Oh yes, I am a lucky woman. As Lords of Cudworth we have a responsibility to provide an heir to the Cudworth estate and keep it in the family.' She touched her stomach again, as if she were pregnant, but something about her expression made Elizabeth think she wasn't.

'Of course, an heir must be important for you.' Elizabeth said.

'Indeed. But anyway, before I go on is there anything you would like to know? Perhaps you would like to hear some news of the people back home?'

'Actually, yes. I wonder if you have any news of Mother Pannell?' Elizabeth bit her lip in anticipation.

'I'm sorry, I don't know if she's still around—she keeps to herself.' Molly said. 'Is there anything else?'

She shook her head.

'Then let us proceed.' She lowered her voice. 'I want my mother to pay for what she did to my father.'

Elizabeth gasped.

'What I need you to do is gather evidence and witnesses. I cannot be seen to be investigating this. You will need to interview the servants.' She finished her wine and her voice quickened. 'It's been ten years, but she has not changed the household. The staff are mostly the same as before. They will talk to you. They will recognise you. I am certain some of them will help you—she's not well liked.'

'Molly—'

She did not allow her to interrupt. 'I want her tried and executed for killing my—' she sniffed before continuing, 'for killing such an upstanding member of this community. I will testify to whatever you need. Sir Henry will listen to me.'

'But Molly—'

'I know my mother is guilty, but she will never be tried of such a crime without firm evidence.'

Elizabeth nodded.

'If you agree to help me with this, I will give you money. You never need work again. If you would like, I can give you work to do for one of my charities, or I can arrange a marriage for you. We can discuss all of that later. But you must tell nobody of my involvement. Not Mary, not her daughters, nobody. Do you agree to my terms?' Molly's voice was stern. It was surprising, especially for a young woman. But it suited her.

It struck Elizabeth that Molly must be very used to getting her way. She did not allow Elizabeth to interrupt her, even to offer help or advice. She had made up her mind and so had Elizabeth— she would do whatever was necessary.

'I do.'

35

KIPPAX – ELIZABETH

Kippax, West Yorkshire, 1603

Elizabeth recognised where they were once she caught sight of the river. The morning was still dark, but the moon lit up the tips of the long grass. This is where she played as a child. Her memories of being here with Mother Pannell played out in her mind.

'Mary?' She called. Mary rode up beside her.

'Are we nearly there?'

She nodded. 'I used to run around on these riverbanks.' She slowed down her horse and took the reins with one hand. She gestured towards the edge of the river. 'And this is where I learned to swim.'

'Did Mother Pannell teach you?'

'Yes.'

Elizabeth kicked her horse and rode ahead. The outline of the two huts eventually took shape.

'Mother, is that our old house?' Bess's voice sounded from behind Elizabeth.

'It is. Do you not recognise it? It is light enough.'

'It's been so long, that's all.'

The last time Bess was here, she and her sister thought they had escaped Sir Henry for good. They were going to make a new start in London. If only she had known what was going to happen.

'Is that Mother Pannell?' The silhouette of an old woman, hunched over, surveying her herb garden, took shape. Her long, white plait hung down the middle of her back like always.

'She looks older.' Elizabeth said simply. The guilt was building up inside her. Her breaths sped up. What was she going to say?

As they got closer, she saw them. She walked a few steps in their direction before putting a hand to her lower back and watching.

'How old is she now?' Mary asked.

'Eighty-six.' Elizabeth replied, trying to keep her voice steady. She hadn't expected to find her mother alive.

Mother Pannell shouted at them before they were within earshot.

'What is she saying?' Bess asked.

'Scolding us before we have even returned.' Elizabeth muttered.

'There was no reason for you to return,' she continued. Her croaked voice was raised, and she pointed her finger aggressively as she spoke. 'I was doing fine here; the girls had already left. You're going to ruin everything. Why you have returned I do not know—'

'Mother!' Elizabeth shouted back. 'Please. Give us a minute.' She dismounted her horse and hurried towards her. 'We have been riding for days. We're exhausted.'

She scoffed, turned her back on them and went inside. There wasn't space for all of them, so only Elizabeth followed her. She felt in her pocket for Mother Pannell's book she had given her before they left for London. Elizabeth so desperately wanted to share what Mary had told her. About Mother Pannell's family and her husband. But she couldn't face it. Mary had broken her trust by telling Elizabeth everything. She decided not to say anything.

'Light the fire and make yourselves something to eat.' Mother Pannell called. 'I don't know why you've returned—we'll need to make a plan, figure out what to do next.'

Elizabeth took a loaf of bread from the shelf. 'We have a plan,

Mother.' She tore off a piece for Mary and Bess and went out to give it to them. 'I'll see you soon.'

Bess hurried off, but Mary pulled Elizabeth into an embrace.

'I'll be careful,' she whispered.

Elizabeth pressed her lips against Mary's. Mother Pannell sighed loudly from behind her.

'We'll figure this out. I promise.' Mary kissed her again, this time lingering. Elizabeth didn't want her to stop. Her heart beat faster and she kissed her back, more passionately this time. Mary's hands found their way to Elizabeth's waist and she let out a quiet moan.

Mary's lips were soft, and her hands were gentle. The sensation crept from her lips to her waist to all around her body. She almost forgot where they were. The kiss kept going. Mary's cap came off as Elizabeth's long fingers ran through her hair, pulling gently.

Mary pulled away. 'I have to go.' A longing struck Elizabeth.

'Goodbye,' she managed. Elizabeth stroked her cheek, and then she was gone.

36

ROMANCE – BESS

Bess ran all the way to the Middletons' farm, but she wasn't as fit as she used to be. When she arrived, she had a sharp pain in her belly and sweat dripping down her face. This wasn't how she wanted to greet Matthew. But there was no time to think about it. She saw his boots, tatty as ever, before she stood up straight to see him grinning back at her.

'Bess!' He pulled her close. 'You're back.'

His touch was warm and spread from the spot where his fingertips brushed against her back all over her. She squeezed him tightly. 'I didn't know if you'd—I wasn't sure if I'd find you—' she sputtered.

'Are you well? Where have you been? I tried to find you, even managed to get down to London for a job. But I couldn't see you anywhere.' He cupped her face in her hands. 'Talk to me.'

By now a small crowd of her former co-workers, and some new, younger ones, had formed around the pair. Bess's cheeks flushed red, and she led him away. 'Not here.'

He looked behind him. 'Oh. Of course, I'm sorry.'

She smiled. She had missed his voice.

'What are you all looking at? Don't you have work to do?' Matthew shouted. 'Come on,' he whispered to Bess. 'Let's go.'

'I don't want to get you in trouble,' she started.

'Don't be silly. Follow me.' He took her by the hand and led her to the old barn where he used to sleep. He pushed her against the far wall.

Bess gasped. 'What are you—'

'Shh,' he whispered. 'they'll hear us.' He brought his face close to hers. 'I've missed you so much.'

'Me too. I'm sorry. I wanted to write. I was going to, but—'

'It's fine. You're here now.' His lips were soft on hers, pressing gently at first.

She pressed back. Her fingers ran through his hair, pulling him closer. 'We shouldn't—'

'I've dreamed of this moment for years,' he said.

Bess moaned softly, teasing her tongue into his mouth. 'So have I.'

He pushed her down onto a pile of hay.

Bess's heart beat faster. She wanted to let him carry on. More than anything, she wished she could do what she wanted, for once. But there was no time. 'Matthew, we can't.'

He stopped. 'I know, we shouldn't—I'm sorry.'

She pushed him off and sat up straight before adjusting her dress.

Matthew grinned. 'You're even more beautiful than I remember.'

Bess knew this wasn't true, but she didn't argue. 'Matthew, I need your help.'

He frowned. 'What's wrong?'

'It's not over. I should have said, before. I just got caught up in the moment when I saw you.'

'Me too.' He pulled her into a hug again and kissed the top of her head. 'Don't worry about it. Tell me what's going on.'

'I need to find as many people as possible who will testify against Lady Witham.'

He raised an eyebrow. 'Bess, think of what you're asking. To stand up to Lady Witham? She employs half the town!'

'Please.' She looked him in the eye. 'It's our only chance to clear Mother's name.'

37

GIVING UP – MARY

Mary knocked at the front door of Ledston Hall. It was exactly as she remembered it. Why wouldn't it be? This place had been here for years, would probably still be here for years to come.

William opened the door. 'Mary!'

She blinked, taken aback. 'William? You're still working here?'

'Come here, give your old brother a hug,' he said.

She let herself be held.

'Now tell me what the devil you're thinking, coming back here when Lady Witham's out for your head?' William whispered.

Mary broke down sobbing.

'What's this for? Stop crying, right now.'

She hadn't meant for this to happen. 'I'm sorry, I just—I think I'm going to die.'

His eyes widened in alarm. 'You came back here just to die? Get out! Go, right now. I'll distract Lady Witham.'

Mary shook her head and sniffed, wiping her face with her sleeve. 'No. I'm not going anywhere.'

Before he had a chance to argue with her, Lady Witham appeared behind him. More skeletal than Mary remembered, Lady Witham's collarbone showed through her dress. Her harsh cheekbones only served to accentuate her wrinkles. She looked much older. With a smirk, she revealed all of her black teeth. Mary tried not to gag.

'Look who's come to visit!' She put her hands on her hips. 'Alice! Send for Sir Henry.'

The children's old nursery maid stared at Mary, mouthed, 'run', then pushed past her to run into town.

'You've come to confess?' Lady Witham asked.

Mary opened her mouth to speak, but she didn't have a chance.

'Never mind. I don't care. What matters is that you will finally be convicted. Get her inside, William.'

He looked from Lady Witham to Mary and shook his head. 'I'm sorry, ma'am. I don't think I can.'

Mary narrowed her eyes at him. 'Don't be stupid. Do what she says.'

William grabbed her arm and bent down to whisper, 'what are you doing?', but Mary ignored him.

'Put her in there and lock the door. We'll wait here for Sir Henry. I'm going to get a drink, to celebrate.'

Mary rolled her eyes.

'Stop making light of this, I beg you!' William muttered, through gritted teeth. He closed the door to the drawing room and pointed to the windows. 'That's your best chance of escape. You'd better go now. I'll think of something to tell them.'

'William, you don't understand. I came here to turn myself in.'

He shook his head. 'But why?'

'It's the only way to keep my daughter safe.'

He tilted his head. 'Daughter?'

She nodded. 'Bess. She's all I have left. Agnes is dead.'

'Mary please. I know you must be upset, but don't give yourself up just because you're grieving.'

'I'm not giving up. I'm sacrificing myself.'

'What's the difference?' William shouted.

'Shh,' Mary whispered. 'Lady Witham will hear you.'

'I don't care! What are you thinking, coming here like this? I won't sit and watch while my sister has herself killed. It's foolish and reckless. I won't let you.' He pushed open a window. 'You're getting out of here.'

Mary shook her head. 'I tried running—it didn't work. Sir Henry found us, all the way in London. If I confess, at least I can end this here. They only went after my girls because Lady Witham wanted my confession. It's the only way to save them.'

'Does Elizabeth know you're doing this?'

Mary bit her lip.

'What does she think is happening here?'

'She's trying to clear my name.'

William's eyes lit up. 'Yes—let's do that!'

Mary sighed. 'It's not that simple.'

'I don't care. You have to try. If you're going ahead with this, letting them arrest you again, just promise me you won't confess.'

She didn't answer.

'You know they'll hurt you? They'll have another three days with you.'

'I can handle them.' Mary had dealt with their questioning already. If it meant her daughter would be safe, she would go through it all again.

'What about this—how do you know they won't arrest Bess as soon as you're dead? The daughter of a witch is as good as a witch, isn't she?'

Mary hesitated. 'No, Sir Henry didn't want her. He only wanted to go after me.'

'That was before. You don't know what it's been like since you've been gone.'

Mary's eyes widened in alarm.

But before she could do anything, a key turned in the lock and Sir Henry stood with a smirk. 'There you are.'

38

NAÏVE – ELIZABETH

Elizabeth looked at Mother Pannell. She looked even older up close. The lines on her face were more pronounced than before. Her long white hair was styled as it always was, in a long plait down her back, but it was more wiry and messier than before. Her expression of disappointment in Elizabeth was unchanged.

'I'm sorry,' was all Elizabeth said. She wanted desperately to ask her about her past—to ask more about her mother and the rest of her family. Why didn't she ever tell her they left her alone in a foreign country to marry a stranger? But Elizabeth thought about all the things she hadn't told Mother Pannell. She never spoke about her feelings for Mary, and she certainly didn't talk about intimate topics like marriage. No, it was best to leave it unsaid, to keep her secret.

'Elizabeth, I only ask you the meaning of this. You know that Lady Witham will have Mary arrested! She has been after her for years. Ever since she lost her boy. Why have you returned?'

She groaned. 'We didn't have a choice! They found us, even in London.'

Mother Pannell waved a hand dismissively. 'You could have fled somewhere else.'

Elizabeth raised her voice. 'They would have arrested her, eventually. Her daughters, too.'

'What happened, anyway? To the other one?'

'Oh.' Elizabeth hesitated. 'Agnes—well, Agnes died.'

She frowned. 'How?'

Elizabeth picked at her nails. She didn't want to disrespect Agnes's memory, but she couldn't lie to her mother either.

'I said, how did she die?'

'There was nothing we could do,' she muttered.

'Elizabeth, you had better tell me exactly how the girl died.'

'What does it matter?'

'Tell me.'

She took a deep breath. 'Bess and Agnes, when they got to London, they didn't know anyone. They had nowhere to go for help, no money at all, and they were so young. Agnes was such a pretty young girl.'

'Go on.'

'It wasn't her fault.'

Mother Pannell's expression darkened. 'Oh no, she didn't—?'

'She didn't have a choice. She did what she had to do to survive. Bess didn't know—she was distraught.'

'And she caught something? Off one of the men?'

Elizabeth nodded.

'When did it happen?'

'Only days ago. Well, she'd been ill for a long time. We were in the same city for years, but didn't find them until it was too late.'

'How did Mary take it?'

'How do you think?'

'Elizabeth, you can never understand her pain. She's a mother who has just lost her daughter.'

'Of course I understand. I know Mary better than anyone.'

'Come over here, sit down.' Mother Pannell's voice was soft, like she was speaking to a child.

She sat down.

'Mary's gone to turn herself in?' Mother Pannell asked.

Elizabeth nodded.

'She's not going to clear her name.'

'Yes, she is.'

'No. Think about it.'

Elizabeth shouted, 'no, it's you who doesn't understand. We can call witnesses—'

'No.'

She reached into her pocket and held up the leather-bound book. 'What about this? You held on to the accounts of women accused of witchcraft for all these years. Why? Don't you think it's wrong? Mary doesn't deserve to be hanged.' She threw the book to the ground and the loose sheets flew into the air. 'None of these women did.'

Mother Pannell sighed and collected the sheets. 'Listen to me.' She slotted them back into the book and tucked it into Elizabeth's pocket. 'It's not as simple as telling people she's innocent.'

'But there's more to it than just that. We have a plan. Molly—you remember Molly Witham—she's on our side, and she's going to help us.'

'No, Elizabeth.'

'She is! Not only does she know Sir Henry, but she knows what her mother did. Molly said she'll make sure they let Mary go.'

Mother Pannell shook Elizabeth by the shoulders. 'Listen to me. Stop being so naïve. I've seen the fallout of you all fleeing to London.'

Elizabeth froze.

'Sir Henry is under a lot of pressure at the moment. He was already in trouble for losing you, and then there were all those trips to London to find you. If he gets Mary into custody again, I promise you, he won't let her go.'

'You're wrong.'

'Trust me, please. I love you more than anything, and you need to prepare yourself for what's going to happen. You should never have left London.'

'We had to! They found us. Look, the only way to clear Mary's name, and her daughter's too—was to come back here, face up to it.'

'Face up to what? What do you think you're going to be able to do? You never could think straight when it came to that woman.'

'This is Kippax! We were born here; the whole town knows us. Half of them have worked at Ledston Hall at some point. We'll be able to get witnesses to testify for Mary. Nobody would believe Mary's remedies would hurt anyone.'

Mother Pannell shook her head. 'Have you not grown up at all in the ten years you've been gone? You sound more naïve than ever.'

Elizabeth pursed her lips.

'Lady Witham has more influence than you know.'

'I know we can do this.'

'This won't work, I promise.'

'Why can't you just trust me?'

Her mother stood there staring at her, after all these years, and all she could do was criticise her. It wasn't fair. 'I'm a grown adult and I have been for a long time. You're just bitter now that you can see I don't need you anymore.'

39

TRIAL – MARY

City of York, 1603

His Majesty King James's Justice of the Peace, Sir Henry Griffith, sat on a tall wooden chair, on a raised platform, in the large courtroom in the city of York. He cleared his throat. Those who had gathered inside stood from their chairs.

'We stand here today ready to hear testimony and evidence against the accused, one Mrs Mary Pannell.' His voice echoed around the courtroom; it had tall ceilings and no soft furnishings. Even the windows did not have curtains.

Mary stood, unmoving, her gaze pointed downward so that nobody could see her eyes filling with tears. Everybody else sat down. Mary looked for Elizabeth but she wasn't there, and neither was Molly.

'She has been accused of witchcraft ten years since, at which point she was apprehended for the murder of Sir William Witham of Ledston Hall, in the West Riding of the county of York.'

Suddenly the crowd was silent. Sir Henry went on, reading from a sheet he held in front of him, 'The charges are as follows. The first charge is that you did place a charm on Sir William Witham, taking him to your bed.'

Whispers and nods spread around the onlookers.

'Second, you are charged with bewitching him to death, that is the premeditated murder of Sir William by poison.'

Mary kept her head down.

'Next is a charge of common malefice: that you did knowingly place a disease on his son, Master William Witham, being five years of age.'

A gasp passed around the crowd.

'Finally, another charge of charming and premeditated murder: that you did mix and administer a so-called "cure" for the boy, in full knowledge that it would bring about his death. It is the purpose of this trial to examine all available evidence, question the witnesses and come to a decision. If the accused is found guilty, I will also pronounce the sentence.'

Mary breathed quickly. In, out. In, out. Stay calm, she told herself.

Lady Witham wore an ugly scowl. Her lips were pursed into a tight pout and she was looking down her nose at Mary. Sir Henry gave her a knowing look.

'The key witness today is Lady Eleanor Witham née Neale, wife of the late Sir William Witham.'

He gestured to where she sat, and all eyes in the room followed. Mary looked around, searching for a familiar face, but the room was bright and crowded. She couldn't see Elizabeth. Lady Witham made her way to the front of the courtroom and looked to Sir Henry for instruction.

'If you would relate the events to which you bore witness, Lady Witham.'

She nodded once. With a frown, she held her chin high and narrated a clearly rehearsed sequence of events. To hide her black teeth, she took a handkerchief from her skirts and held it in front of her mouth. Mary raised her eyebrows. She used to enjoy showing off her teeth—it was evidence of her copious sugar intake, much like the Queen. Someone must have finally told her the truth about them. It was a pity, it would have been useful for Mary if the courtroom had turned away from her in disgust. 'It was in 1593. God help me. The last year I saw my dear boy alive.'

With her mouth closed, she dabbed at her cheek with the handkerchief, though there were no tears.

'He was the most beautiful boy. Ever since the day he was born he was my favourite. I have been blessed with eleven children, eight of whom are still alive today.'

She sniffed. Mary saw that the people gathered in the court-room appeared to be taken in by this performance.

'I am a lucky woman, to be sure. My late husband, Sir William Witham, was a good man and a good husband to me. But as a woman, my true joy comes from the love of my children.'

The other women nodded in agreement, their minds flitting to thoughts of their own children. The men present also nodded along, imagining their own wives. They would want them consumed with thoughts of protecting their children too.

'I always treated my servants with respect. I keep a modest household and ensure everybody is adequately provided for.'

Mary scoffed.

'This is why it pains me so that a member of my household, someone whom I had taken under my own roof, would go to such lengths to hurt me, a good Christian woman.'

Every person in the room seemed to nod along as she told her side of the story.

'That woman.'

She pointed to Mary, at which point all eyes in the room burned her with their gaze.

'She forced my husband into an extramarital affair.'

A forced sob emerged from Lady Witham.

'A good man, tempted by the devil. The woman has the devil within her, I have seen it. Nothing short of that would entice my husband.'

Once more, the crowd nodded along.

'I prayed to our Lord God in heaven. I looked after my dear children and put my trust in God Himself.'

Sir Henry cut in at this point. 'Onto the matter at hand, Lady Witham.'

'Yes, of course.' She sniffed once more. 'That woman has been practising witchcraft for years, and one day she brewed a witch's potion.'

Silence spread across the room immediately.

'Not only did she feed it to my husband, causing his own unfortunate death—'

A collective gasp.

'But she lied to me, forced me, made me feed the poison to my own little boy.'

The sob she let out this time actually seemed real. Mary assumed though that this was out of guilt, rather than sadness. Either way, the crowd was nodding along with everything she said. People kept scowling at Mary. They believed Lady Witham over her already. She wracked her brain for what to do, what to say when it was her turn to speak. How could she convince them to believe her? Looking around the room frantically, she could not see Elizabeth, nor Molly, nor any of her friends from home. Could it be that they had abandoned her?

Sir Henry Griffith allowed Lady Witham to finish her story before calling upon Mary to speak. Only she was not afforded the same freedom to speak as Lady Witham.

'Mrs Mary Pannell.' He frowned. 'If you would advance to the front of the room, I have some questions for you.'

'But please, may I—' Mary tried to speak, with no luck.

'No. You will answer my questions, that is all. Understood?'

She nodded.

'Is it true that you were a servant in the household of Sir and Lady Witham in the year 1593?' Sir Henry asked.

'Yes, Sir.'

'And you admit to being in charge of the care of the young boy, Master William Witham?'

Mary had not realised the questions would be like this. What chance did she have to defend herself? 'Yes, but—'

'Enough. Did you, or did you not, bring in the poison that eventually killed the boy?'

'It was not poison!' Mary exclaimed.

An uproar arose. The crowds stood up. Voices chanted various taunts. Some people even threw things at her. Mary winced. She held her hands up to her face to protect herself.

Sir Henry held up his hand. 'Order. Order in my courtroom!' He shouted. Mary hurried back to her seat.

When the shouting had finally subsided, he spoke in a low voice.

'Mary Pannell, I have no further questions for you at this stage —you may sit down.' He then addressed the courtroom once again. 'We have now heard testimony and questioned the accused. The last piece of evidence will be the results of the examination, carried out by my trusted medical team.' He gestured to an old man on one of the benches, who stood up and walked to the centre of the courtroom.

He took a piece of paper from inside his cloak and read aloud, all in one, disinterested tone.

'In humble obedience to your Lordship, I declare that I, along with a team of surgeons and midwives, have made diligent searches and inspections on the woman who stands here accused, brought up lately from the parish of Kippax. We have found on the body of Mary Pannell two things which may be called teats.'

He folded up the piece of paper. He waited for a nod from Sir Henry, at which point he returned it and sat back down.

'Understood. For those who may not be aware, a witch's teat is a raised bump on their body, from which they have allowed the devil to feed. These teats are tangible, ostensible and insensitive to pain. That two of these devil's marks were found on the body of the accused is further evidence that she has been doing the work of the devil.'

The audience whispered among themselves.

A woman cleared her throat near the back of the room. It was a heavily pregnant woman in her twenties, leaning on a man that must have been her husband. Mary recognised her from when she worked at Ledston Hall. Of course, back then she had been a sixteen-year-old young woman, with her nose always stuck in a book and her cheeks always covered in spots. Mary had liked her straightforward nature, although they had never been friendly.

'Excuse me, Sir Henry?'

He frowned. 'Yes?'

'My name is Anne Bygges, née Witham. I would like to speak in support of Mary Pannell.' A hush spread around the crowd. She continued, 'My father was the late Sir William, and since I was still unmarried and living at Ledston Hall in 1593, I bear witness to the fact that she did not commit these offences. I trust you to see that the woman in front of you is innocent.'

Mary looked again and realised the man was not her husband, but her brother. He was a few years younger than Anne; Mary could not remember his exact age.

'I, Henry Witham, agree with my sister. Mary Pannell is not the guilty party. We have known her for years and can speak to her strong moral character and loyalty to the family. Never have we suspected her involvement in any kind of sacrilege.' He helped Anne to sit back down. Mary was shocked that even Henry had come to defend her. He probably didn't even remember her.

'Hmm.' Sir Henry said. He said nothing back to them.

Mary tried to catch their eyes to mouth a word of thanks, but their eyes were firmly fixed on their mother in anger.

'I understand that several of the defendant's neighbours have also come to speak in her defence.' Sir Henry read from the list in front of him. 'First, we have Alice.'

When Alice stood up, a murmur spread around the crowd. Her face always shocked people who weren't used to it. She cleared her throat. 'Yes, sir.'

'What is your connection to the case?'

'Sir, I am the nursery maid in the Witham household, and Mary's neighbour.'

'How long have you known her?'

'All her life, sir.'

'Have you ever known her to mix remedies?'

Her eyes widened.

'Alice, I asked you a question. You will answer, please.'

'Sir, she means well. I have never heard of her remedies being harmful. In fact, she helps many of—'

'Enough!' Sir Henry called. 'Sit down.'

Alice stared at Mary, her expression full of regret—but there was nothing she could do now.

Sir Henry read from the list in front of him. 'Another servant from Ledston Hall,' he sighed. 'Dorothy?'

Mary gasped—Dorothy had come to speak in her defence? They had never been close, had never even really spoken. In fact, Mary had always thought Dorothy was a bit too friendly with William while he was married.

Dorothy had more lines on her face and now wore a wedding ring on her finger. 'Yes, sir.'

'You have known the family for—'

'Fifteen years. Mary was a good worker and I can assure you, she didn't hurt anyone. Not Sir William and not his son.'

'Very well.' Sir Henry gestured for her to sit back down. 'Next, we have Matthew. Do you also work for the family?'

He stood up and gave Mary a nod, as if to reassure her that she would be fine. 'No, sir. I am a farmhand for the Middletons, and a neighbour of the Pannells.'

Sir Henry sighed, evidently bored. 'How long have you known the family?'

'Ever since I was a boy, sir. I promise you, Mary would never harm a soul.'

Mary's heart jumped. One by one, her old neighbours from Kippax spoke in her defence. Sir Henry tried to catch them out, like he had done with Alice, but they stood their ground. They told him how Mary helped the town, and explained that she never made mistakes and as far as they knew, had never hurt anyone.

'Mary Pannell, please stand.' Sir Henry surveyed the crowd, where all the witnesses sat. 'Do you know these people who have spoken in your defence?'

'Yes, sir.'

'Have they given a fair representation of how they know you, and of who you are as an individual?'

'Yes, sir.'

He narrowed his eyes. 'First, Anne and Henry—remind me who they are.'

'They were both residents of Ledston Hall while I worked there.'

'Hmm.' He checked through his notes. 'They were children at the time they knew you?'

'Yes, but—'

'Please simply ask the questions put to you.'

'Yes, sir. They were children.' Mary didn't want to appear rude, but she wanted to give her side of the story.

'Part of your job was to take care of these children, yes?'

'Yes, sir.'

Sir Henry grinned triumphantly. 'Well then, the children will have had a misplaced loyalty in the woman who had cared for them! I will have to disregard their testimony. The same goes for their nursery maid, Alice. I cannot assume she isn't speaking on their behalf too. They could be lying to protect you.'

Mary's face turned red in anger. She raised her voice. 'Sir, please. Anne and Henry Witham are both adults now, as is Alice, and I have no relationship with them.' She tried not to let her voice falter. 'They have no reason to lie today, and I beg you to listen to them. I am an innocent Christian woman, accused of an awful crime. There is no solid evidence against me and in fact, I ask you to abandon the entire case and set me free.'

Sir Henry bashed his hand on the wooden desk in front of him. 'Enough! I will have quiet in my courtroom!'

Mary stopped talking. She took deep breaths. She had said all she needed to say, and she could see some members of the audience nodding, even agreeing with her. Had she managed to convince them of her innocence?

'As for the other witnesses, the defendant's neighbours had no knowledge of the crimes, but I heard no evidence that they were even there on the day of the alleged murders.'

Mary gasped.

'The only actual witness with any actual evidence was Lady Witham, whose testimony was clear.'

Whispers spread around the room.

'Please, sir, she's lying!' Mary shouted.

'Silence!' Sir Henry once again commanded. 'You will all disregard this last comment. The fact is, we have gathered and presented to you today a multitude of evidence against this woman, known in her community to cast spells and curses. We have medical evidence proving the fact that she has lain with the devil, and still she denies this. This woman is a proven liar who seeks to defend her life and refuses to come clean, even to God Himself.'

The onlookers now glared at Mary. Despite all those who had spoken in her defence, some people were still looking at her as if she really were a witch.

Sir Henry continued to speak, summarising the results of the findings and eventually asked Mary to come forward once more. She staggered back to the front of the courtroom, her face flushed red and streamed with tears.

'In light of the evidence presented here today, I hereby pronounce you guilty of the crimes of witchcraft and two counts of murder. I sentence you to be hanged by the neck until dead, and thereafter your body will be burnt at the stake.'

She bent over. A gasp turned into a sob. She screamed.

'Take her.' Sir Henry called to two men who grabbed her by the arms and dragged her from the room.

Mary continued to scream, bent double as they dragged her from the room. She didn't even notice Elizabeth running towards the door of the courtroom, sweat dripping down her face, the guard blocking her way in.

40

EXECUTION – ELIZABETH

Pannell Hill, Kippax, 1603

Elizabeth rode ahead of Bess and Matthew. 'Hurry, we're almost there.'

Mary was to be executed on the very hill she had walked up every day to go to work at Ledston Hall. It must have been Lady Witham's idea of a sick joke. Elizabeth tried not to think about it. For now, she just had to get there. She'd find a way to set Mary free.

'Matthew,' she began. 'Have you ever been married?'

'No, ma'am.'

Bess blushed and muttered, 'Elizabeth!'

She ignored her. 'You don't have any children?'

'Not yet, ma'am.'

'But you have been seeing Bess a lot recently?'

He nodded.

'Is that why you're here today? For Bess?'

'Yes, ma'am. Bess loves her mother very much, so I'm here to support her any way that I can.' He held his reins in one hand, and reached over to pat Bess's shoulder with the other hand.

'You don't think Lady Witham's claims of witchcraft are true?'

He shook his head. 'No. Not at all.'

'How do you know? You didn't know Mary, did you?' She narrowed her eyes at him.

'Please, Elizabeth. I know Bess well enough. We worked together for years before she left. I know she would never be involved in something like this, and when she tells me her mother is innocent, I believe her completely.'

Elizabeth was impressed. He seemed to care about her. Even so, she wanted to make sure. 'When Bess left Kippax, were you angry?'

'No. Not angry. Though I missed her terribly.' He paused to consider his words. 'I urged her to leave—they were going to arrest her. I couldn't let that happen.'

Bess smiled back at him.

He went on, 'when you all left, people started to talk. Lady Witham was angry, and she was spreading stories about Mary. But none of us in town believed them. Mother Pannell and Mary have always helped us. We knew Bess and Agnes were innocent.'

'Good.' Elizabeth stole a glance at Bess, who was avoiding her gaze. She must not have told him about Agnes. 'It was such a shame to have lost Agnes to the Plague.'

His eyes darted to Bess. 'The Plague?'

'Yes,' she mumbled. 'The Plague. Terrible disease.'

'I had no idea—I'm so sorry.'

Elizabeth changed the subject again. 'Did you ever tell Bess how you felt about her, before she left?'

Bess blushed again, but said nothing this time.

'No, ma'am. It's my biggest regret.'

'Well, don't wait too long. Life is too short.'

He nodded. 'I know.'

It was getting dark, and the crowds were growing. People had come from all over to see the hanging. Further ahead, a group of men were hammering pieces of wood together, building the gallows. They were almost finished. Elizabeth shivered. She wore only a thin cloak, and her arms had goosebumps.

Elizabeth had not imagined the wooden structure would be so tall. The place where the accused would stand was on a central wooden platform. There was a set of steps made of uneven planks of wood, slightly too far apart to climb easily. Mary would struggle to get up there. No. Elizabeth interrupted her own thoughts. No, Mary would not have to go up there at all—Elizabeth would find a way to help her.

The wooden structure was connected to the platform with a series of triangular attachments to keep it steady. There was a noose hanging from the centre of the overhead wooden beam. It was ready to execute someone. Elizabeth stared as she pictured the horrific event happening to Mary.

No. She would save her. More people had gathered in the area, trying to find somewhere they could watch the execution.

At this point, her thoughts were interrupted by Molly shaking her shoulders. 'Elizabeth, quick. Sir Henry's in here.' She directed her to the man who sat on a piece of wood near the gallows, drinking whisky.

Molly began. 'Sir Henry. I hope you remember me. Molly Witham, daughter of the late Sir William Witham, wife of Mr Thomas Jobson, of the Cudworth Estate.'

He nodded, swaying as he did so. 'Yes, I remember. But as I told you yesterday, I simply will not have Lady Witham arrested. You should go home.'

Elizabeth's heart sank.

'Sir, please. She is guilty—ask anyone.'

He laughed and rolled his eyes. 'She warned me you might do this. If you don't stop these accusations right now, I'll have to arrest you for working with the witch. Perhaps you are a witch yourself!'

Elizabeth's eyes filled with tears; it was hopeless.

Molly sighed. 'Very well. If you won't accept Lady Witham as the guilty party, I can give you another name. I assure you, you have the wrong woman. You cannot execute Mrs Mary Pannell.'

Elizabeth frowned. Another name?

'It is too late.' He gestured around, where crowds were gathering more and more by the second. 'The people have come to see a witch hang, and that is what they will have.'

A voice interrupted him. Elizabeth recognised it.

Mother Pannell said, 'but they can. I will go in her place. I am the one who mixed the potions. Both for Sir William and his son. I planned for all of this to happen.'

Elizabeth gasped. 'Mother, no!'

'This is her choice,' Molly said.

'How could you?' Elizabeth never thought Molly capable of this. 'She's my mother!'

'Please, my girl.' Mother Pannell put a hand on her shoulder. 'You don't need to protect me. I'm here to tell what I've done, and I'm sure Sir Henry will hear my confession.'

At the word confession, Sir Henry blinked. 'You're here to confess?'

Elizabeth knew this was what he wanted all along. It was the strongest piece of evidence he could have, and it would give validity to the whole execution. He would certainly be keen to hear what she had to say. But how could she let her own mother hang?

Mother Pannell pulled Elizabeth into a hug and whispered, 'don't fight me on this. Just make sure they let Mary go. I know how much she means to you. I love you.'

Elizabeth's eyes welled up with tears. She felt for the book in her pocket and took a deep breath. Mother Pannell had seen witches executed years ago. She'd written all about it—and now she was about to die the same way. Was Elizabeth really going to let this happen?

Before she had a chance to think about it, Sir Henry called his men over. 'Arrest this woman and take her confession. It looks like she's the one we'll hang.'

They dragged her away.

Elizabeth sniffed. 'Wait—you have to let Mary go!'

41

EXECUTION – BESS

Sir Henry's servant returned with Mary. Confused, and covered in blood and dirt, she was barely recognisable.

'You may release her.' He commanded.

Mary ran to embrace Elizabeth and Bess. 'I thought I would never see you again. Why have they let me go?'

'Mother, you're back!' Bess hugged her tightly.

'I'm here. Come on, let's get out of here.'

Bess shared a look with Elizabeth but she shook her head. Now wasn't the time to explain what Mother Pannell had done.

'Mother, what have they done to you?'

She had an open wound on her arm, and there was blood running down her leg.

'And what are you wearing?'

Her dress was ripped to pieces, barely allowing her any modesty. Elizabeth took off her cloak and wrapped it around Mary.

'Don't ask so many questions, Bess.'

'Mary, I'm so pleased you're back,' Matthew said.

Mary span around to look at him.

'Mother, this is Matthew.' She held his hand.

Mary nodded. 'I see.'

'Please, ma'am, I wanted to ask you a question.'

'What is it?'

'I would like to ask you for the honour of your daughter's hand in marriage.'

Bess gasped.

Mary looked over to Elizabeth, who nodded her approval. 'If Bess wishes to marry you, I'm happy.'

He grinned and dropped down on one knee. 'Bess, will you marry me?'

She squealed and squeezed him into a tight hug. 'Yes! Of course I'll marry you.'

Bess bit her lip. 'Mother, there's something you need to know.'

'Not now, Bess.' Elizabeth hissed. 'Mary has enough to be thinking about.'

Mary looked from Bess to Elizabeth, and then at the scene around her. 'No, something's wrong. Why isn't the crowd dispersing? Haven't they told them the hanging is off?'

Bess shook her head. 'It's not.'

'Bess!' Elizabeth shouted. 'Don't.'

'Elizabeth, don't lie to me.' Her voice shook. 'Are they coming back to arrest me?'

'God, no!' Elizabeth wrapped her arms around Mary. 'You're safe now. Don't worry. I'll never let anything happen to you again.'

Mary winced.

'I'm sorry—we'll get you bandaged up as soon as we get home.'

Mary pushed her away. 'Elizabeth, tell me what my daughter is talking about. Who are they hanging tonight, if not me?'

'Bess, you and Matthew need to leave. You shouldn't be here for this.'

42

EXECUTION - MARY

Once they were alone, Mary screamed at Elizabeth. 'What is happening?'

The people around them turned to stare.

'Tell me why we're still waiting here!'

Elizabeth avoided eye contact. 'It was her choice, I couldn't stop her.'

'Who? Who are you talking about?'

'It's Mother Pannell.'

Mary gasped and put her hands to her mouth.

'She said it was all her. She's given them a full confession.'

'No!'

Elizabeth sobbed. 'I'm so sorry. I tried to find another way, but there was nothing. Molly knew about it too. I think she went to see Mother Pannell behind my back.'

Mary could feel her own tears welling up. Mother Pannell had been like a mother to her all her life, and today she was going to die for her. 'Elizabeth! Is that her?'

Sir Henry's men were leading someone towards the gallows. There was a black hood over their head, but from the hunched back to the crooked way of walking, there was no doubt it was her. Her long white plait poked out of the bottom of her hood.

Mary could see why Sir Henry had agreed to it. His role was to appease the people and ensure somebody unimportant, preferably a woman, was executed today. In this respect, he had succeeded.

Mother Pannell struggled to walk up the steep steps. How did they expect her to get up there when she couldn't even see? She tripped on the first step and instinctively tugged at her hands to break her fall, but they had been tied behind her back. The men either side of her dragged her back up onto her feet. She tried to stretch her leg up to the next step and tripped again. Her grunts were loud, but she didn't say anything. Maybe they had gagged her.

Eventually she was standing right under the noose, in the centre of the platform. Sir Henry Griffith stood next to her. He was much taller than her and stood up straight. He addressed the crowd. Hundreds of people stood in front of him, watching.

'Today we have all come to witness the execution of The Pannell Witch. She used to inhabit the nearby parish of Kippax. After a recent trial and a multitude of evidence, I have sentenced her myself.' The speech seemed incredibly short to Mary. After such an incredible life, it didn't seem fair that this was how it was going to end.

He gestured to the executioner, who wrapped a noose around Mother Pannell's neck, and pulled the knot tight. She groaned as her back was pulled up straighter than was comfortable, waiting for them to kill her.

'We thank God for teaching us how to deal with such a being. We pray we can rid ourselves of such evil before it is allowed to spread. Today is the day we kill the witch!'

There was an uproar in the crowd. It was like the people were glad this was happening. Mary grabbed Elizabeth's hand and squeezed it tightly.

'You know, most people will think it was you they hanged.' Elizabeth said.

Mary gulped. It was true, nobody had really seen them release her. 'But they'll see me in Kippax and realise—'

'Mary, please. All the court records say you were found guilty. There's no guarantee they'll make a note of Mother Pannell's confession. Sir Henry won't arrest you or Bess now that the execution has taken place, but you have to understand that we cannot stay in Kippax.'

Mary said nothing as she thought it over. They stared up at the platform for a long time, waiting.

'It should be Lady Witham up there,' Mary said. She glared at the woman who stood right in front of the gallows, staring up at the platform.

'Yes,' Elizabeth agreed. 'But look at her. She's devastated. She'll live the rest of her life knowing that she's the reason her baby died. That's punishment enough.'

'It's not enough. We should do something. I'm going over to her.' Mary walked over to where Lady Witham stood, pretending to dab tears from her cheeks with a silk handkerchief.

'No.' Elizabeth was firm. 'You're not speaking to her.'

'Why not? She deserves it.'

'Are you forgetting what happened the last time you confronted her?' Elizabeth raised her voice, but the crowds paid no notice. With a hanging about to take place, the crowd was excitable and everyone was busy with their own conversations.

Mary sighed. 'It's not the same.'

'It is,' Elizabeth insisted. 'People like that will never have to face up to their crimes. It's always people like us who pay for it.'

Mary bit her lip. Elizabeth was right.

'Don't make Mother Pannell's death mean nothing. If you anger Lady Witham, she might demand your death too.'

Mary nodded. 'I suppose.'

'Anyway, as far as Lady Witham knows, it's you being executed today. She thinks you're about to die! This is the best chance we can have at living our own lives, because she won't be there to come after us anymore. She has to think she's won. Please, don't go over there.'

'You're right. I'm sorry. But it's not fair. Mother Pannell shouldn't have to pay for this with her life.'

'I know.'

Mother Pannell stood on the platform, the noose around her neck and her hands tied behind her back. Although her eyes were covered, Mary could feel them on her. She knew she was in the crowd, watching her die in her place.

The executioner pulled a lever, and the platform gave way. Mother Pannell's body dropped straight down through the gap. Her legs flailed wildly in the air. Mary tried to listen but the cheers of the crowd were deafening. There was a mixture of cheers and shouts. The people were eager to see the so-called 'witch' die and they couldn't contain their excitement.

It was as if they had come to the theatre in London. Here was the stage, and this was the climax of the play. Everyone was eager to find out what would happen. Eventually, her body stopped moving. The shouts died down as the onlookers stared at the corpse. Once they realised it was all over, people began to talk once more. The chattering became louder as they left, pushing against each other as they did.

Mary had tears streaming down her face. Could she have stopped this? No. Mother Pannell gave her life for Mary. She and Elizabeth walked towards the gallows, where a group of men were discussing how to take down the body.

Mary shivered. It was a cold evening, and now that it was getting dark and the hanging was finished, the crowds had dispersed. The mist rose from the damp grass and seemed to enclose them in the space with Mother Pannell, as if there was nobody else around.

In the distance, Mary could just about make out the outline of Ledston Hall. She pictured Lady Witham. She would be home by now, staring out of her upstairs window, waiting for what she thought was Mary's body to go up in flames.

The crunch of the men's footsteps on the icy grass as they piled up wood to make the pyre was all Mary could concentrate on. She stared, not even aware if Elizabeth was talking to her anymore. Her mind was racing, like she wasn't even here anymore. It should be her about to be burned.

The wave of heat on her face was the first sign that the pyre had been lit. Then the crackling of the flames. Loud crashes of wood on wood sounded as men threw more logs onto the pyre.

Two men cut down the noose and carried the body. One by the

shoulders and one by the ankles. The head fell back. Was the neck broken? The angle looked wrong. They grunted in time with each other and threw the bony corpse onto the fire. It looked too small to be a person. Not just any person, but Mother Pannell. How had her life been reduced to this?

The light of the fire finally reached her eyes. It fought through the fog, itching to be seen. Mary forced herself to watch Mother Pannell burn. This was her punishment.

She found Elizabeth next to her and pulled her close. They did not say a word to each other. There were no words. Here and now, on the hill that would be come to known as Pannell Hill, was the last day they would ever spend in the village of Kippax.

CONNECT WITH ME!

I love hearing what readers have to say about my books so please leave me a review.

As an indie author, reviews are really helpful for me. Thank you so much for all your support!

For more about the English Witch Trials, you can read the articles on my website:

melissamanners.com

Read the prequel, **Becoming The Pannell Witch**, available now.

To be the first to hear about my next book,
The Witham Witch, sign up to my mailing list on my website.

I really love to hear from my readers, so follow me:

facebook.com/melissamannerswrites

twitter.com/melissamanners

instagram.com/melissamannerswrites

amazon.com/author/melissamanners

goodreads.com/melissamanners

EPILOGUE

Although this telling of the story of the Pannell 'witch' is a work of fiction, it has its roots in reality. Mary Pannell (née Tailor) did exist. She was born in the parish of Kippax, West Yorkshire, and married John Pannell in 1559. She did have two daughters, Elizabeth 'Bess' and Agnes, and a brother William Tailor, though of course the details of their relationships cannot be assumed. The characters of Mary 'Molly' Witham and George Chapman were also taken from reality and are some of the most historically well-known characters of this novel.

Molly Witham

The fascinating character of Mary 'Molly' Witham is not my own invention. She was born in 1579 when she lived at Ledston Hall with her family. It is not known whether or not she had a relation-ship with Mary Pannell, a servant in her home, but her apparent execution when Mary Witham was just 14 years old is bound to have affected her. She got married twice, first to Lord Thomas Jobson of Cudworth at the age of 15, then after being widowed, she married Thomas Bolles of Osberton in Nottinghamshire, when she was 32 years old. She had two children with each husband. In 1635 King Charles I made her a baronet in her own right, something which was unheard of in England at the time and for the majority of the time since. She was granted the baronetcy of Nova Scotia, and Dame Mary Bolles proudly signed her name 'Baronetesse' from then on. She has been described as charitable but eccentric, and when she lived at Heath Hall, near Wakefield in Yorkshire, she apparently erected a water tower to pump fresh water, which still stands, to her household via a water wheel. During the English Civil War, she may have supported the troops, though there is some disagreement around which side she supported. It may even be that she supported both the royalists and the parliamentarians at times. It is not known whether she changed sides during the war or if she secretly supported the parliamentarians all along. Her close relationship with the King meant she was expected to support the royalists, but when the parliamentarians came into power they placed no sanctions on her, like they did many royalist supporters. She died at the old age of 83, when she was buried in Ledsham Church, the church local to her childhood home of Ledston Hall, where she may have been friendly with Mary Pannell. She must have cherished the first fifteen years of her life that she spent there where her funeral monument still stands today. It is a marble altar-tomb, with the effigy of the lady represented as wrapped in a shroud, leaving the bold features of her face exposed. The inscription reads:

'Here lyeth interred the body of Right Worshipful Dame Mary Bolles, of Heath Hall, in the County of York. Baroness, one of the daughters of Wm Witham, of the ancient family of the Withams, of Leadstone Hall, Esquire, who married to her first husband Thos Jobson, of Cudworth, Esq. had issue Thos Jobson. To her second husband Thomas Bolles, Esq she had issue Anne, who married Sir William Dalston, Bart., the same Dame Mary Bolles being over 80 years of age.'

In her will, Mary left money to various charitable causes and provided for a lavish two-week funeral, to which everyone was invited. It is said that the will also requested that the room in which she died should be sealed. After fifty years somebody opened up the room, at which point Dame Mary is said to have come back to haunt the surrounding heath.

George Chapman

George Chapman did exist, though there is no evidence of his being related to the Chapmans of Yorkshire. He was brought up in Hitchin, Hertfordshire, though there are not many records of his early life. He attended the university of Oxford in 1574, where he gained an extensive knowledge of Greek and Latin.

Later, he worked for a prominent nobleman, Sir Ralph Sadler, from 1583 to 1585, after which time he served in the military in the United Provinces, now known as the Netherlands. On his return to London in 1594, though there is no evidence of him housing an Elizabeth or Mary Pannell, his writings are well documented, beginning with the Shadow of Night. His politically dangerous literary group, sometimes called the School of Night (although the idea that Shakespeare coined and used this term is now widely discredited) was made up of its patron Sir Walter Raleigh, the poets Christopher Marlow, Matthew Roydon and William Warner, mathematician Thomas Harriot, 9th Earl of Northumberland Henry Percy, the Earl of Derby, Sir George Carey and many others. The group was said to be atheist or in league with the devil, which at this time was a dangerous position to take. They may have discussed modern topics such as theology, philosophy, astronomy, geography, chemistry and general unorthodox scientific and religious beliefs. These were against the church and the monarch and as such were treasonable matters.

Sir Walter Raleigh was a favourite of Queen Elizabeth I, and when granted a royal patent to explore America, he is said to have named Virginia after his beloved virgin Queen. He fell out of favour with the Queen when he secretly married Bess Throckmorton, one of her ladies in waiting, in 1592, for which he was briefly imprisoned. The following year he was imprisoned again for an expedition, and he was later made an MP. King James I had him executed for treason in 1618.

Towards the end of the 1590s, it is true that Chapman's plays were not doing so well, leading him to relinquish his claim to the family estate and falling victim to a fraudulent moneylender, leading to his short imprisonment. It is also true that when James I came to the throne in 1603, Chapman was offered a position in the household of Prince Henry, with whose patronage he was able to compose more plays, including the comedy Eastward Ho, co-written with Ben Jonson and John Marston. The play was seen to be anti-Scottish and to insult a number of James I's policies and so Chapman was once again imprisoned. Upon his release, he continued to write plays though they were tragedies.

Chapman's love of Greek and Latin never seemed to fade and his poetic translations of Homer's Iliad and Odyssey are available to read today. Prince Henry had promised Chapman a pension, though on the prince's death in 1612, his father did not keep his promise. Chapman was able to find a new patron, the Earl of Somerset, but when his marital scandals led to his having to leave his career at court, Chapman was once again in financial difficulties. He struggled financially until his death in 1634, aged 75, when he was honoured by the elite. Chapman's friend and famous architect Inigo Jones designed his Romanesque funeral monument, in Holborn, London. After his death he has continued to be remembered, including in a tribute in a sonnet by Keats in 1816, 'On First Looking Into Chapman's Homer'.

The Plague

The plagues of England in 1593 and 1603 were not as severe as the Black Death, but there were outbreaks in which residents were told to stay at home across the country.

Mary Pannell

As for Mary Pannell, she did work for William and Eleanor Witham at Ledston Hall, where they lived with their children. Part of Mary's duties involved caring for the young Master William Witham. How he died at the age of five is somewhat of a mystery, though the theory presented in this novel is one that has been widely assumed. The story goes that, in 1593, Mary introduced into the household a lotion of some kind to be spread on the sick child's chest, which was subsequently fed to him in error. This caused the tragic death of the boy, whose father died the same year.

Mary was blamed for the boy's death and was apparently tried for witchcraft, found guilty and executed in 1603, some ten years later. The details of her trial, including the evidence of her questioning, examination and reports from neighbours, is based on records from accused witches of the same time period, as Mary Pannell's records have been unfortunately lost. It is said that her trial and hanging took place in York, before her body was taken to what is now known as Pannell (also spelled Pannal) Hill in the parish of Kippax, near Castleford, to be burned in the woods there, in view of Ledston Hall.

This retelling of the story presents a possible explanation of why it took ten years to bring Mary to trial, though there is no evidence of her escape to and return from London.

Mother Pannell

There is no evidence that Mother Pannell ever existed. However, at this time in 1500s England, it was common for a small village to have an old woman referred to as a 'wise woman', known by the title 'Mother' rather than 'Mrs'. A 'wise woman' would often live in isolation and provide much needed services for the community, such as midwifery and herbal remedies. The ignorance of science at this time meant that these women were feared and often blamed for unfortunate events, such as a death in the community or a failed harvest. It might have been claimed that the woman (or sometimes man) in question was in league with the devil and was even a witch, a criminal offence at the time. With a wealthy, powerful family like the Withams supporting the prosecution of Mary Pannell, it is unlikely that Mary had any chance of being acquitted. I have supposed that Mary did all she could to help the young boy, and that his death was a tragic accident.

A woman in a position of power such as Eleanor Witham is unlikely to have been blamed for witchcraft. The women most often blamed were the older, unmarried women, especially if they were known for dabbling in midwifery and herbal remedies. This is where the character of Mother Pannell comes in. For all we know, this is exactly what happened all those years ago. The ghost of Mary Pannell is said to haunt Pannell Hill, but I like to think Mary is at peace.

ABOUT THE AUTHOR

Melissa was born and raised in London where her book obsession began. She would take a book everywhere she went (she still does this, and probably always will). Her writing career started at the tender age of eight when she wrote her first 'book': a folded booklet summarising the story of Persephone.

Her love of Greek mythology continued into adulthood, as did her love of storytelling. She spent her teen years writing angst-ridden fanfic until she found NaNoWriMo, which she entered year after year.

It was not until she was in her twenties that she found her love of historical fiction. The historical period that most stuck out was that of the English Witch Trials—horrifying, yet fascinating. The treatment of women in particular (but also a range of other people seen as 'different'), is what Melissa wanted to address in her own writing.

She loves to reframe the narrative that has been passed down to us, mostly by men, and allow stories to be told from a new perspective. It's a shame we don't have many records from this period, but through historical fiction we can give those neglected members of society a voice.

BECOMING THE PANNELL WITCH: A PREQUEL

CHAPTER ONE - DINNER

Kippax, West Yorkshire, 1556

Mary chopped the carrots in front of her and ran over the words in her mind. She wanted to be ready to explain to her father exactly why she was ready to look for work.

'Put the pot of potatoes over the fire,' Mary told Ellen, pointing to the glimmering flames in the middle of the room.

Ellen was fourteen now, old enough to be cooking for the family. She sighed. 'Can't you do it? I'm waiting for someone.' She was kneeling on the bench by the window, eyes fixed on the path that led up to their door.

Mary put the water on to boil herself and narrowed her eyes. 'Who are you expecting? Have you invited over a guest? Did you ask Father's permission?' She didn't want one of Ellen's friends coming round and spoiling her chance to speak to him. He didn't often join them for dinner, and he was in a good mood today, so it was the perfect opportunity.

'Don't worry, he knows,' she giggled.

She added the carrots and once they were soft, she dished them out onto plates. Then she took the chicken out of the oven and used a sharp knife to carve it for them.

Ellen shrieked and ran over to look out of the window.

'Will you keep it down?' Mary asked.

'He's here,' Ellen said.

A tall, slender man with a head full of dark hair was heading towards their small house.

'Father? Are we having a guest for dinner?'

Their father emerged from his room yawning.

'Father?' Mary repeated.

He rubbed his eyes, just woken from a nap. 'Well yes, young John Pannell will be joining us this evening. Didn't I say?'

Mary tutted. 'No, you didn't. I'll serve up another plate.' There weren't quite enough potatoes left, so she picked one off each of their plates and added to the last one. 'Ellen, set out the tablecloth, and bring the extra chair from outside. Oh, and go and fetch us some wine.'

She grinned, and this time did as she was asked without arguing.

'Father, you can't greet a guest like this—go and put a shirt on. And comb your hair.' He raised his eyebrows but did as Mary told him. His head was mostly bald, but his grey hair stuck up in the air like he had just been running around in the wind.

Mary combed her own hair and had just enough time to change her dress before she heard the knock on the door. Mary stepped into the main room with a deep breath.

Her father invited the man inside and introduced him to his youngest daughter, Ellen. 'You know my son, William, of course— he's working tonight. And this is my eldest, Mary,' he said with a wide smile.

He couldn't have been older than twenty. His silky hair was pushed back, emphasising his high cheekbones and broad jawline. He was clean shaven and wore undamaged, uncreased clothes. None of the men in town took care of themselves like this. 'Pleased to meet you.' He gave a slight bow of his head. 'Let me see you.'

Mary stood up straight, hands held behind her back, eyes on the ground.

Ellen smirked. 'Turn around, then! And do it slowly.'

Mary's cheeks burned, but she took hold of her skirts and twirled in a small circle.

'You'll do just fine.' He ran his eyes over her, then spoke to her father. 'She's not too plain, not too thin. In fact, she could even be considered beautiful.'

Ellen gasped.

Her father grinned. 'Like her mother.'

He went on, 'I'm John Pannell. I actually grew up in Kippax but I've been away for a number of years, working. You don't need to know about all of that.' His voice was deep and smooth.

There was no denying that he was an attractive man, but so far, everything he had said made her uncomfortable. She smiled politely. 'Thank you for joining us. Please, sit down,' Mary gestured to the table, where her family were already sitting. Ellen was sitting in the garden chair—she had left her normal seat, next to Mary's, for John.

Mary brought over the plates, serving John first and herself last.

John stood and pulled out Mary's chair for her to sit down, brushing her shoulder as he tucked her under the table. Mary wasn't sure if it was on purpose, but his touch made her shiver.

Their father thanked God for their food before they ate. 'It's good to see you again, John. How's your mother?'

John finished chewing and wiped the corners of his mouth before answering. 'She's better, thank you. Still misses my father, of course. But glad to have me back in town, I think.'

He grinned. 'Good to hear.' He addressed his children. 'I knew John's father as a boy, you know. We worked together for years before he had the accident.'

Mary knew what he was talking about. A few years ago, there was a mining explosion which killed a lot of the men in Kippax. Mary's father worked on the farms and was one of the men called to the search and rescue operation, but the mine had collapsed, burying most of the miners underground. Afterwards, a lot of young sons were sent to the mines in their father's place to support their families. They were lucky their father hadn't been a miner— they would have had nobody else to look after them. John didn't seem too affected by it now, but Mary knew exactly what it was like to lose a parent, regardless of how much you might hide your feelings.

'Yes, it was my mother who suggested I look you up, actually.' John gazed at Mary, though he was talking to her father. Then he added, 'the food is delicious, by the way. Almost as good as that of a professional cook.'

Mary knew she was better than that—she had always excelled in the kitchen. But she didn't want to be rude to a guest, so she bit her tongue. 'Thank you.'

Her father gleamed with pride. 'She'll make a great wife one day.'

'Not for a while, I'm sure,' Mary added, avoiding his gaze.

Her father almost said something but John held up a hand. 'Of course. Not until the right man presents himself.'

Mary let out a breath, relieved. She returned to her dinner.

'She's done such a good job taking care of Ellen all these years, and William too. She'll be a great mother,' her father added.

Mary's jaw tensed up again.

John shook his head. 'It's nothing for you to worry about. Women love motherhood, trust me. I'm sure you'll take to it quite easily.'

How could he be so confident about how she would feel? She looked sideways at his big green eyes. It was difficult to work him out. 'Are you looking to get married soon?'

Ellen hadn't eaten a bite of her dinner. Instead her eyes were glued to her sister and John, desperate to hear their conversation.

'Who doesn't want to fall in love?' He locked eyes with her. Despite his behaviour, he did seem to like her. He hadn't looked at anyone else since he arrived.

Mary's father cleared his throat loudly, making Mary jump.

'Oh!' She ran her eyes around the table. 'I'm sorry. Are you all finished?' She piled up the plates and took them away, before refilling the wine cups.

'Ellen? I need to talk to you. Come outside for a minute,' their father said.

Mary's eyes widened.

As soon as they were alone, John took her hand in his. 'You should know, I'm planning to ask your father for your hand.'

Mary took a deep breath in.

He scooted his chair closer to hers and reached over to whisper in her ear. 'There's something between us. I know you feel it too. Say you'll marry me.'

The hairs on the back of her neck stood on end. She hadn't realised he was going to propose—at least not tonight. They had only just met, and she knew almost nothing about him or his family. She wanted to explain this to him and ask why he was asking so soon. Maybe they could discuss it and he would see what an unreasonable request this was. But the words didn't come out. Instead, she whispered, her voice shaking, 'but we're so young.'

'We don't have to marry right away, if that's what you're worried about. I'll happily wait days, even weeks, for your hand.'

Mary bit her lip, not sure how to respond.

John kissed her hand before releasing it, searching her eyes for an answer. It didn't come, but still he went outside to speak to her father.

When John left, her father came back in with a wide grin on his face. 'I think we all know what happens next.'

Ellen slumped down at the table.

'Now I suppose you'll want weeks to plan the wedding? And money, too. Hmm.'

'When will I get our room to myself?' Ellen added.

'I'll need to have a word with the priest,' their father mumbled.

'Stop!' Mary cried.

The room fell into silence.

'I can't marry him.'

Her father glared at her. 'Out,' he ordered Ellen. She hurried outside, shutting the door behind her, though Ellen's hair was visible by the window—she was still listening.

'I want what's best for you,' he started. 'You know that don't you?'

Mary nodded.

'Haven't I always been good to you?'

It was true, he was a good father. They had sometimes struggled financially, but what family didn't? He never laid a hand on them, and he never forced them to accept a stepmother they hated. Mary didn't want him to be offended. She whispered, 'please. Don't make me marry him.'

He shook his head. 'Make you marry him? Didn't I see how well the two of you got on? He's young, handsome and has the means to support you. He has even agreed to take care of your brother and sister, should I die before they can take care of themselves. What could you have against that?'

'Nothing. It's not that. I like him, really I do. But I thought now that I'm eighteen, I could finally have some freedom. Ellen and William could pitch in around the house. I could stop doing everything around here.'

'Everything?' He raised his voice. 'You say you do everything around here?' He stood and paced from one side of the room to the other. 'Do you realise how much I've sacrificed for this family? How many men do you know who raised a family on their own? Ever since your mother died, I've done whatever it takes to keep this family going. How could you have the audacity to walk away from us now?'

Mary shook her head vigorously. 'No, Father. It's not that. I'm truly grateful for you. I just need some time—'

He interrupted her. 'Time? No. I won't accept it. You've put off marriage for years, but you can't keep it up forever. Girls marry. That's all there is to it.'

'Not everyone marries,' she muttered.

He took her hand. 'My dear, don't be nervous. There's no reason you shouldn't be married. You're a fine-looking girl with good manners. Why shouldn't John want to marry you?'

'It's not that.'

'What then?'

'Just because it's the normal thing to do, it doesn't mean I should have to do it.'

He sighed. 'There's nothing wrong with the man, and I know you like him. It doesn't have to be immediate, but within a matter of weeks, you'll marry him.'

'Father!'

'I mean it.'

Mary tried to stop the tears from falling but it was too late. 'I won't let you force me to marry.'

'You know it's best for everyone.'

'Please.' Mary dropped to her knees and reached for her father's hands. 'I'm begging you, don't make me do this. Don't punish me. It's not my fault Mother died. I should have never had to take up all her responsibilities so young. All these years I've been stuck here.'

He brushed her hands away. 'Stuck? Stuck with your family?'

Mary knew she shouldn't have said that, but it was too late.

'If that's how you feel, you can sleep somewhere else tonight.'

'But Father—'

'Get out, now.'

———

To continue reading, buy Becoming The Pannell Witch now!

Printed in Great Britain
by Amazon